Jimmy Stokes spent his working life teaching and trying to resolve young people's problems. Having worked with secondary pupils in a variety of schools, Jimmy strived to ensure that each one aspired to fulfil their potential. During his career, he worked with pupils from ethnic minorities. He recognised that outside influences could prevent these students fulfilling their potential. Understanding this problem led to him ensuring that these youngsters received the appropriate level of help to do justice to their future prospects.

Disappointingly throughout a long career, Jimmy only worked with one person of colour and this individual was a supply teacher. *Blood on Their Hands* is a novel which helps explain this dearth of people from ethnic minorities in the teaching profession and other walks of life.

Jimmy Stokes

BLOOD ON THEIR HANDS

AUSTIN MACAULEY PUBLISHERS™

LONDON • CAMBRIDGE • NEW YORK • SHARJAH

A CIP catalogue record for this title is available from the British Library.

ISBN 9781035818174 (Paperback)
ISBN 9781035818181 (ePub e-book)

www.austinmacauley.com

First Published 2023
Austin Macauley Publishers Ltd®
1 Canada Square
Canary Wharf
London
E14 5AA

I would like to thank Algy Foster and Graham Murrell for their cooperation and contribution which enabled me to write this book. We have been friends for half a century which has given me a window into the prejudices they have had to face and overcome to succeed in their chosen profession. I truly admire what they have achieved.

A big thanks to Linda Vale (nee Murrell) for her help in producing this work.

A huge thank you to my wonderful family for their support and a big welcome to my new twin granddaughters, Sophie and Lottie.

Table of Contents

Foreword

Algy and Graham are the two principal characters in *Blood on their Hands*. I met them in 1971 when we began teacher training at Cardiff College of Education. During this and in subsequent years, I became aware of the struggle they faced at times against discrimination.

Algy Foster is black, his father travelling from St Kitts to Britain on the Empire Windrush. Graham Murrell is mixed race, his grandfather having come to Britain from Barbados to fight in the Great War. Looking at Graham, it would be easy to mistake him for somebody who is white. This presented difficulties for him when he faced racist conversation which he found abhorrent and understandably he was intolerant of such talk.

During the 1960s, 70s and 80s, discrimination in Britain was rife. Organisations which should have been pillars of society were institutionally racist. In this story, South Wales Police quite rightly face justifiable criticism for their attitude on occasions towards Algy and Graham.

However, it was their investigation and subsequent treatment of a group of men of colour in Cardiff's Butetown area that was particularly despicable. Their case represented probably the worst miscarriage of justice in British legal history.

Since the 1980s, there have been significant improvements in police forces throughout the country. Nevertheless, some forces are still being let down by rogue individuals who have acted in a way that demeans their position in society. While the book highlights the policing problems of the past, it would be remiss of me not to pay tribute to the brave men and women who do sterling work to protect the British people and in particular to those who have lost their lives in the course of doing their duty.

Having spent three years together training as teachers, I was able to appreciate the position in which Algy and Graham found themselves. Being able to empathise with their situation has empowered me to write the book through their eyes. Both have been happy with the interpretation of their families' story.

Reflecting on a teaching career which spanned nearly forty years in Wales, I realise that I only ever taught with one person of colour. This discredits a system which should have promoted greater diversity. Led by educators from ethnic minorities people are working hard to redress this problem. Statistics today show that people of colour are still badly under-represented in education.

There has to be greater diversity within the teaching profession if the workforce is to truly reflect British society today. It would provide youngsters from ethnic minorities with the desire to succeed.

During recent times, the church has not always been the luminary it should have been. From Biblical times, slavery was accepted as a necessary part of society and seemed to be missing the basic religious tenet of Christianity, that there is equality in creation. Jesus's compassion for the underdog seems to have been bypassed when people of African descent were perceived as members of a different species.

Algy, one of the two main characters in the book, was a victim of discrimination by members of an organisation that should have been setting an example to society. Today, church attitudes have improved and they now aspire to act as the guiding light they always should have been. In the Catholic Church, African priests are now helping to solve the shortage of vocations to the priesthood throughout Europe and the United States.

Television programmes during the 1960s, 70s and 80s portrayed people of colour as an inferior species. The reader should try to discern between what is fact and fiction in the book, as Algy and Graham look for the root cause of racism.

My story is not an updated version of 'Roots.' Instead, I've tried to show how my two friends struggled against adversity to become successful in the field of education, at a time when there were many barriers for people of colour. They drew inspiration from a black woman who grew up and lived all her life in Butetown, Cardiff. These momentous achievements have led to her being immortalised in bronze at Cardiff's Central Square.

Betty Campbell's achievements have culminated in her being the first Welsh woman to be honoured in this way; a remarkable achievement for a woman of colour. This is where my tale begins.

Although, my story is set in Wales, it is my sincere hope that every young person of colour draws inspiration from my narrative and aspires to be a Betty, Algy or Graham, whatever their chosen field.

Prologue
Wednesday, 29 September 2021

Graham and Algy were strolling along St Mary's Street in Cardiff on their way to Central Square. Today, this redeveloped area by Cardiff Central Train Station was to be the site of a significant occasion in Welsh history. The unveiling of a statue would resonate around the British Isles.

Not only was this the first statue of a named female in Wales but Betty Campbell was a black woman who'd managed to transcend racial and social difficulties to become the first black Headteacher in Wales.

Betty's father was Simon Vickers Johnson, a Jamaican who had arrived in the Principality when he was fifteen years of age. He married Betty's mother, a Welsh Barbadian. In 1934, Betty was born and was christened Rachel Elizabeth Johnson. Unfortunately, her father was killed during the war, causing her mother to struggle financially.

Steadfastly working hard to make ends meet, Nora as she became known, did all she could to provide for the family. Rachel universally known as Betty was very able and diligent in school.

From a young age, she was determined to break down barriers and enter the teaching profession. At eleven, Betty passed the eleven plus exam enabling her to take a place at Lady Margaret High School. At seventeen years of age, while studying in the Sixth Form, Betty became pregnant and left school to marry Rupert Campbell.

Betty's resolve was such that she was still hell bent on teaching. In 1960, Cardiff College of Education voted to admit women and offered teacher training places to six females. Betty, who in the meantime had given birth to three children, applied and the college granted her a place. Her quest to enter the teaching profession had been made even more difficult when one of her schoolteachers told Betty that it was no good her wanting to teach because she was black.

Heartbroken by this prejudiced, insensitive statement, she became even more determined to succeed and could not be deterred from fulfilling her ambition. Her drive not only enabled her to achieve her lifelong goal but innovative teaching gave rise to Betty becoming Headteacher of Mount Stuart Primary School in the Docks. At the time the area was universally known as Tiger Bay. Betty lived in the Tiger Bay community and following her retirement became a councillor for Cardiff's Butetown Ward.

Her commitment to education, local politics and the Commission for Racial Equality ensured Betty became an icon within the Tiger Bay community. Betty's work gained credibility throughout Wales and she became a totemic figure for people from ethnic minorities particularly those who wanted to teach.

Betty's outstanding work resonated with many people in the United Kingdom. Following her death in 2017, Carwyn Jones, Welsh First Minister, described Betty as a real pioneer and a catalyst to other black and ethnic minority people. Pressure was applied for a statue to be erected in her honour.

Eve Shepherd a renowned sculptor was commissioned to create the work. Today was a pre-eminent occasion as the statue was to be unveiled by members of the Campbell family. Betty had been an inspiration to Graham Murrell and Algy Foster. There was no way they were going to miss this auspicious occasion.

As the two friends sauntered past Cardiff Market, there were large groups of people walking towards Central Square. Women were in the majority because this awe-inspiring female had broken down many barriers to become admired and achieve great status in society. Whereas many people are affected by fame, Betty always stayed true to her roots.

People truly respected her because of it and many women were given a shot in the arm through the work of this pioneering headteacher. The majority of modern women refused to cower to a patriarchal dominated society and were motivated to break free from the shackles constraining them in the same way as Betty Campbell had. Both their own lives and society at large were enhanced by this new attitude among women.

Algy reflected on this male dominance in society and spoke, 'Gray, do you realise that only a fifth of all statues in Britain depict a woman?'

'I didn't know that but it's an awful statistic and a terrible indictment on society.'

'This is a particularly momentous day. Not only was Betty female but her burden was made even worse by her being a black woman. Could you ever imagine a statue of a black person being put up in Cardiff when we were young, let alone one of a black woman? If anyone had mentioned that in the 60s or 70s, people would have said they were mad.'

'You are definitely right, Algy. Discrimination was rife. Look at some of the television programmes which were racist. Most people just accepted it and thought it was okay.'

'Just look at the discrimination in our own city in sport. Rugby players like Billy Boston and Clive Sullivan were fantastic but they had to go to the North of England to play Rugby League. Rugby Union clubs in South Wales didn't want black players in their teams.'

'Just think about this, Algy. Betty's father fought in the war and lost his life in the struggle for freedom in Europe but he couldn't have played rugby in South Wales. Worse still he made the ultimate sacrifice along with other black military men but he still would have been discriminated against because of his colour.'

Algy became exasperated and blurted out, 'It just doesn't make sense. When we were young in church we were taught "All men and women are created in God's image". Yet many white people saw themselves as superior to black people and even today a significant minority still hold racist views.'

The two friends turned into Central Square where they could see the Betty Campbell statue concealed by a cover ready to be unveiled. Designed by one of the best sculptors of her generation the work had been kept a secret. Algy and Graham knew this statue would be very special befitting a woman who had achieved so much in her life.

'Algy, she broke down barriers by being the first black person to go into teaching from Cardiff College of Education. You're right. We really owe her. She was a role model for us. We knew it could be done because she'd accomplished it and Betty's inspiration was the main reason we applied to train to teach at the same college.'

'Cardiff College of Education was fantastic giving her that opportunity at the beginning of the 1960s. What a significant move on their part, as it opened the way for other people of colour to become teachers.'

'I really don't think we'd have gone there if it hadn't been for Betty. Her presence in the Docks community really energised us to achieve without us knowing it.'

'You're right, Algy, because when she went there at twenty-six, she already had three children. Betty's commitment was second to none.'

'How right you are. Look how we've benefitted from a long teaching career and we're now on a good pension.'

'You never know, Algy, they might even build a statue of us.'

'Aye, they'd probably put it where the Top Rank night club used to be because we spent so much time there.'

'We were definitely the best dancers in our year group in college.'

'Trouble is with all that contact sport we've now got a job to walk properly let alone dance!'

'I wouldn't have changed it for the world but that's the trouble with all that physical activity, it catches up with you. Never mind if I had my time over again the result would be exactly the same.'

Drawing closer to the statue the two friends chuckled.

'My mother would have loved to be here today to witness this,' exclaimed Graham.

'Yes, Betty and your mum were really good friends, Gray.'

'Quite right, mate. The two were genuinely close but by God could they bicker.'

'You know why. They were both determined women and steadfast in their beliefs.'

'Nevertheless, they were great friends and woe betide anyone who said anything bad about either of them. Mam and Betty Campbell would have their guts for garters.'

'Changing the subject, Gray, hasn't it been an incredible year and what happened in Benin was supernatural.'

'I was agnostic until then but what happened there has definitely strengthened my belief in God.'

'Me too. I was very sceptical about whether there's a God or not. I'm trying to be as good as I can because we're approaching the red zone.'

'What do you mean by that?'

'We're in our late 60s, so how much time have we got left?'

'Take it from me. I'd say we were in the green room. Just about ready to go on.'

The friends laughed at these casual comments and Algy changed the subject.

'I've just had a thought. Do you think John and Tony will turn up?'

'Hopefully,' exclaimed Graham.

Part 1
The Door of No Return

Chapter 1

Ibadan, South-West Nigeria, 1780

Adedamola and Akin were both young Yoruba tribesmen who'd grown up living in adjacent huts in the same Nigerian village. The tribe had created a clearing in the forest for twenty huts but the canopy of the forest towered over the village. This ancient ecosystem of trees provided the Yoruba with everything needed to survive. Generations of the tribe handed down knowledge acquired throughout the centuries about plants which were good to eat and those containing healing properties. The forest contained abundant animals providing meat for the tribe. Water was plentiful because of the heavy rainfall in the jungle and the rivers were teeming with fish. Being near the equator the climate was constantly hot and steamy and the Yoruba were fully acclimatised to this. Nearby was a troupe of macaque monkeys who chattered and screeched all day. The Yoruba loved these primates and although they would have been good to eat, they never hunted them. On occasions the macaques would naughtily tease the Yoruba by throwing fruit at them but nevertheless the Yoruba would find their behaviour entertaining and the two groups lived in harmony. The Yoruba realised that the monkeys were a natural alarm against intruders, dementedly screeching if there was a hint of danger. Countless bird species inhabited the rainforest canopy providing the Yoruba with harmonious birdsong. At night the tranquillity of the forest was interrupted by the constant chirping of crickets. All these animals created a plethora of noise that the Yoruba were accustomed to.

Both men slept on straw mats next to their young wives. Adedamola was married to Abedi a woman who was two years his junior and they had a two-month-old baby. Akin and his wife Bimpe were expecting their first child but nobody would know as she was in the early stages of her pregnancy.

Outside the hut dawn had broken allowing bright shafts of sunlight to penetrate the small gaps in the walls. Speedily sun rays began to strike the faces of the occupants. Impotent at first these sunbeams swiftly developed into a fierce heat even capable of burning tribespeople who were accustomed to such temperatures. Being in the tropical rainforest further relief would come from hefty rain showers which helped alleviate the heat of the day. During the hottest part of the day the Yoruba would seek the shade of the forest to prevent their bodies being ravaged by the burning west African sun. Adedamola was the first to stir. His nostrils were filled with the sweet pungent smell of smoke emitted by the fire he'd banked up the night before. The rainforest contained many different species of wild animals, some capable of threatening the Yoruba's safety. A good fire would keep any intruding animal away from the village. Moving his hands upwards Adedamola contacted his face to rub the sleep from his eyes. Initial blurred vision was immediately replaced with clarity enabling him to see his young wife Abedi and their young son Adedayo. Brimming with pride at having produced a son Adedamola hoped this would be the first of many children. The more children in a family the more pairs of hands there were to work. Sons would be taught how to hunt because there was an abundance of animals in close proximity to the village and the streams teemed with fish. Girls were excellent around the home but when they married it became expensive for any Yoruba family because a dowry had to be paid. This would be crops or animals paid to the husband's family. Pushing any negative thoughts from his mind Adedamola gave thanks to the Great Forest Spirit for the gift of a wife and son to perpetuate his family line. Akin was unaffected by the morning light and he and his wife Bimpe remained asleep. Being childless meant they didn't have to deal with a little one. In the future that would change once their child was born.

Suddenly there was a commotion, the macaques going berserk and bringing everyone in the village out of their huts. Akin and Bimpe were rudely awoken by the pandemonium taking place outside. A once peaceful, organised Nigerian village was swiftly reduced to chaos. Peering through their hut door Adedamola and Akin could see that the village had been invaded by a large group of men. Casting their eyes on these marauders Adedamola and Akin's hearts were pounding in their chests. Both men feared the worst. Stories circulated the local Yoruba villages of other west African tribes being employed by white Europeans and armed with guns to capture rival tribes. Yoruba weapons were no match for guns which could kill from a distance. One Yoruba tribesman bravely tried to defend his wife from one of the interlopers. Another of the renegades pointed his gun and a loud bang followed causing the Yoruba man to drop lifeless onto his back. A significant portion of his skull was missing with blood oozing from this gaping hole. Adedamola and Akin could see tribal markings on this invading bunch enabling them to identify the group as Edo tribesmen from Benin. Horrified at the thought of losing their lives to these mercenaries who were rounding up Africans for money the Yoruba complied with the Edo demands by assembling in front of their huts.

Adedamola and Akin comforted their wives. Clenching little Adedayo to her chest Abedi wanted to protect him from these men who were disloyal to their west African heritage. A small group of these trespassers huddled together in conversation. What followed this hastily arranged conflab beggared belief. One of the group strolled over to Abedi then roughly snatched Adedayo from her. As any father would, Adedamola reacted to protect his son but one of the Edo put a gun barrel to his head and screamed at him. Although using a different tribal dialect, Adedamola already having witnessed the death of one of the villagers knew what would happen if he continued to resist.

Forcibly retreating Adedamola couldn't believe what was to happen next. Abedi was screaming crying. Akin grimaced and Bimpe covered her eyes. The treacherous Edo tribesman drew a pistol from its holster and shot the baby in the head. Brave Yoruba tribespeople let out ear piercing screams at the inhumanity they'd just witnessed. A despicable murderous action had been carried out by men who were motivated by money and showed no concern for their fellow Africans. Next the little corpse was bundled into a sack. Abedi's heart raced causing her to gasp for breath. Her palpitating heart gave rise to her chest visibly moving up and down. The barbarism she had just witnessed caused her breathing to quicken until she was panting and gasping for air, her body secreting copious quantities of perspiration. Such inhumane treatment prompted her legs to buckle and she collapsed screaming. A final ignominy occurred when the Edo man tied up the sack and threw it into the fire. Driven on by the promise of financial reward from their European masters for this consignment of slaves had precipitated this ghastly behaviour. Little Adedayo was seen as surplus to requirement being too small to make such a long journey from the forest to the coast. Consequently, he met a gruesome end at the hands of this avaricious group. Baby Adedayo paid the price for this group's greed and willingness to ignore the importance of the sanctity of human life.

Taking a lead, Adedamola and Akin although in a state of shock regained a measure of composure, knowing they had to calm their wives, or they could all lose their lives. Such wicked humans would have no compunction about killing more tribespeople who couldn't be controlled. Adedamola picked Abedi up and whispered encouragement to her. Likewise, Akin spoke under his breath to Bimpe. Both women calmed and they gathered with the other Yoruba. Abedi as any mother would was distraught and nauseated at the loss of her precious infant. She was finding difficulty processing the inhumanity of what had just taken place. Although emotionally scarred Abedi had to control her anguish. Forlorn and with her mind in turmoil from the excruciating pain inflicted by the Edo's tyranny, she had no choice but to conform to the Edo's demands if she wanted to stay alive.

Although Africans, the Edo wore European clothes with belts of musket balls crossing their chests. Spears, bow and arrow and clubs were no match against such lethal weapons provided by their European masters. Conforming was essential or they'd meet the same fate as little Adedayo.

Varied tribal dialects meant the Yoruba could not understand the Edo leader but his screaming and gesturing left them in no doubt that he wanted them to conform to his dictates. Some of the Edo forcibly turned the Yoruba sideways. Angrily foaming at the mouth, the Edo leader was anxious to shackle the Yoruba captives ready for the march to the coast. Motioning for them to put their hands in front of their torsos the other Edo manacled the group. A single chain with collars along its length was applied to the Yoruba. People used to the freedom of the African rainforest had fear etched on their faces. Adedamola and Akin although sick to the pits of their stomachs continued to encourage Abedi and Bimpe who were also traumatised by Adedayo's death. Although as emotionally scarred as their wives the two men acted pragmatically. One life had been lost but did it need to be five more deaths because Bimpe was in the early stages of pregnancy. Fully restrained with the coffle made escape impossible. Such an inhumane tethering of the Yoruba demeaned their captors who were willing to sell their fellow Africans into slavery at the hands of Europeans.

Stories told in the Yoruba villages spoke of Ouidah in Benin as a great trading centre for African slaves. Yoruba and other tribes were betrayed by their fellow Africans and put on ships sailing to distant lands where once-free Africans were forced into a life of servitude. Perverse behaviour such as this reduced these slavers to the level of animals. These men were willing to capture and sell once-freemen. African traitors were handsomely remunerated for their treachery and this prevented white Europeans from having to enter the rainforest where they were at risk of falling foul to tropical diseases from which they had no immunity. The rainforest was thought of as being so dangerous it became known as the white man's grave.

Adedamola was manacled and coffled at the front of the group with his wife Abedi behind him. Akin and Bimpe were tethered in Abedi's wake. African slavers did all they could to keep slaves alive on the journey because of the substantial financial reward. Yoruba always stayed in the vicinity of their village and although very fit from hunting and growing crops this march to the coast would be a severe test of their resilience. Discomfort from being tethered together in the exhausting heat would drain the Yoruba. Adedamola, Abedi, Akin and Bimpe continually encouraged each other. Abedi needed to be regularly uplifted following Adedayo's death and all the villagers whispered words of inspiration to her. Being at the front Adedamola would occasionally have a gun barrel pushed into his back to keep the Yoruba moving. Uncertain as to their destination the Yoruba knew they were marching to a new way of life. Greedy Edo tribesmen were responsible for this mistreatment of their fellow Africans and had blood on their hands.

Chapter 2

Ouidah Benin, Ten Days Later

Following an arduous ten-day march restrained by coffle and manacles, Adedamola, Abedi, Akin, Bimpe and the other Yoruba glimpsed the ocean for the first time in their lives. Living in the rainforest they'd encountered numerous streams and rivers but this was not like any other expanse of water they'd ever seen. The water extended as far as the eye could see, making them wonder where the other side was.

In the rainforest, they'd used canoes and small boats with tiny sails but the boats they could now see were enormous with gigantic sails billowing in the ocean breeze. Europeans were marching Africans onto the decks of these vessels and they disappeared into the boat. Stunned by what they were witnessing, the Yoruba thought people were being swallowed by a huge beast.

Already traumatised by what they were observing, the Yoruba were to be the victims of heartrending cruelty. Their foot slog finished, the Yoruba could see scores of Africans being treated more tortuously than any animal. Any self-esteem the Africans possessed was being eroded by the inhuman treatment of the traders. Men and women who'd known the freedom of the African rainforest were now tethered like livestock.

The Yoruba had arrived at the Ouidah slave market in Benin and their fate was now sealed. Adedamola, Abedi, Akin and Bimpe now faced a life of bondage where they'd be forced to do their master's bidding or lose their life. Being young meant they were a valuable commodity whereas older Africans were surplus to requirement. Younger slaves would produce offspring who in turn would face subjugation and a lifetime of work.

Chastisement on the journey had been kept to a minimum because a marked slave would fetch a lower price at the auction. Nevertheless disobedience would lead to a slave being disciplined with the whip. Absolute defiance could lead to a slave being beaten to death.

These Europeans knew that another raid on an African village would occasion a less confrontational character being enslaved. There was an endless supply of victims making the European traders unconcerned about the odd African refusing to conform. Beating one served as an example to the others who despite the situation, they found themselves in still valued their life.

Days on the march ensured the Yoruba were caked with dust. Any who had been whipped had weals on their flesh making them a tasty proposition for blood thirsty insects. Totally restrained on the march the Yoruba were helpless to alleviate the irritation caused by flies allowing these infuriating insects to feast at will on them.

Dumbfounded by the sight greeting their eyes, Adedamola whispered to Abedi, 'Just do as they tell you. Don't upset them in any way, we have to stay alive.'

'I'll do whatever it takes. After seeing what happened to Adedayo, these people are so bad, they'd be prepared to kill us without giving it a second thought.'

Although, the Yoruba were shackled, the Edo traders kept physical punishment to a minimum because they were determined to maximise their financial gain. Desperately fatigued following a long journey, their physical appearance would be dire if they were constantly punished, pushing their market price down, consequently lowering the Edo cut of the money. Wherever Adedamola looked he saw Africans tied like animals.

He could see Europeans checking Africans for good stature. Pliancy in the limbs and joints was essential if a slave was to work diligently. A slave in poor physical condition would produce inferior work.

Adedamola and Akin's humiliation was complete when a trader put his hand inside their loin cloths, roughly grabbing their penises to check for venereal disease. This demeaning act caused once proud Yoruba tribesmen to wince through the indignity of their action.

Removal of the restricting coffle was welcome but the horrors of the slave market made it difficult to appreciate release from this confinement. Slavers manacled the Yoruba around the ankle with enough length of chain allowing the slaves to walk with a shorter stride. Any chance of escape was impossible but the Yoruba were able to talk to each other.

'I'm really frightened, Adedamola,' exclaimed Abedi.

'So am I but we must stay strong. It's important we stay alive.'

'Do you know what they're going to do with us?' Akin asked.

'If they were going to kill us, they'd have done it in our village. It looks like they're going to sell us,' remarked Bimpe.

A distraught Adedamola looked around, and said, 'This is a marketplace for human beings. It looks like we're going to be sold. Information circulating in our local villages tells of men and women being sold separately and put on different boats.'

'We need to do as we're told and hope they allow us to stay together,' replied Abedi.

Coffle removed, the Yoruba were able to turn around and see a market-place full of frightened and distressed Africans. Tribespeople were being paraded on a stage in front of European sea captains as a precursor to being sold. Akin's voice quivered at the thought of being separated from his wife.

'It looks like we'll be lucky to stay together Bimpe because the men are being separated from their wives.'

Adedamola could see a man dressed in black with a white collar watching the slave traders work. In a stuttering voice Adedamola said, 'It looks like he's supervising what's going on.'

Bimpe shook with fear, and whispered, 'They're using a red-hot iron to brand their skin.'

Daunted by what she saw Abedi stuttered, 'How sickening. You can see the smoke coming from their bodies where they are being burnt.'

Ear splitting screams resonated around the marketplace as the branding iron impacted the ebony flesh.

'They're using a branding iron to imprint a cross on their bodies,' proclaimed Adedamola.

The Yoruba tribespeople's inexperience of European religious traditions meant they failed to understand the significance of what was taking place. In time, the slaves would come to realise that the men in black were Roman Catholic priests supervising crosses being seared into each African's flesh. Catholic clergy at the time were convinced that God wanted them to do this because the imprinted crosses were being used as a baptismal symbol.

Searing flesh was considered a substitute for baptism by water similar to baptism by blood in the early Christian Church. A person in the early church who had not been baptised and was then martyred for their faith was thought to have been baptised with blood. This form of baptism involved the complete forgiveness of sin guaranteeing immediate entry into heaven.

Branding Africans with the cross, the church believed these tribespeople were being initiated into Christianity. At the time the church taught there was no entry to heaven without baptism. Catholic clergy thought they were doing Africans a favour but they totally disregarded the rich culture these people were born into where they lived in harmony with their environment.

Catholic priests were guilty of supporting the slave traders who were treating the Africans as a commodity to be kidnapped and sold. The desecration of their humanity was a fate the Yoruba would now have to face from their fellow human beings.

Witnessing this ignominious scene, Adedamola, Abedi, Akin and Bimpe began to quake with terror at the thought of being branded. Very shortly it would be their turn.

'When we get to the stage, we need to walk across swiftly to avoid being whipped,' Adedamola pointed out.

The general hustle and bustle of the marketplace including instructions being shouted and the clanking of manacles and chains prevented Adedamola being heard. Abedi, Akin and his wife Bimpe were nervously sweating at the prospect of what they would have to face.

'I don't know whether I've the courage to put up with the pain,' exclaimed Abedi in an agitated voice.

'I feel exactly the same,' agreed Akin.

'And me,' whispered a worried Bimpe.

Adedamola decided to encourage his fellow Yoruba proclaiming, 'We all feel the same way but I'm going to call on the Great Forest Spirit to give us strength. Then I'm going to grit my teeth when they brand me hoping I can bear the pain.'

Answering in a faint voice, Abedi said, 'You're really courageous, Adedamola, but I don't think I've got it in me to be so brave.'

Swiftly interjecting, Akin declared, 'We can only hope the pain of the branding passes quickly.'

Abedi knew that they were trying to lift her spirits in the face of such an horrendous ordeal but if she were to survive this hell, she needed to display a fearlessness as she drew near to the branding iron, despite quaking with fear inside.

As the four Yoruba were getting closer to the trader with the branding iron, screams emitted by Africans already being imprinted grew louder. Any background market noise was superseded by the screams of burnt human beings. Growing ever more agitated Bimpe whispered again,

'The line is moving quickly and it'll soon be our turn. That vicious looking man at the table seems to be in charge.'

Just as Bimpe finished speaking, a grossly overweight European with a cruel face and a purple bulbous nose addressed the callous individual sat at the table. Stoney faced and lacking any compassion both men were expressionless, morose and concerned with making as much money as possible from African slaves. Accumulating wealth by buying and selling their fellow human beings stimulated these grotesque traders.

Consuming excessive quantities of alcohol and food had certainly disfigured the overweight European. Ill-gotten gains from human trafficking while not illegal in the eighteenth century certainly broke any moral code where human beings should be treated equally. Cruelty was the norm for the one in charge sitting at the table. This marketplace misery just washed over him, having no effect at all on him.

In a gruff voice, the man with the purple nose spoke to the overseer at the table, 'Senor de Sousa, the next group consists of Yoruba from Nigeria. They're physically impressive and their arms and legs have been examined. There's no venereal disease and they'll make good workers. They're sure to fetch a top price.'

Adedamola let out a shudder when he heard the overseer's name.

'Listen to me the three of you. That man is Felix de Sousa.'

'What do you mean?' Bimpe exclaimed.

'Many of the tribes living near our village have spoken fearfully about this trader. His name strikes fear into the hearts of Africans because of his cruelty.'

Akin wanted to know more about this de Sousa so Adedamola enlightened him.

'De Sousa is a monster who shows no concern for African people. We are just a means for him to make money and through his cruelty he has become very wealthy. He's Portuguese and we need to keep our voices down because we're getting close to him and the marketplace noise will not cover our voices. We can't afford to be heard.'

Reaching de Sousa's table, he glanced at Adedamola and Abedi and without a flicker of emotion he blurted out, 'Sell these two as a pair because they're married and will fetch a top price. These Africans will just breed year after year and the plantation owner in the New World who buys them will have a bargain.'

'We don't usually do that. Men and women are sold separately and to hell with their marriage,' retorted the man with the bulbous nose.

'This couple is going to be an exemption, Big Nose.'

Looking beyond, Adedamola and Abedi, de Sousa's eyes glimpsed Akin and Bimpe. A hint of a smile rolled across his face and the left side of his mouth curled, distorting his face and making him appear even more threatening. This dark intimidating character's withering look struck fear into Akin and Bimpe.

Again, in a snarling voice, he growled, 'Same for these. Sell them as a pair. They'll also be good value for any plantation owner because of their breeding potential. Look at their physiques. It's easy to see how hard they could be made to work. Make sure they're sold to different captains. We want them on different ships.'

'As you say, Senor de Sousa, we'll make sure it's done.'

'Oi, don't forget different ships. That's important.'

Felix de Sousa had migrated from Brazil which was a Portuguese colony. Reputed to be the greatest of all slave traders, de Sousa monopolised the slave trade in Benin. De Sousa was reputed to be a Roman Catholic but the rumour mill in Ouidah claimed he dabbled in voodoo calling on dead spirits to answer his prayers.

Along with practising voodoo he was thought to have a harem of eighty women, mostly Africans, for his pleasure. Single minded and motivated by money his only concern was to get African slaves to the sea captains in the best condition possible to achieve a top price. On the surface he appeared not to be cruel but this was a veneer. De Sousa didn't have an iota of compassion in his body and if he had to kill an African to achieve compliance from others then he wouldn't hesitate.

'What type of man would sit by and watch fellow humans being branded,' thought Adedamola.

Quite simply de Sousa was an abhorrent man who was prepared to countenance heinous crimes against other human beings. De Sousa most certainly had blood on his hands.

One of de Sousa's assistants tied the Yorubas' hands behind their backs and with their feet manacled, Adedamola and Abedi shuffled across the stage. One of de Sousa's henchmen gestured with a whip for them to stop, giving Portuguese, French and British sea captains a chance to examine these men and women before they started bidding. Felix de Sousa announced the starting price giving the captains an opportunity to begin.

A top price was expected for the two couples because of their breeding potential. This would interest the sea captains because when these slaves were sold on in the New World, they in turn would achieve a good profit. Their whole persona was riddled with greed making them the most distasteful of men. Professing themselves to be Christians was laughable.

These men were in league with the Devil. Bidding for the four Yoruba was high. Capt. Barber, an English sea captain, raised his hand sealing the fate of Adedamola and Abedi as slaves. They were destined for slavery on a Caribbean Island under English control.

Akin and Bimpe were doomed to a life of servitude on an island under French dominion. A French captain named Capt. Badeau outbid all other suitors. Concluding the deals Felix de Sousa bellowed at the top of his voice, 'Brand these pagan savages. Baptise them in the name of the Lord.'

Adedamola and Akin whispered encouraging words to their wives for them to be brave at the prospect of the horrendous ordeal in front of them. The four Yoruba tried to put on a brave face but their stomachs were turning somersaults. Both women appreciated their husbands efforts to embolden them but there was an inevitability about what they were feeling.

Branding a person was nothing short of barbaric behaviour making a mockery of human intelligence. Causing pain on the level the Yoruba would experience contradicted Jesus's teaching. Yet these men were anxious to express their affiliation to Christianity. Jesus taught, 'Do unto others as you would want done unto you.'

Would Felix de Sousa and these evil sea captains have wanted to face being branded? Their actions were the work of the Devil and aligned to greed.

Tribesmen immediately in front of them were dragged kicking and screaming to the branding iron. Adedamola, Abedi, Akin and Bimpe outwardly concealed their fear but their minds were awash with the thought of their flesh being seared. Stepping forward first Adedamola hoped that any mark would be on the torso, not their faces. Disfiguring people in this way would be a callous, vindictive act.

Facing Adedamola was a grotesque looking human being ready to inflict a mark which in the slave trader's eyes would provide a rite of passage into Christianity. This creature had a scar running the length of his left cheek. Surely this was a trophy gained in some drunken knife fight. Walking towards Adedamola, he glared at him with his cold as steel, piercing blue eyes exuding pure evil.

Here was a life form completely devoid of any care or concern at all. Many of his teeth were missing and any remaining ones were rotten, further marring his looks and making him look more evil than any human being the Yoruba had ever seen. All this monster cared about was the money coming his way for imprinting a burning cross on another human. Moving closer to Adedamola his beard touched Adedamola's face.

Refusing to flinch, he was determined not to be intimidated by this money grabbing sadist. His breath reeking of alcohol, mingled with decomposing food caught in the remains of his teeth would make anyone feel sick. Standing on the right-hand side of this man was a Catholic priest. Dressed in black, he appeared as an earthly manifestation of the Angel of Death not a man of God who in line with Jesus's teaching should have been promoting support for the underdog.

He and many other clergy like him had allowed such sadistic practices to contradict the Christian teaching that God is love. Fixing a stare on the man about to perpetrate a horrible crime, Adedamola bravely held his ground. Appearing outwardly courageous, his insides quivered at the thought of his body being violated with a branding iron.

Wincing with fear and sweating profusely at the thought of what was going to happen and already weakened by a long foot slog, resistance was impossible as the preceding man was dragged by two men to the heartless villain who stamped a cross on his shoulder. As he did, the priest made the sign of the cross saying, 'I baptise you in the name of the Father, Son and Holy Spirit.'

These actions sealed the man's entry into Christianity believing that tribespeople would be saved from burning in hell. The actions were misguided and an insult to an all-loving God.

It was now Adedamola's turn and he approached his fate with fortitude, all the time glaring at Scarface. His courageous stance antagonised the monster. Determined to exact revenge he lifted the branding iron towards his neck holding it just above his ebony flesh. Adedamola determined to maintain his composure could feel the heat radiating from the iron but he still refused to flinch.

Continuing to goad his victim, Scarface moved the iron towards his face. Suddenly, the priest realising that an unnecessary disfigurement driven by revenge was about to take place shouted, 'Stop. On his shoulder.'

Seeing that the intimidation had gone too far, the misguided clergyman prevented Adedamola from being ruthlessly maimed. Although, church teaching was deluded in its thinking about the cruelty of this form of baptism the priest had shown he was capable of a shred of kindness by preventing an unspeakable grisly branding. Gritting his teeth and clenching his fists although they were tied behind his back, Adedamola waited for the moment of impact.

A horrible grin came over Scarface as he sadistically forced the iron into Adedamola's left shoulder. The putrid odour from Scarface's mouth was replaced by the nauseating stench of burning flesh. Again the priest made the sign of the Cross, and completed the baptism by referring again to the Christian Trinity. This iniquitous behaviour would definitely have drawn the harshest rebuke from Jesus.

Stoically, Adedamola absorbed the pain refusing to be detracted by the smell of charred flesh. At the time of his branding Adedamola failed to understand the symbolism of being marked but he would now carry this imprint to the grave. Having absorbed the pain Adedamola's thoughts turned to Abedi, Akin and Bimpe. A young, beautiful Yoruba woman, Abedi, would be next to undergo this harrowing ordeal.

Adedamola invoked the Great Forest Spirit to help his wife cope with her dire situation. When the branding iron had contacted his skin, Adedamola experienced an intense burning, causing pain to radiate from the wound, eventually pervading his whole body. Knowing Abedi to be a mentally strong woman who would show fortitude, his great love for her meant he would share in her suffering.

Once more Scarface displayed no emotion as he branded Abedi's left shoulder. Watching her face contort with pain she made no noise but Adedamola grimaced letting out a shriek. The priest concluded this dreadful excuse for a rite of passage initiating Abedi into Christianity by repeating the prayer. Less defiant than Adedamola, Akin was unable to blank out the pain and he emitted a loud scream when the iron touched his shoulder.

Last to approach Scarface was Bimpe who had a steely determination on her face as he imprinted her with the cross. Impressively courageous, she gritted her teeth barely emitting any noise at all. All the Yoruba were resolute in the face of the mistreatment they'd received. Unfortunately, this was only the beginning of their nightmare.

Still manacled to their respective partners the four Yoruba had been bought by different sea captains. Adedamola and Abedi were forced to stand with the slaves bought by the Englishman Capt. Barber whereas Akin and Bimpe were led away to stand with the slaves bought by Capt. Badeau, the French slaver. At this point, these lifelong friends realised they would never see each other again.

Business having been completed the slaves were marched to their respective ships. In one way they had been lucky because men and women were usually separated, the slavers showing no sensitivity towards married couples and partners who were sent to different destinations. Fearful at the prospect of going onto such a large vessel, they were consoled at having each other's company; a small mercy in these dire circumstances.

Intuition told them that these ships would be their home for months. Adedamola prayed that he and Abedi would be resilient enough to cope with the journey's rigours. Being guided to the gangplank of their particular ship fear made the slaves reticent about boarding. This led to a whip being cracked and the slaves scurried aboard.

Fearful at the prospect of entering an environment so totally alien to the west African rainforest or being killed for disobedience, the whip provided the impetus the slavers were looking for.

Once aboard their vessels the crews opened the hold making once free tribesmen wonder how so many people could fit in a confined area. Suddenly, confronted with a pokey hole being their home for the foreseeable future the slaves tried to control their breathing to prevent them panicking. Despite this, their fear became tangible sucking the breath from their mouths and terror washed over them.

Manacled, there was nowhere to run and the slaves became resigned to their fate. Both couples on their respective ships were determined to survive in the knowledge they were fortunate enough to have their partner with them. During the many low moments over the coming months, they could console each other.

Now fully loaded with human cargo, the hold on each ship was sealed and the sails unfurled ready for the journey. Soon their African homeland would be a distant memory. Adedamola and Abedi began their journey aboard the British ship, with Akin and Bimpe on the French vessel.

Part 2
The Murrells Arrive in Cardiff

Chapter 3

Bridgetown Barbados, 14 July 1914

Europe had just descended into chaos by entering into a world war and even though it was the wet season in Barbados the island was experiencing a beautiful day. Heavy downpours at this time of the year would result in parts of this stunning West Indian island having up to 60 inches of rain each year. Nevertheless, temperatures on a July day could soar into the mid-eighties Fahrenheit.

Located in the hurricane zone, Barbados could potentially experience one of those devastating climatic events with the capability of being catastrophic for the island. Sixteen years ago, was the last time Barbados had experienced one of these cyclonic incidents.

Purposefully striding along the harbourside was Joseph Albert Murrell who was born in 1893 and could just about remember this calamitous meteorological event. Like many other West Indians, he was anxious to join the great struggle taking place in Europe. By participating in the war, Joseph would be able to prove his loyalty to the King.

His parents were both committed supporters of the monarchy, even giving Joey, as he was called, the middle name Albert, after Queen Victoria's husband. Fervent Christians, the Murrells were staunch supporters of the Anglican Church. Six days each week, Joey's family worked on a sugar cane plantation but on a Sunday, production was halted for them to serve the Lord. Men in each family would don their best suits and women their delightfully patterned frocks as a mark of respect to Almighty God.

Joey was twenty-one years of age as he made his way towards a British tramp steamer named the SS Pontwen owned by a Cardiff based company. Slung over his left shoulder was a kit bag containing all his worldly possessions. A tenaciously resolute character, Joey was determined to work his passage on the Pontwen to play his part in the Great War and "do his bit" for King and country.

He'd heard Cardiff was a port in Wales which had become world renowned. This small principality was producing more coal than any other country on the globe. Subsequently, this boom led to Cardiff the capital of Wales becoming an important port city to export this much sought-after commodity around the world. As he approached the Pontwen, Joey could see a sailor on deck and he yelled,

'Hey man, are there any jobs on the ship for a man who wants to serve his king.'

'Butty, there's always jobs going on here for those who don't mind hard work. Come aboard to meet the captain,' replied the sailor in a Welsh accent.

'I'll be up there now.'

Anxiously climbing the gangplank, Joey was determined to secure the job giving him passage to Britain. Climbing aboard he thought to himself, 'None of this "hey man" for the captain. I must remember to address him as "Sir".'

Never one to bow down or scrape Joey was desperate to impress this man so he could have a job. He was quite prepared to do anything on board to get to Britain. The sailor he'd spoken to introduced himself as Dai.

'Man, I've never heard of that name before.'

'It's short for David. I'll take you to see the captain. He's on the bridge.'

Joey followed Dai to the bridge in order that he could be assessed by the main man.

'Sir, this is Joey Murrell from Bridgetown. He wants to get a job aboard so he can get to Britain.'

'I'm Capt. Jones and I suppose you want to join the war effort, Murrell.'

'Yes, Sir.'

'We'll see what we can do because we need new crew. You're the first to ask for a job but there'll be plenty of others like you. Over half the ship's company will be Barbadian by the time we sail in two days.'

'Oh that's good, Sir.'

'Mind you we don't want shirkers only hard workers. We'll all have to pull our weight on here.'

'Sir, what jobs have you got.'

'There's jobs going as firemen, trimmers and donkey men.'

Joey was familiar with all these jobs. He knew they were all hard work. The job of fireman was particularly back breaking. They needed to shovel five tons of coal each day into the furnace. Also called stokers these men kept the engines going. A fireman would be a knackering job so if Joey could avoid stoking the furnaces he would.

Mind you a trimmer wouldn't be too bad. It would be much less physical but he'd have the responsibility for ensuring huge quantities of coal were evenly distributed throughout the ship. Getting this wrong meant that the ship could list. There was always the possibility if this happened that the ship might sink. His top choice would be a job as a donkeyman.

Doing this job would mean he was in charge of a donkey engine. This was an auxiliary engine supplying power to winches controlling the cargo hoists. It could also be used to provide additional power for the propellors. Joey had had experience with this type of machinery on the sugar plantations.

'Murrell. you're first to ask for a job so you've got a choice.'

'Well, Sir, I'd like to be a donkeyman.'

'Fine choice, Murrell. A man with a brain. That's what I would have chosen but remember I need those engines to be ready at all times.'

'Looking forward to it, Sir.'

'Able Seaman Jones will show you where you sleep.'

'Thank you, Sir.'

Joey followed Dai and remarked, 'Are you called Jones as well?'

'Yes, Joey. Jones is a very common name in Wales.'

'That's interesting. I don't know anyone called Jones in Barbados. Until we were set free from slavery, we always took our owner's surname. Us Murrells kept ours.'

Taking Joey towards the bow of the ship, Dai said, 'Here's your quarters, Joey. There'll be a lot of others sleeping here with you. See that trunk over there? You'll find a hammock to sleep in. Don't think we've got nice soft beds aboard this vessel. In the meantime, you need to get accustomed to the ship and in particular the engines you'll be looking after.'

'Thank you, Dai.'

The next two days saw more Barbadian men join the ship all with the same intention as Joey. Serving King and country in the war was their primary aim. Joey had started work straight away using the donkey engine to load a cargo of

41

sugar cane onto the Pontwen. He would then use the engine to increase thrust to the propellors.

It would be important to maintain maximum propulsion. With a full complement of crew aboard, the Pontwen set sail for Cardiff. Joey Albert Murrell was about to start a new chapter in his life.

Chapter 4

'For all you men coming to Britain for the first time that is the Pembrokeshire coast over there. Welcome to Welsh waters but we've got about 100 miles to go before we get to Cardiff,' declared the captain.

It was 30 August, exactly a month after the Pontwen had left Barbados. Joey knew it was late summer in Britain but the morning air had an autumnal feel to it. A cool breeze blew into Joey's face so totally different to the warm Barbadian breezes. He had never experienced this type of weather before.

Although, Barbados was always warm, he knew Britain had four distinct seasons. Acclimatising to the British weather would take time but he was determined to adjust. He'd certainly need a good overcoat otherwise Joey would freeze in the winter. He thought to himself, 'Never mind I'll get used to it.'

30 minutes after telling the West Indian crew members that they could see the Welsh coast the captain spoke again.

'We're now entering the Bristol Channel and on the port side you can see Milford Haven. Being at war the Royal Navy is using this natural harbour to assemble convoys for Gibraltar. Merchant ships are the main target for German U boats making these vessels dangerous places to work.'

Standing nearby was one of the able seamen.

'What are U boats?' Joey asked.

'They're submarines.'

Having lived in the Caribbean, Joey was relatively naïve about these things and enquired, 'What are they, Sir?'

'They go under the sea and fire torpedoes at vessels on the surface.'

During his time in Barbados, Joey had seen a few guns but by comparison his life was unsophisticated and he again asked, 'How do they work, Sir?'

'They're like a fish with an explosive device on the front, Murrell.'

'That means they must have a propellor to cut through the water.'

'Quite right, Murrell, and the Germans use them against merchant ships. They do it to stop food getting into the country.'

'Sir, I don't mean to be rude but we're carrying sugar cane. That's food isn't it.'

'Don't worry. Once we were in the Bristol Channel, we were safe. There's been no sinking here by a U boat.'

'Man, if I knew we could have been sunk, I'd have thought twice about sailing. Why hasn't there been any sinkings in the Bristol Channel?'

'We'll go into Cardiff on the high tide but most of the time the channel's too shallow for U boats. There are lots of sandbanks here which have led to many other boats sinking.'

'Gee it's good to know we're safe.'

Joey could see another large town on the port side and exclaimed, 'Able Seaman is that Cardiff?'

'No, Murrell, that's Swansea the second largest settlement in Wales. It's only about 35 miles to Cardiff so we'll be docking in about 4 hours.'

As the Pontwen had entered the Bristol Channel, Joey had noticed that the sea was blue. Nothing in Joey's mind could compare to the sea in the Caribbean which was beautifully warm with a green blue hue close to the shore. Further away the sea was sapphire blue and when he was at home in Barbados, he would swim every day.

In many ways home was a paradise but he was desperately anxious to serve the King and he hoped to make more money in Wales. Sailing ever closer to Cardiff Joey noticed the sea's colouration altering dramatically. He exclaimed, 'Sir, the sea's gone brown. It looks dirty.'

'The channel has become polluted with sewage.'

'Ugh that's nasty, Sir.'

'That's not the only reason it has a brown colour. The channel is shaped like a funnel and has a huge tidal range stirring up the mud and sand which mixes with the water making it look muddy.'

'That means it must have bad currents.'

'It can be dangerous and is the reason why ships have sunk here.'

The City of Cardiff came into view and Joey started to understand how big a city Cardiff was. Bridgetown Barbados's capital was tiny by comparison, so a big city was going to be an eyeopener for Joey. Glancing to the starboard side, he could see two islands one very steep and the other equally as flat.

Intrigued Joey asked, 'What are these two islands called?'

'Steep Holme and Flat Holme.'

'I can tell which is which.'

'Murrell, you don't need to be a genius to work that out.'

Even though the able seaman was in charge of the West Indian sailors generally he was very respectful towards them. To his credit, he refrained from making derogatory comments about black people and treated them fairly. He didn't get fed up with answering their questions, and Joey asked, 'Do any people live on these islands.'

'Steep Holme has many colonies of sea birds whereas Flat Holme has an isolation hospital.'

'Isolation from what, Sir?'

'Infectious diseases, Murrell. There have been cholera outbreaks so rather than keep infected people in the community they are sent to the island.'

'That's a really serious illness.'

'It would go rampant through the city, so people have to be isolated.'

'I can see the sense in that.'

'However, Flat Holme is a famous island because an Italian named Marconi sent the first wireless signal across the water from there to Lavernock Point on the mainland which is just off our port side.'

Joey would never have been able to envisage the hustle and bustle of a port like Cardiff but as the tramp steamer approached the dock, he was about to experience the frenetic nature of this vibrant dock area. There were countless warehouses and winches to load cargo onto vessels and more ships than he'd ever seen before. God willing, he would be able to serve the King and earn a decent wage, subsequently raising his standard of living.

Thankfully, there was ample work in this port city because it was the coal capital of the world. Rail links had been developed to Cardiff from the Welsh valleys allowing 10.5 million tonnes of coal to be brought to the port for export around the world. It was Joey's aim to work on merchant ships supporting the war effort.

Originally, it had been his intention to sign up to go to the front line to fight in Europe against the Germans. Although, 16,000 men from the Caribbean volunteered to fight, they were initially prevented from going into combat against white Europeans. Joey found it unbelievable that the colour of his skin prevented him fighting.

What a bizarre way for an ethnic group to express their superiority over another. British soldiers were killing Germans but blacks were prevented from fighting alongside them even though they were on the same side. Fighting aside, Caribbean men were assigned very dangerous jobs on the European front.

Black soldiers carried ammunition, built roads, railways and dug trenches. German snipers would target Caribbean men and they were also well within range of enemy artillery.

Although, the British Government would not allow black men to fight, they eventually decided to enlist these men into the British West Indies Regiment founded in 1915. True to the discriminatory nature of British society, the regiment's officers were all white. Joey decided to serve the British war effort in the best way he could by enlisting in the Merchant Navy as a donkey man.

It quickly dawned on him that this was no soft option; Joey would be working in the engine room, the area of any ship targeted by German U boats. Always below the surface German torpedoes would slam into a ship's hull devastating the engine room, invariably sinking the ship. If these merchant ships failed to bring in food the British people would starve.

Arriving in Cardiff, the crew of the Pontwen assembled on deck to be paid for their service. Having packed up his kit bag, Joey slung it over his shoulder and joined the ship's company. Approximately, half the crew were black and they'd been aboard four weeks. One of the able seamen paid the crew 35 shillings per week.

Joey was paid 140 shillings in seven one-pound notes. Having been born into a poor home in Barbados Joey had never possessed much money. Always optimistic Joey thought he would have no problem finding lodgings in a boarding house in a port as busy as Cardiff. Looking at the countless ships moored at the quayside Joey was confident he'd always be able to work. Securing his money in a belt, Joey left the Pontwen which had been his home for four weeks.

Chapter 5

Joey Murrell headed along the dockside passing numerous tramp steamers as he went. Such high numbers of vessels substantiated the claim that Cardiff was one of the largest coal exporting ports in the world. In front of him was a distinctive large red brick building so Joey decided to head in that direction.

Two thoughts were occupying his mind. Lodgings were a priority because whereas you could sleep outside in the Caribbean this was not an option in Cardiff if one wanted to remain healthy. Thought also had to be given to finding work because although, temporarily financially secure Joey would have to continue supporting himself. Walking towards Joey was another seaman.

Being much lighter in colour Joey knew this man was surely Arabic. Dressed in traditional clothes he wore an ankle length white gown with long sleeves and sported a turban. Joey knew this to be the traditional garb for a man from the Middle East. Joey approached the man greeting him politely, 'Good day, Sir. Are you a sailor?'

'I am and I've lived in Cardiff for a few years.'

'Is there plenty of work here?'

'Most of the time there's no problem getting work.'

'Oh, that's good to hear.'

'I've never been to the Welsh Valleys but coal comes in on the trains from the mines and tramp steamers then take it to different parts of Europe.'

'By the way, I'm Joey Murrell and what's your name?'

'Just call me Abdul. I take it you've just come from the Caribbean in the hope of supporting the King in the World War. I'm from Aden in Yemen.'

'Quite right, Abdul. I realise that I can't go to the frontline to fight but I can work on merchant ships.'

'I'm not really interested in the war even though Britain has affiliations with my country. I just want to work. By the way, Joey, working on ships is very dangerous because German U boats sink many of them.'

'I'm determined to serve the King so let's hope I keep out of trouble.'

'Let me tell you, Joey, the coal business is massive in Wales. There are over one hundred coal exporting businesses in Cardiff with three hundred ships.'

'That'll suit me fine. I was heading towards that red brick building.'

'You mean the Pierhead Building where the Bute Dock Company are based.'

'Man, that's a stunning building.'

'Some man called the Third Marquis of Bute built the dock and he was believed to be the richest man in the world.'

'That's unbelievable, Abdul. I wouldn't mind a bit of his wealth.'

'Aye, there's a lot of others like you.'

'Not that many years ago, this was a really posh area with so many merchants and bankers working here. Because of this the elaborate buildings you see were built and Mount Stuart Square was developed.'

'Are they still here?'

'Na they moved to the suburbs and while this might not be the posh area it used to be, people are very contented and get on well together. We've got so many different nationalities living here.'

'How many?'

'About fifty.'

'That's amazing.'

'It is. We've got Somalis, Yemenis, Spanish, Italians, Irish and lots of people like you from the Caribbean. You'll be okay here.'

'That's great to know.'

'They call this area Tiger Bay.'

'Why?'

'Well, it was a name first used in London's East End and to the best of my knowledge it was popular slang used by sailors about any notoriously dangerous dock area. Just north of the old east London docks were Blue Gate Fields which was a slum area. They used the name Tiger Bay here.'

'Blimey, it's still a strange name.'

'Aye, you've got to understand the original tigers of Tiger Bay were the prostitutes earning their living close to Bute Street. Sailors would go up to Charlotte Street and Whitmore Lane to pay for these women's services.'

'I'll have to look out for these girls and give them a wide berth. What I need at the moment are lodgings.'

'You'll be spoilt for choice. There's loads of lodging houses in Bute Street.'

'Thanks, Abdul.'

'By the way, Joey, the best one is run by Annie Sleeman, a girl from some place in the valleys called Mountain Ash. Be careful not to miss it because it's above the General Store. Go through the door up the stairs and Annie will be there.'

'All the best.'

Kit bag over his shoulder, Joey negotiated his way out of the docks and came to the bottom of Bute Street. There were numerous shops, many with boarding houses above them. Barbados had bars but for the first time, Joey could see British pubs. He walked past one called the Packet, which was packed with seamen who were loud and boisterous.

Beer flowing freely had released their inhibitions. Joey thought who could blame them when they were risking their lives at sea to export Welsh coal. These were not normal times. The Great War had started meaning German U boats were the scourge of merchant seamen.

A few hours in the pub gave them a chance to unwind from the unbearable tension of their job. One sailor staggering in the doorway shouted, 'Come on in, Sailor Boy.'

Timidly Joey replied, 'I'm looking for a boarding house.'

'Ah, that can wait. Get in here on the beer with us.'

Joey had never been one for excessive drink. He liked a few beers but getting sloshed was not the Joey way. Politely, he replied, 'Thanks very much but I need to find a bed for the night. I'm looking for Annie Sleeman's boarding house.'

'Sailor Boy, she's the best-looking filly in Tiger Bay. She's a Welsh girl but treats us well. Just go up those steps over there.'

Crossing the street, Joey knew he had to be switched on to the traffic on the road. There was little traffic in Barbados making the streets a place where one did not need to be cautious. An old horse and cart with food and bottles of beer was making its way up the street. Wealthy bankers and merchants drove cars which people had to look out for.

On the other side of a high wall was a train with numerous trucks carrying coal. Grey, white smoke billowed from the funnel, helping to create a temporary smokescreen. Joey had seen a railway in Barbados where the engine was much smaller than this one. The train in Bridgetown was a narrow-gauge line used for transporting some passengers and moving sugar cane.

Crossing the road, Joey was oblivious to the tram coming towards him until the driver rang the bell, causing him to scarper to the other side of the road. He reflected that being hit by this vehicle would not be a good start to life in Cardiff. Nevertheless, it missed him but it was a very close call. Averting his gaze, he could see the general store and the open door to the side of it.

Poking his head in, he climbed the stairs to a door with a sign, 'Knock and wait.' Any carpet left on the stairs was threadbare and the walls were painted a dark green. Appearing dowdy, Joey hoped that the rooms were an improvement on the passageway. Following the instruction on the door, Joey waited for someone to answer.

Inside Joey could hear a shuffling noise and someone came to open the door. An older man with a limp appeared in the doorway. In a distinctive voice, which in time Joey would come to realise was a Cardiff accent, he said, 'Oh, Sailor Boy, are you looking for lodgings?'

'I was surprised when you answered the door. I thought this place was owned by Annie Sleeman.'

'It is, mate. I do odd jobs for her. At one time I used to go to sea but after a winch crushed my foot I've had to stay ashore.'

'That's unlucky.'

'Yeah, I had my foot chopped off and I've got a false one. It's better than nothing.'

'Oh, I'm sorry to hear that.'

'I don't enjoy sympathy, so I'll get Annie.'

He coarsely shouted 'Annie' at the top of his voice. Immediately, she came to the door. Joey was astounded when this young woman who was probably a little younger than he was stood in front of him. Stunningly beautiful with blonde hair, her good looks mesmerised Joey.

At first, he stood open mouthed bewitched by this drop dead gorgeous youthful female. He had been expecting someone much older to own a boarding house rather than a young lady. He was startled by how attractive she was, and it took his breath away. Suddenly, Joey came back to earth when she said, 'Are you looking for lodgings?'

'Yes, I've just got off a boat from the West Indies.'

'I can see where you're from. I've been working here long enough. We get sailors from all around the world.'

'How much is a bed?'

'One night is 2 shillings, but if you stay a week, it'll cost you 12 and six.'

'That's fine by me. I've just been paid, so I'll pay for the week.

'What's your name?'

'Joey Murrell, ma'am.'

'No need for the ma'am, just call me Annie.'

'Okay, Annie.'

'You need to know I take the money up front. There's four to a room and you must make your bed. We've got a bathroom with a toilet but you'll have to pay for a bath.'

'So how much is that, Annie?'

'Threepence to cover the cost of heating the water.'

'That seems okay.'

'I think it's very fair. Some of the other boarding houses charge more.'

'What about breakfast, Annie?'

'It's sixpence for breakfast. There's always bread, cheese and pressed ham. Occasionally, we have boiled eggs.'

'Count me in, Annie.'

'Oh, by the way, there's no drinking alcohol in the room and you're not allowed to bring women in.'

She escorted Joey to his accommodation. When she opened the door, he was pleasantly surprised. Joey could see four beds in a well decorated room. This delightful environment was in stark contrast to the dowdily decorated stairway. A comfortable bed with clean linen brought a smile to his face.

He was certain this would be a good place to stay. Joey was anxious to keep on Annie's good side and said, 'I'll keep my bed tidy. Could you tell me where the nearest Anglican church is?'

'That's St Mary's Church at the top end of Bute Street. Why did you ask that?'

'In Barbados my whole family went to church every Sunday. The English brought the Anglican church to Barbados and many Barbadian people attend services weekly.'

'That's good to hear because many of my clients spend all their time in the pub and use the local prostitutes for sex. They are forever spending their time in Whitmore Lane and Charlotte Street.'

'I would never go to one of those women.'

'Well, I can tell you, Joey, there's Bible study tonight at 7:00 pm.'

'Would they welcome a stranger.'

'All are welcome in the Lord's House.'

'I need to put my possessions in my bedside cabinet.'

'Just a word of warning, Joey. Don't leave your money there. Some men wouldn't think twice about stealing it to spend on drink or women of ill repute.'

'Thanks, Annie, for the advice.'

Leaving the boarding house at 6:30 pm, Joey made his way along Bute Street. Passing some impressive buildings on his way to the church, he became aware that coal had brought great wealth to some businessmen in Tiger Bay. The Packet pub had been named after the packet ships carrying mail to and from British outposts. In Bridgetown, Joey had never seen structures like the Cory Building.

This was built by very wealthy brothers with extensive interests in the coal trade. Pillars on the building had been splendidly decorated with grand designs on them. Taking time to look at this impressive work caused Joey to ponder how some people in this area had established themselves as wealthy businessmen.

Just as Joey was studying the faces on one of the wondrous pillars a woman stepped out of the shadows. She was scantily dressed and with heavy makeup. Her intention was to snare a sailor who had been at sea for weeks and was looking for sex.

'Sailor Boy. Would you like me to show you a good time?'

'It's not for me, thanks. I'm on my way to church.'

'Surely you'd prefer to have fun with me, luv.'

'My family have always followed Biblical teaching, so the answer has to be no. It's important I remain true to my beliefs.'

This Tiger Bay prostitute solicited for sex and on nearly every occasion would have been successful with men who could have been at sea for months. On this occasion, she was perplexed at this refusal and was dumbstruck for a few seconds.

'Are you sure you're not one of them. Those men who doesn't like women?'

'No worry on that score but I was brought up in the church in Barbados and we're expected to act morally. Nothing against you, Madam, but the answer has to be no. Besides, I'm on my way to Saint Mary the Virgin Church. Am I going in the right direction?'

Deciding it was no good persisting with this sailor boy, she replied, 'You are,' and went on her way.

Walking for another 15 minutes, Joey could easily pick out the church. It was much larger than the Anglican churches in Barbados and had obviously been built to cater for the burgeoning population in this area of the city. Business brought people into the area and their spiritual welfare needed catering for.

Joey knew this would be a diverse worshipping community because so many different nationalities had arrived in this thriving port. Opening the door, he was not disappointed because inside was a large group of people of all creeds and colours, including Annie Sleeman. Tiger Bay inhabitants had learned the importance of living together in harmony and in Joey's mind this was a model for the world to follow.

World War I in Europe had just started and it seemed to Joey that people would always find something to argue about. As he looked at the group harmoniously studying the Bible together, Joey was heartened by their love for one another.

For a while Joey stood at the back until the vicar saw him and called, 'My son, come join us.'

Annie Sleeman turned around and said, 'Joey's in my boarding house. He can come by me.'

Up to this point, Joey had only seen one side of Annie. She was a businesswoman but in this different environment she showed herself as a caring individual, welcoming Joey with open arms. Over the next few months, Joey managed to get plenty of work at sea, enabling him to stay long term at Annie's boarding house.

As their relationship developed, she began to divulge more information about herself. Having been born and brought up in Mountain Ash, a mining village in the South Wales valleys, she was left some money by a relative who had died. Ever the businesswoman, she decided to move to Cardiff because it would be financially beneficial. Annie saw relocation as an opportunity to amass money by buying a boarding house and renting out rooms.

It was not long before the relationship blossomed. Joey had been struck by how attractive Annie was the first time he met her. What he didn't know at that initial meeting was how handsome she thought Joey was but more importantly he was a kind soul with a loving heart. These were characteristics she was looking for in a lifelong partner.

Fortunately, she found these qualities in Joey Albert Murrell and on Saturday, 20 January 1917, the couple decided to endorse their love for one another by marrying at St Mary, the Virgin Church Butetown.

Chapter 6

Happily married Joey and Annie lived in rooms by the boarding house in Bute Street. Merchant seamen of different nationalities visited Cardiff ensuring Annie had a thriving business. This provided a steady income but Joey's passion involved going to sea, even though this could be a dangerous occupation. German U boats continually preyed on British merchant vessels to stop food and other commodities getting into the country.

Being an island there was a benefit to being surrounded by water, making it difficult for an enemy to invade. The detrimental side of this was that the only way goods could be brought in was by ship. Germany decided to sink as many merchant ships as they could in an effort to deprive the British people of food.

On 17 July 1917, Joey Murrell left his rooms in Bute Street and went to the dock gate, looking for a berth on a ship. This was early morning on a summer's day. It was pleasant with mist swirling in the air. As Joey stood with other men waiting for the ship's owners to begin recruiting, some men were talking about the night before in the Packet, while others spoke about their visit to the red-light area.

Being married, Joey realised through his marriage vows that he'd made a commitment to Annie. He avoided being drawn into this frivolous conversation by his contemporaries. Being completely dedicated to Annie, nothing would deter him from fulfilling his marital obligations. Besides, he was hoping that she was pregnant, bringing even greater responsibility.

Although, pleasantly mild, as Joey exhaled his breath condensed producing a light cloud which very quickly dissipated and eventually disappeared. He could see a ship's owner and Able Seaman approaching the group hoping to be recruited. Reaching the assembled men, the Able Seaman said, 'We need a donkey man for the SS Llanover. It'll be taking coal to Norway.'

Joey shouted out, 'I'm your man. I was a donkey man on the Pontwen.'

'The job's yours. What's your name?'

'Joey Murrell, Sir.'

'Murrell, make your way to the wharf over to the right. You'll be responsible with a bloke called Andy for the donkey engines. You'll be winching the coal on board and then later in the engine room operating another donkey engine to produce auxiliary power for the propellers.'

'I'm on my way.'

'Murrell, are you a bit slow? You haven't asked about wages. Does that mean you don't want to be paid?'

'Sorry, Sir.'

'You'll earn 21 shillings.'

'That's good pay, Sir.'

'We're going north to the Scottish coast which is particularly dangerous. There's a lot of U boats that'll be looking to sink us.'

'That's okay, Sir. I understand the dangers. I'll start loading the coal.'

The other potential recruits looked disappointed. Many had children and no work meant no food. Joey was aware that some men were desperate and on occasions, he'd stood aside for other sailors with families to work. This time he was the only donkeyman at the gate, so he was guaranteed the job.

He still felt compassion for the others who were desperate. Joey climbed the gangplank to be greeted by another able seaman, 'Follow me. I'll show you where you'll be sleeping. You can leave your kit here and report on deck.'

'I'll be there shortly.'

'Don't hang about. We need to get the coal aboard.'

As quick as a flash, Joey was on deck. He was keen to create a good impression. Joey thought the ship might employ him again if he did a satisfactory job. He immediately started the donkey engine to give the winches enough power to start lifting coal.

'Well done, Murrell, you're a good worker.'

'I pride myself on my reliability, Sir.'

'That's a good trait in your character, Murrell.'

'Thank you, Sir.'

'When you're finished here, we need you in the engine room to use a donkey engine to give additional power to the main propellers. We need to make good speed.'

'No problem, Sir.'

'By the way, you'll be working shifts with another donkey man. We need to keep the engines going flat out 24 hours a day. Don't worry, you'll be earning your money.'

'I've got it, Sir. By the way, what's his name?'

'His name is Andy Jones. You'll be like ships passing in the night because you'll be so busy.'

Joey went to the engine room to meet Andy. Entering the room, a gigantic man strode forward and put out his hand for Joey to shake. His whopping hand easily swallowed Joey's little mitt.

'What's your name and which island are you from?'

'My name's Joey and I'm from Barbados. I came over on the Pontwen. What about you?'

'I'm from Jamaica. We'll be working 12 hours a day each. Now we can work six on and six off, which would be better than working 12 hours straight off.'

'I agree with that, Andy. It means we'll be able to maintain concentration more easily.'

'We'll toss a coin to see who starts a 6-hour stint first.'

Andy took the coin from his pocket, placed it in his hand, turning it over to prove it wasn't a double header.

'I trust you, Andy. I'll have heads.'

Tossing it into the air Andy caught it and put it on the back of his hand.

'Tails, Joey.'

'That's fine.'

'Well, I'll begin at 6:00 pm tonight because that's the time we said. Until then, we'll work together on providing power for the winches.'

From the beginning of their relationship, the two men appeared to hit it off. Blending well meant there was a smooth transition at each shift change over ensuring no flatlining in power. This could only happen if the donkey engine maintained maximum throttle.

Tuesday, 17 July 1917, the SS Llanover departed on its journey to Norway laden with coal. The ship was heading for Oslo on the southern Norwegian coast. Initially, sailing into the Bristol Channel at high tide, they headed for the Pembrokeshire coast, then turned north towards the West Coast of Scotland. Leaving the British Isles behind, the Llanover would turn northeast to Norway.

It was 6:00 pm on the third day at sea when Joey went to the engine room for the changeover. The Llanover was sailing off the West Coast of Scotland in

Faslane Bay when the donkey engine developed a minor fault which Andy corrected. Before departing for a well-earned rest, he pointed out the problem to Joey.

On deck the watch spotted a torpedo heading straight towards the Llanover. A German U boat had launched the weapon as part of its policy to sink British merchant vessels and like a fish coming at high speed the Llanover was an easy target. Travelling below the surface, the ship's watch could see this potentially destructive weapon designed to disrupt the supply lines to and from Britain. Ship's watch rang the alarm but it was too late.

The weapon detonated against the ship's hull. As the men went to the rear of the engine there was an almighty explosion. An incredible boom resulted in a jolting sensation unlike anything the men in the engine room had ever experienced before. Germans saw merchant vessels as fair game and decided to sink it.

In the early part of the war, the German policy had involved giving the crew a chance to use the lifeboats to leave the ship. Then the sinking would take place. As the war progressed, fighting in Europe had become more bitter and acrimonious, so allowing a crew to man the lifeboats had been replaced by a sink on sight blueprint.

The Llanover had been hit with a torpedo to the portside. Being below the waterline the engine room took a direct hit. Suddenly, a busy workplace, which was a hive of activity, was no longer able to function. An almighty explosion had opened a huge hole in the hull of the ship.

Voices of trimmers, firemen and mechanics eagerly working as a team were replaced by screams. Manically hysterical noises overwhelmed Joey's senses. Severed limbs and horrific blast injuries were testament to the destructive power of this lethal weapon. Joey and the others were not soldiers but brave merchant seamen carrying out an imperative and unquestionably dangerous job.

Even though they were unarmed these men were considered fair game in war. Alongside the explosion, fires broke out and the Llanover's fate was sealed. A sinking was inevitable. Copious quantities of water were passing through the cavity, causing the ship to list. Voices on deck could be heard screaming.

'Man the lifeboats,' bellowed the captain.

'Forget the engine room, those fellas didn't have a chance. Every man for himself because we'll sink quickly,' screamed an able seaman.

Frantic activity followed as crew fought to get the lifeboats into the sea. In the ensuing panic, men jumped into the water, and unless they could get into a lifeboat quickly, they could well become a victim of hypothermia. If it had been the winter months, a relatively short period in the water would have killed them.

Pandemonium followed as efforts were made to lower lifesaving vessels into the water. Time was at a premium because the Llanover wouldn't float much longer.

In the engine room, Joey and Andy had gone behind the donkey engine to inspect the problem just as the torpedo hit the ship. This action had saved their lives because the donkey engine had taken the full force of the blast. Both men were faced with an appalling situation. A huge cavity in the hull allowed water to pour in.

Thinking quickly Joey called out, 'If we try to leave through the blast hole, the force of the water will wash us into the boat and probably kill us.'

'We've got no chance, Joey.'

'There is a chance. Just give the hole time to fill with more water. Then if you were like me in Barbados, we used to swim underwater for a long time looking for lobsters.'

'That's right but the water was warm. The water is freezing here.'

'It's our only chance. We go under the water when the blast hole is completely covered and swim out of the cavity. We then need to make sure we get away from the ship as fast as we can because it will sink quickly and drag us under.'

Both men climbed onto the donkey engine waiting for the torpedo hole to be covered with water. Timing was the key if they were to swim through the hole. Waiting for the water pressure to equalise was incredibly stressful. Joey shouted, 'All the other boys in the engine room will drown.'

'Yes. Some of them are so badly injured they've got no chance.'

'Just wait now Andy and I'll give the word.'

'It's your call, Joey.'

Joey waited and watched for the hole to cover. To enable them to swim both men removed their shoes as the ship's hull filled. Their legs were in the water. Waiting and watching Joey could see the hole begin to disappear. He shouted, 'Deep breath now, Andy.'

Inhaling deeply both men went under the water. It was lucky that this was summer because the sea was still cold but not icy as it would be in the winter months. The two men gasped as they went under the water. At least they were giving themselves a fighting chance.

Adrenaline coursed through their veins, producing the determination needed to succeed. Hopefully, there'd be some lifeboats in the water to take them to safety. For the time being skills learned underwater in the Caribbean saved their lives. Resurfacing they could see lifeboats hanging about 20 feet above the water.

In calm conditions, lowering lifeboats would normally be a straightforward procedure but in the ensuing panic mistakes were made causing lives to be lost. Some seamen were killed when they were smashed into the side of the vessel by the force of the water. There was one lifeboat in the water with two men in it. Hurriedly swimming to it, Andy and Joey were hauled from the sea.

Blankets stored in the boat were wrapped around both men as they sat and watched the Llanover completely fill with water and finally submerge beneath the waves. A donkey engine had saved Joey and Andy. Only four men were left alive from the whole crew. As the men in the lifeboat sat and pondered their salvation they gave thanks to God for their deliverance from death. They would be going home but many families would be left fatherless.

Chapter 7

A bigger lifeboat picked up Joey and his fellow survivors. Andy and Joey both realised that if this sinking had happened in the winter, the sea would have been too cold to survive. Andy was grateful for Joey's knowledge about water pressure. Letting the hole in the hull cover with water saved their lives.

Although, stressful waiting for this scientific phenomenon to occur, he realised any impetuosity would have meant they were washed away. Being able to climb onto the donkey engine, which was at a higher level than the hole in the hull, had contributed to the men being saved. Thankfully, both were going home to Tiger Bay.

This unique society in Cardiff had started to become a melting pot of different cultures and whatever your creed or colour, people were welcome here. Annie was white and Joey black which was not unusual in this unique society.

News had reached Cardiff that the SS Llanover had been sunk by a German U boat and there were only a few survivors. Annie pessimistically assumed Joey was lost with the ship and had already dressed in black as a mark of respect for her husband's sacrifice. Many families had suffered the loss of loved ones due to the horrific fighting in Europe, so Joey would just have been another casualty of the harrowingly gruesome World War.

Arriving in Cardiff by train, Joey walked down Bute Street, climbed the stairs to the boarding house and knocked the door. Annie opened the door and there in front of her stood Joey. She was flabbergasted and at first Annie was speechless. It was as if she'd seen an apparition.

She knew most of the crew were lost, but everyone in Tiger Bay was aware of the danger confronting those working in a ship's engine room. This led her to assume there was no way Joey could survive. Bursting into tears she exclaimed, 'I took it as read that you were one of the deceased.'

'You're not getting rid of me that easily.'

Annie flung herself at Joey, hugging him with such a force that he thought he was not going to be able to breathe. Overjoyed at seeing her husband, she couldn't contain her emotions. She blurted out, 'Joey Murrell, I love you.'

'I feel exactly the same way about you, Annie.'

Reunited with Annie, Joey knew he'd have to go back to sea in the future but for the time being the couple were thrilled to be able to enjoy each other's company.

'You're not going anywhere, Joey Murrell.'

'Well not for the time being in any case.'

Hostilities between Germany and the Allies ended on 11 November 1918. Although, going to sea was still dangerous Joey would no longer have to worry about being blown to smithereens. Welsh coal had brought many different nationalities to Cardiff.

People from all corners of the globe looked for work in the Docks area, making it a truly cosmopolitan society. In 1914, there were 700 black people living in Cardiff but by April 1919, the numbers had increased to 3,000.

During the war, black seamen had been employed on ships because the shipowners could undercut wages by employing foreign sailors. Following the conclusion of hostilities in Europe, many men of African, Arab and Asian descent were discharged from the army, significantly increasing ethnic minority numbers further. Docks trade picked up exponentially but not enough to absorb all those who wanted to work there.

Employers gave preference to white men, though there were still many without work. A housing shortage was created causing many whites to scapegoat non-whites who'd bought houses to fill with lodgers. Antipathy towards non-whites who married white women also increased.

Tensions in Tiger Bay came to a head on 11 June 1919, between white soldiers returning from the Great War and non-whites living locally. This created a pernicious effect within the Tiger Bay community. Annie and Joey were caught up in this developing animosity towards ethnic minorities.

Determined to protect Annie and their property, Joey declared, 'Annie, we need to protect the house.'

'How do we do that?'

'We'll board it up.'

'You're right, because Bute Street houses have had their windows smashed.'

'We also need to arm ourselves.'

'With what, Joey. We haven't got guns.'

'We'll make clubs and hide in the basement.'

'I heard that the occupants of a Malay shop have had to climb on the roof to protect themselves.'

'It's disgraceful, Annie, because sailors and soldiers from ethnic minorities more than did their bit in the war.'

'I'm really frightened.'

'I'll break up one of the wooden dining chairs and shape it into a good club. If anyone comes in the house, I'll hit them on the bonce. That'll give them something to think about.'

'Please look after me, Joey, I'm a white woman and these people hate mixed marriages.'

'I survived a sinking ship so don't worry, if they come near you, I'll sort them out.'

Rioting continued for three days and although two men broke into Annie and Joey's place, he dementedly confronted them with his homemade club. These two men were hell bent on driving out Joey because he was black and had employment. One was tall and the other shorter with cross eyes. Both were unshaven and would invoke terror and menace in most people.

The taller one shouted, 'Get out of this town and go back to your own country.'

While the shorter one screamed, 'You married a white girl. You dirty black bastard.'

Here were two intruders who'd bitten off more than they could chew. Joey Murrell refused to be intimidated by these interlopers and he manically swung his club, catching the taller man a glancing blow to the shoulder. Experiencing Joey's determination to hold his ground, the shorter, cross-eyed one exclaimed, 'This one's mad. Let's go.'

Holding his shoulder, the tall man bid a hasty retreat, closely followed by his short friend. Joey had told Annie to take cover under the table. She was incredibly grateful for her husband's courageous stance.

'Thanks, Joey, you're so brave.'

'There's no way I'll cower down to these people.'

Three days later, the riots were over in Cardiff. Two members of the ethnic community were dead and white and black people were arrested. The law in Britain should have been seen to treat people as equals but on this occasion, blacks were dealt with more harshly. The die had been cast in 1919 and this discrimination against ethnic minorities would be a scourge on British society for the foreseeable future.

1921 was a momentous year in the lives of Annie and Joey Murrell. Annie gave birth to a son and the couple named him after his father. Both parents considered Joey Junior a real gift from God who'd hopefully continue the Murrell family line.

Young Joey was christened in Saint Mary the Virgin Church, Bute Street maintaining the family tradition of belonging to the Anglican faith. Young Joey attended Mount Stuart School from 1926 until 1935 after which he left at fourteen years of age.

Acquiring employment at this time was difficult and young Joey was sent to stay with his aunt Mary in London. The capital was becoming more ethnically diverse and it would be easier for Joey to find work there. Although, guaranteed lodgings, he would have to stand on his own two feet. His aunt's home was in Poplar a part of the Tower Hamlets Borough in the East End.

Joey was anxious to find employment and to help with this he purchased the Evening Standard newspaper. During the evening, he would forensically trawl through the job vacancies. He realised that his dad earned good money when he was employed but working as a seaman was really unpredictable. Joey wanted regular work, subsequently giving him a steady income.

After a few weeks, he saw what he was looking for. A world-renowned hotel, the London Hilton in Mayfair, was looking for a bellboy and Joey applied, successfully gaining a post. His work on the door was really important giving him the opportunity to meet eminent dignitaries from around the world. Young Joey appreciated the importance of his job because a bellboy could create a favourable first impression for guests.

In October 1935, Joey was still quite naïve when a car drew up outside the hotel. A well-dressed dapper individual with a perfectly trimmed moustache, sat in a car waiting for his chauffeur to open the door. A more mature individual called Jimmy manned the door with Joey.

'Look who it is,' exclaimed Jimmy.

'What do you mean?'

'It's Johnny Hughes.'

'Is he important?'

'He's one of the richest people in the world.'

'Which country is he from?'

'Where else but the USA. All the wealthiest people come from there.'

'What does he do?'

'He's a business magnate and he's worth millions.'

Joey was immaculately dressed in a light brown coat with dark brown edges and a top hat. Standing as erect as he could made him look taller than he actually was. This was a significant front of house job, making it mandatory that Joey created a favourable impression for clients who were paying a fortune to stay at the hotel.

'Do I look okay, Jimmy?'

'You look top drawer. Americans always tip. This one's really generous.'

Leaving his car, Johnny Hughes climbed the steps and walked towards Joey.

'Good day, Sir.'

'It's been an excellent day young man.'

'Oh that's good, Sir.'

'Yes, young man the stock market's performing really well. Shares in my company are at an all-time high.'

'Oh I'm really pleased, Sir. You're not looking for someone from Cardiff to run one of your companies are you,' asked Joey in a cheeky voice.

'Not at present, Son, but you'll go far. Can you take my bags to the room?'

'I'm on my way. Nothing's too much trouble.'

'I'm in room 101.'

Joey picked up the cases and went to reception for the key. Knowing that room 101 was a plushily furnished suite Joey thought to himself, 'This one really has lots of money.'

Taking the lift, Joey took the luggage to the room. Opening the door, he was made aware of the opulent splendour enjoyed by the wealthy. This suite had every luxury imaginable. Joey had seen a wireless before but they were basic models compared to the high spec device in the room. Standing tall by the door Joey waited for Jonny Hughes to arrive.

This business magnate strolled confidently along the corridor. Behind him was a large entourage of assistants. As he entered the room Joey said, 'Here's your room, Sir.'

'Young man, you've been excellent and when the manager pops up later on, I'll be telling him how good you are.'

Joey was impressed with Jonny Hughes because he'd heard terrible stories from the US about a white supremacist organisation called the Ku Klux Klan who torture and kill blacks. Here was a man who seemed fair, treating all ethnicities as human beings.

'Thank you, Sir.'

Mr Hughes reached into his pocket taking out a £1 note and handed it to Joey. At this moment, Joey understood the phrase "hot under the collar". Feeling flushed with excitement, Joey had just been handed the equivalent of two days wages.

'Well done, Son. You're an excellent employee.'

'Thank you so much. I'm indebted to you.'

Joey left and returned to his position at the front of the hotel wondering which other famous people might turn up.

Chapter 8

In February 1939, Joey decided to return to Cardiff. A four-year stint in London had been good for him. Having been forced to stand on his own two feet Joey became independent and matured into a hard-working individual. Meanwhile, Hitler had risen to power in Germany and he became chancellor in 1933 with the sole aim of taking revenge for his country's defeat in World War I.

In March 1936, Hitler regained the Rhineland which the country had lost as part of the harsh reparations paid after the Great War. Recouping this land provided the desperate German people with much needed employment.

By embarking on this course of action, Hitler pushed foreign appeasement to the limit. Neville Chamberlain the much-maligned British Prime minister was the man most strongly associated with appeasing Hitler. He signed the Munich Agreement without questioning Hitler's demands that the Rhineland was rightfully German.

Many British people lacked the stomach for a fight following the terrible human cost during the Great War. Politicians such as Winston Churchill were regarded as warmongers through considering Hitler to be a real threat to world peace. Hitler continued to push his luck in Europe and in March 1939 annexed Czechoslovakia having totally disregarded the Munich Agreement.

A line in the sand was drawn that if Hitler invaded Poland Britain would declare war. It had only been twenty-one years since the end of the Great War and the continent was now facing another significant conflict.

Joey was eighteen in 1939 and thought it safer to return home to Cardiff. London would certainly be a prime target for German bombers. Cardiff would be targeted by the Germans due to the importance of the docks but it would still be significantly safer than London. Little did Joey know that a letter had been despatched to him arriving in Bute Street on 12 September 1939. Picking it up, he hurriedly opened it and read the contents.

He cried out, 'Mam, Dad, I've had a letter telling me that Parliament passed a law on 3 September giving the country the legal right to conscript me into the armed forces.'

Suddenly, Annie was perturbed blurting out, 'Who can be conscripted?'

'All men 18 to 41 years of age.'

'Oh no, that means you'll have to go.'

'I want to fight for my country'

'Your father left Barbados to join the war effort during the Great War but so many men died.'

'Mam, Hitler's got to be stopped.'

'Is the loss of life really worth it.'

Just as Annie finished speaking Joey senior came home from work at the docks.

'It looks like I'm going to be conscripted into the forces,' exclaimed young Joey.

'You'll have to go because Hitler's a real threat to world peace.'

'From my point of view, I don't want to lose my son. Look how many boys died in the Great War.'

'Love, there's no choice because if Hitler's not defeated, life won't be worth living.'

'When do you think I'll be conscripted, Dad?'

'It'll be a while but this war's going to go on for a long time.'

'That makes it worse because the wireless has been saying how Hitler has built up his armed forces,' exclaimed Annie.

'Let's hope the Americans come and help us because they'll have the equipment to sort it out,' proclaimed Joey senior.

'Mam and Dad, enough of any negative talk. Let's have a cup of tea and worry about it when I'm conscripted.'

Every morning, Joey Junior would wait anxiously by the door for the postman to arrive. War had been waging for eight months and although old enough, Joey had still not been drafted for service. The passing of each day brought a higher degree of consternation.

On the one hand, Joey wanted to fight having been regaled with stories from World War I but he realised there was a good chance he might not come home again. Waiting by the door on 24 May, a letter in a brown envelope with the letters MOD (Ministry of Defence) dropped through the letterbox. Surely this was it. With a mixture of emotions, Joey opened it to learn he was not going into the army but the RAF.

Annie heard the letterbox go and shouted, 'Is there anything there for you?'

'Yes, Mam. There's a letter from the MOD.'

'What does it say?'

'I've been drafted into the RAF.'

Joey Senior arrived on the scene blurting out, 'When do you start training?'

'I'm going to be a navigator.'

'Where are you going to train?'

'Pengam Moors in Tremorfa.'

Relieved Joey senior said, 'That's RAF Cardiff.'

Annie's anxiety level dropped realising that her son was going to be close to home for the time being. Her relief was obvious as she said, 'That's good. At least we'll get to see you when you're training.'

Ever the realist, Joey senior exclaimed, 'Being a navigator in the RAF is no less dangerous than being in the army. The Luftwaffe have excellent planes and will be trying to shoot you down.'

Trembling at this prospect, Annie in a quivering voice exclaimed, 'They'll give you training, won't they?'

'The training schedule's here, Mam.'

'Read it out. I'm starting to get really nervous.'

'Obviously, it has to be done quickly or the war would be over.'

'Hopefully, they won't cut any corners because you're precious to me, Joey.'

'Mam, you'll be a nervous wreck if you carry on.'

'I can't help it, Joey.'

Joey senior could see how stressed Annie was getting. He attempted to calm the situation and said, 'Let the lad explain what's going to happen.'

'The letter says there will be 500 hours of ground instruction, which will be in the classroom.'

'What's that in weeks?'

'It'll be about ten weeks. Then there's 100 hours in the air, which will be another three weeks.'

Maths was not one of Annie's strong points and with her anxiety levels at fever pitch, even the simplest sum was beyond her.

'How many weeks is it in total?' She asked.

'Well thirteen, Mam.'

That's an unlucky number. Oh no!'

Joey senior intervened, 'Annie, use your head because you're making this worse than it need be.'

Just like any mother, Annie couldn't help worrying and asked, 'When do you start?'

'Monday, 27, Mam.'

Employing his sense of realism, Joey Senior proclaimed, 'We need to get a move on then. Let me tell you the indomitable Murrell spirit will not be found wanting.'

Joey Junior went off to RAF Cardiff to begin training on Monday, 27 May 1940. Assembling with the other recruits, Joey was fitted for his RAF uniform and then sent for a regulation haircut. He was sure his parents would be immensely proud of him.

Remembering his childhood, when his father had told him he was stopped from fighting on the frontline in World War I because it was thought improper for blacks to kill Europeans, Joey reflected that race relations in Britain had improved slightly and he was proud to serve the king. Although, mam was a bag of nerves, Joey knew she and dad would be overjoyed that their son was in uniform.

Training was intense and no time was wasted getting recruits ready for battle. Joey learned to use a map and compass, which would be the main tools in the fight against the Germans. However, the instructors were quick to point out that intuition was the most essential ingredient if a navigator was to be successful.

Joey completed his basic training and learned that he was going to be deployed to Egypt. He would be fighting in the North African conflict, not in Europe. On 21 September 1940, Joey was given three days leave before his deployment to North Africa. Annie was overwhelmed to see Joey.

Greeting him with a big kiss she asked, 'Where will you be going, Joey?'

'I've been deployed to Egypt. We leave in five days. We'll be providing support for the Eighth Army.'

'I didn't know we were fighting in North Africa,' exclaimed Annie.

As far as she was concerned, the sooner this war was over, the better. However, Joey Senior had taken a greater interest in proceedings, pointing out, 'Annie, North Africa is a major battlefield in the war. Although, Egypt is an independent country, the United Kingdom has a major influence there.'

'Why have we got anything to do with Egypt? It's miles away. Besides most of it is sand,' exclaimed Annie.

'Mam, Britain intervened in Egyptian affairs in 1882 and it's unfortunate because the relationship between the Egyptians and British has created the growth of nationalism in Egypt. This has caused relations to deteriorate.'

Quick to defend the British stance in Egypt, Joey Senior pointed out, 'The treaty made in the last century means Egyptians have to play host to British troops but they remain neutral in the war.'

Annie was really perturbed at this point, exclaiming, 'Well, I don't know how you can welcome British soldiers and claim to be neutral.'

'Don't worry about it, love. All these political situations are complicated. We've just got to do our bit. Let's enjoy these couple of days with Joey.'

The Axis Powers originally called the Berlin Rome Axis was a military coalition responsible for starting World War II. In Europe, Italy and Germany were the two countries who formed this evil consortium. It was the Italians who first invaded Egypt in 1940, initiating a response from Britain who succeeded in driving the Italians back.

Joey was deployed to Egypt, firstly to deal with the Italian problem by providing air support for ground troops arriving in Egypt. Setting foot on Egyptian soil on 6 December 1940, Joey played a part in the final Italian defeat on 10 December. When the Italians were driven out of Egypt, he was a navigator in a Blenheim aircraft helping to secure the Egyptian border.

Defeating the Italians would not go unnoticed by Hitler. The Fuhrer was anxious to take revenge. An anticipated German response became reality in February 1941, when the Afrika Korps arrived in North Africa. Confronting the British Army at Tobruk in eastern Libya, they defeated the British successfully driving them back.

Joey realised this German army was a different proposition to the Italians. They were led by an inspirational leader named Erwin Rommel. Disappointed by defeat at Tobruk, Joey knew this was not the end of the North African Campaign because Winston Churchill would be desperate to avenge the defeat. British troops in North Africa were now led by General Montgomery.

His men became known as the Desert Rats. Joey knew Rommel would advance into Egypt in an effort to drive Britain from Egyptian soil. He and his RAF mates flew missions, blowing up German supplies, making it difficult for Rommel to refuel his tanks. Montgomery's Desert Rats were to win the day when they defeated Rommel's Afrika Korps in two battles at El Alamein just over the Egyptian border.

Rommel was defeated on 27 September 1942. Joey played his part in the war effort in a completely different way to his father because he had fought on the frontline, whereas Joey Senior had to contend himself in World War I with a role in the Merchant Navy.

Chapter 9

Joey returned home to a hero's welcome in Tiger Bay. Fortunately, the battle of El Alamein had concluded at the end of September, giving Joey the opportunity to have leave over Christmas. On 10 December, his mother stood in the middle of the road with Joey senior by her side. She failed to contain her excitement which led to her scarpering up Bute Street.

She'd never run so fast and no doubt her speed would have increased further because her apron billowing in the winter air functioned as a parachute, taking the edge off her momentum. Reaching Joey, she threw her arms around his neck, plastering kisses all over his face. She shouted, 'My lovely, Joey. You've come home to mam.'

Covered in lipstick, Joey replied, 'Mam, all the neighbours will be laughing. Blimey, you're so embarrassing.'

'I couldn't care what the neighbours think, my boy's home.'

'You could have waited until I got by the door.'

'My war hero's returned. There's no way I was waiting.'

Lovingly putting her arm around her son, the couple walked towards the more measured Joey Senior, who extended his right arm out to shake his son's hand.

'Well done, Son, home safe and sound.'

'I've got leave for a month but then I've got to report back to RAF Cardiff.'

Exuberantly Joey exclaimed, 'Let's make the most of the time we have together.'

Christmas 1942 in Bute Street was vastly different because of the war. Nevertheless, despite rationing the family was able to enjoy jerk chicken and other goodies but in the background was the thought that he would have to go back.

Sunday, 3 January 1943, just over a week before Joey was to re-join his squadron, there was a knock at the front door. Annie answered and standing in front of her was a very official looking man in a dark suit, bowler hat and carrying a suitcase.

'How can I help you, Sir?'

'I'm here with government approval. I've come to see Joey Murrell.'

'There's two Joey Murrells here.'

'We want to see the one who's in the RAF.'

'He's only just returned from North Africa. What's he done wrong?'

'Nothing at all. We just need to speak to him in private.'

'You'd better come in. I don't know what the neighbours will think.'

'You don't need to worry about that.'

'Would you like a cup of tea and I'll call Joey: he's just out feeding the pigeons.'

'That'll be nice.'

Annie walked to the back door and could see the pigeon coop door was open. She screamed at the top of her voice, 'Joey, there's a man here to see you.'

'I'll just wash my hands and I'm there.'

Swiftly washing his hands Joey enquired, 'Where is the man?'

'He's in the front room, but he's very official looking. He's having a cuppa. Do you want one as well?'

'Yes, Mam.'

Tentatively opening the door Joey entered and introduced himself.

'I'm Joey Murrell and very pleased to meet you, Sir.'

'Sit down, Murrell. What I'm about to tell you is highly classified information and must never be spoken about.'

'What do you mean, Sir?'

'If you speak to anyone about what you hear today, it is a treasonable offence.'

'What would happen?'

Suddenly, the man frighteningly gestured with an imaginary knife going across his throat.

Quaking in his boots, Joey blurted out, 'I can be trusted. I'm discreet.'

'You need to be and so will your parents.'

The door knocked and Annie brought in two cups of tea.

'There you are and there's some biscuits on the plate.'

'Very good, Mrs Murrell. Now if you could shut the door and return to the kitchen. I've heard about curtain twitchers and people who can't mind their own business. I'll be having a chat with you and your husband after I've finished with Joey.'

'I'll be in the kitchen.'

'Right, Murrell. This case is highly classified information. When you were at RAF Cardiff you spoke to colleagues about homing pigeons.'

'Yes, Sir. I keep pigeons.'

'You also said your one pigeon was the best in the world.'

'That's Laval.'

'Yes, so we've heard.'

'I went to the town of Laval in France before the war to buy him. He cost me a fortune but he's worth it. I named him after the town where I bought him.'

'We've also been told that he can find his way to Laval and back home?'

'Yes, Sir, that's true.'

'I know nothing about pigeons but you do and you're both coming into our service.'

'What service is that?'

'The Special Operations Executive. We're a secret service specialising in espionage, special reconnaissance and raids.'

'How can I do that? I've got to get back to RAF Cardiff in a few days.'

'You're out and working for us. There'll be no problem.'

'What do I have to do?'

'Laval will leave here and fly to France.'

'But, Sir, his intuition will take him straight to the town of Laval.'

'That's what we want him to do.'

'He was in his home in the market when I bought him.'

'That's where we want him to go. We've got a British spy working in the market who liaises with the French resistance. Because of its location in the centre of France, the spy ring there is going to be involved in the organisation of the invasion of France.'

'What is that, Sir?'

'Enough of that for now. Remember what you were told about classified information? Now let's find your mother.'

Opening the door Joey called out at the top of his voice, 'Mam.'

Hurrying into the room Annie nearly tripped over her slippers.

'I'm here.'

'Right, Mrs Murrell. Joey is going to be involved in classified work.'

'What does that mean?'

'If you or your husband open your mouth, it's treason.'

Annie had heard of treason but wasn't sure what it was. She asked, 'What would happen?'

'You could all go to the gallows.'

The penny quickly dropped realising that Joey would be involved in serious work.

'Trust us. We will do as we're told.'

'Joey's pigeon, Laval, will be taking coded messages to our spies in France and bringing back information vital to the war effort.'

A concerned Annie said, 'What happens if Laval gets shot?'

'The French love pigeons, so he'll probably end up in a pie!'

'Does that mean Joey won't be going back to the RAF?'

'You've got it. He'll be sending the information and picking up the replies.'

'Does that mean he's a sort of spy?'

'Got it in one, Mrs Murrell. That's why you might all get your necks stretched if you have a loose tongue.'

'I've got the message. By the way, what's your name?'

'You don't need to know my name. All you need to know is I'm the man from the Special Operations Executive. We're a secret organisation known by the initials SOE. That's all you need to know.'

Just as the man from the SOE had finished, Joey Senior came in.

'What's that I hear about loose tongues and necks being stretched.'

'I'll tell you when the man's gone, love.'

'Mr Murrell, I'm warning you to take this seriously. A loose tongue in The Packet pub will bring a packet of trouble for you and your family. Got it?'

'Got it in one, thank you.'

Young Joey was desperate to know how he would receive information.

'Sir, how will I receive the information?'

'A motorbike rider will bring the information to you. It will be coded. You will need to dispatch it and the rider will call back four days later.'

'You can trust me implicitly, Sir.'

Joey's life had just taken a turn in an unexpected direction. He would no longer need to place himself in harm's way in a flying tin can in the sky. But in many ways his work with Laval would be essential to the war effort. Military knowledge gained in North Africa taught him that if Britain and America were to free Europe from Nazi tyranny, the foundations would have to be laid through covert operations.

Joey went through the back of the house to the pigeon coop to look for Laval. Finding him, he took the pigeon in his cupped hands, kissed him and said, 'You've got a big future, Laval. I knew when I bought you I had an incredibly special animal.'

Looking straight at Laval, he appreciated this gentle, plump bird with a small bill could well play a part in the destiny of the World War. Laval's inbuilt compass function and his brain would ensure that the SOE's faith in him would be repaid. Flying into the market tower in France would be no problem for such an intelligent animal.

Deep in thought, Joey concluded that flying between his two homes would be no problem for such an astute, intuitive bird. Replacing Laval on his perch, Joey remarked, 'Look out, Adolf! Laval's going to have you.'

Messages began to arrive in Bute Street and Laval was regularly despatched, returning with other messages. These were written on small rolls of parchment and attached to his claws. These few consequential words were some of the most important ever written providing essential information for the resistance in France.

What came back on the return flight was so significant for the War Cabinet in Britain that it gave them the opportunity to plot the invasion of France. On 28 May 1944, the man from the SOE turned up at Joey's house. Joey answered the door and brought him inside.

'Is everything okay, Sir?'

'Yes, Laval's done well. Resistance activity in France has increased and many Nazis have been killed because of the bird's work, Murrell.'

'That's good, Sir.'

'Enough of that. I'm here for a special reason. 4 June is D Day.'

'What does that mean, Sir?'

'The Yanks and Brits will be landing on the Normandy beaches. What I've got in my suitcase is Laval's last message but it's the most important of all.

'Why's that, Sir?'

'Ask no questions, Murrell. Just dispatch it.'

'I will, Sir.'

'You will not see me again, Murrell. Remember, none of this has happened.'

'Of course, Sir.'

'Good day, Murrell.'

That afternoon, Joey attached the message and let Laval go. His homecoming was later than usual on 4 June. Joey was overwhelmingly relieved to see his favourite animal make it back to Tiger Bay. On the 6, Joey turned on the wireless to hear that an allied force comprising British, American and Canadian troops had landed on five Normandy beaches. American troops had landed on beaches nicknamed Utah and Omaha.

At the same time, British soldiers had stormed beaches called Gold and Sword with the Canadian military coming ashore on Juno beach. The reporter stressed that French resistance activity had increased. Europe's liberation had begun with the German Army coming under attack and being squeezed from all sides. Joey's work and more importantly Laval's had ended. It was time for Laval to retire.

On 2 September 1945, World War II ended. Tiger Bay celebrated in the only way they knew. So many different nationalities from all corners of the globe took to the streets to party. Six long years of war were at an end. Joey Junior was able to party hard with his wife a mixed race Filipino and English girl.

Beatrice Lillian Delacruz was a beautiful girl who Joey had married once his work with the SOE was over. They lived in rooms at Annie and Joey Senior's place. Their fortunes were about to change when the man from the SOE turned up once more on 8 September 1945. He knocked the door and Joey was astounded to see him.

'What's wrong, Murrell?'

'Just shocked to see you, Sir.'

'Well done, Murrell. I've good news '

'What's that, Sir?'

'Your bird's been awarded the Dickens medal.'

'Never heard of that, Sir.'

'It's awarded for animal gallantry. Your bird carried vital information changing the outcome of the war. No questions, Murrell, and by the way we paid you a good salary but I've also got a cheque here from Mr Churchill as a reward for your service. Good day, Murrell.'

Closing the door, Joey exclaimed, 'The bird be buggered. He's got a name Laval and as far as I'm concerned, he's the most amazing animal in the world.'

Joey opened the cheque and was startled. His hand began to quiver. He'd been handed a small fortune.

Screaming at the top of his voice, 'Beattie, we can buy the house in Adelaide Street.'

Part 3
The Fosters Arrive in Cardiff

Chapter 10

Ronald Foster left his cabin as the Empire Windrush sailed past Southend on its way to Tilbury Docks. This venture was the biggest gamble of his life. It was 1957 and Ronald had left his wife and young family behind in St Kitts. As the Windrush sailed into the Thames estuary, Ronald was only twenty-six years of age and there was a tear in his eye as he caught his first glimpse of the mother country.

There could be no greater contrast between his home in the Caribbean where the sun shone incessantly. At home, January was the dry season but as he looked towards Tilbury Docks, he was confronted by a low grey cloud hanging like a pall over the dock. It was dark, gloomy and cold, all so hugely different from St Kitts.

A sunless sky meant the temperature was no more than five degrees Celsius, a full twenty-five degrees cooler than St Kitts. As the Empire Windrush drew closer to Tilbury Docks, Ronald's emotions were all over the place. When he felt like this, he would say that he had "a head like a box full of frogs".

During his time in the Caribbean, Ronald had been an academic highflyer. As an eighteen year old, he won a scholarship to the University of the West Indies. There was only one problem, the university was in Jamaica, an island a thousand miles from St Kitts. Such a distance presented poor Caribbean families with a dilemma. Engaging in higher education was a non-starter because of the considerable financial commitment.

In St Kitts, Ronald became the editor of *The Democrat* newspaper based in Basseterre, the capital of the island. He earned his spurs by working as a reporter but possessing a good intellect he was promoted to editor. Any newspaper editor in London's Fleet Street would have commanded an eye watering salary.

Even though Ronald's work in St Kitts demanded an important level of expertise and proficiency, he was poorly paid. It was this that prompted him to come to England so he could raise his family's standard of living. The plan was to move his wife Isabelle and the three children when he found employment and a place to live.

Ronald was immensely proud of being a citizen of the British Commonwealth and totally committed to serving the Queen. This citizenship entitled him to travel to Britain. Following the cessation of World War II, the British government were looking for Caribbean peoples to work in the mother country.

He borrowed money to come here believing Britain to be a land of milk and honey. Ronald was a committed royalist and as a newspaper reporter, he would often write articles relaying information to the St Kitts people about the new Queen and her deceased father King George VI. It was Ronald's opinion that the Royal Family was a wonderful institution and he couldn't understand why a minority of people wanted to end this special tradition.

So great was his commitment that he could often be heard singing *God Save the Queen* when he was showering.

Isabelle would shout, 'Ronald, for God's sake sing something else. You sound like the cats' choir.'

'Isabelle, no one's greater than the Queen. Look what her father did during the war when he stayed in London despite the bombing. By the way, don't forget the Queen Mother who stayed with him.'

'Look, Ronald, I hold the Queen in high esteem but she's not greater than God.'

'I'll give in on that one, Isabelle.'

'Well, for Lord's sake sing a hymn instead or the neighbours will need ear plugs.'

Ronald thought his young family Algernon, Perry and Lynne could only benefit from him emigrating to Britain. The plan was Ronald would establish himself and they'd come to Britain at a later date. At the conclusion of war in Europe, Britain extended an invitation for peoples in its Empire to help rebuild the country after the carnage of World War II.

Ronald further justified his move by telling Isabelle, 'There's no better education system than the British set up. If children work hard in Britain they can go to university. There'd be little chance of the kids going to university if we stayed in St Kitts.'

Isabelle was in full agreement with Ronald's assessment of this aspect of British life.

'I can't disagree with what you're saying, Ronald. Yes, we need to take a punt on Britain.'

This venture would be a new chapter in the Foster family's history but Ronald was still apprehensive. His point of contact was his uncle, William, who lived in Brixton. If he thought too hard about his future prospects, it could daunt him causing him to wonder if he was doing the right thing. It was absolutely vital that a positive mindset was adopted as he started this new phase of his life.

Suddenly, the Windrush began to judder as it docked in Tilbury. The jolting reminded Ronald that he'd made this journey with lofty expectations of raising the Foster family's living standards. Britain had started to prosper following World War II and Ronald wanted to share in this new affluence.

He anticipated life would be radically different from the Caribbean and disembarked with disparate emotions. He was excited by the prospect of a new life but was also trepidatious at the thought of possible bumps in the road.

Chapter 11

Picking up two suitcases, Ronald left the Empire Windrush with mixed sentiments ready to embark on a new life in Britain. At this significant point in his life, Ronald's mind was awash with the desire to succeed. Would Britain be the land of milk and honey that he hoped for? Or would he be an abject failure? Only time would tell but for the time being, Ronald adopted the stance that the mother country offered great hope for the future. Like many Caribbean people, Ronald was religious. Unfortunately, he viewed this grey January day as a portent that he'd fail in Britain. What he failed to realise was that most days in the winter months in Britain were damp and grey.

Many people in St Kitts liked the traditions attached to the Anglican Church. When he was young, Ronald realised that this heritage had found its way into West Indian culture because it had been the place of worship for the white plantation owners who had enslaved Africans. African names had been dispensed with many years ago when the slaves had been forced to adopt the names of their white owners.

Ronald tried to avoid thinking about the tragic circumstances faced by tribespeople in the past and concentrate on his future. His ancestors had been enslaved on a French plantation but later Britain defeated France making St Kitts one of its own colonies. Today he hoped the mother country would provide his family with a prosperous future.

Ronald set off for the dock gate in the hope he could get a taxi to take him to his Uncle William's house in Brixton. Ronald's spirits lifted as he saw a row of cabs. Approaching the first one he knocked the window to attract the driver's attention. His head was buried in the *Daily Mail* newspaper, and being a former newspaper editor in St Kitts, Ronald wondered how many of these papers were sold each day.

He had been told some papers have a circulation running into millions. This was a far cry from his press days in Basseterre where the Democrat had a limited circulation because much of the population couldn't read. The driver wound the window down, and Ronald asked, 'I'm going to Brixton. Is there any chance you could take me?'

'Bugger off, blackie. I don't like blacks.'

Astounded at this taxi driver's reply, Ronald exclaimed, 'I can't believe this because the British government has asked us to come so we can work to serve this country.'

'It's me who decides who rides in this cab not the government. Just find someone else.'

Instantaneously, Ronald's mind switched to the inclement weather greeting his arrival in Britain. Being an educated man, Ronald had studied Shakespearean literature in school. The Tilbury climate caused him to recollect the time he studied Julius Caesar.

On the night before the Ides of March, a storm was raging in Rome. Shakespeare used storms to create a mood of darkness and foreboding in his work. Ronald fixated his mind on the play and began to obsess about the poor weather, equating it with the taxi driver's repugnant attitude.

Disconsolately, Ronald strolled past a line of taxis because he didn't want a second rebuff. Common sense told him that not all whites could be racist. What a start to life in Britain! Ronald couldn't understand why anyone would refuse him a lift on the basis of his skin colour.

Walking a little further, Ronald found a black cab driver. Delighted to see someone of his own colour, Ronald anticipated a positive welcome and knocked the window. Winding down the window, the driver exclaimed, 'Man, where are you going?'

At last Ronald had met someone who made him feel welcome. However, he wondered how much business this driver would get. Was the racist taxi driver a one off or was he the norm? Ronald was sure he would soon find out.

'Can you take me to Strathleven Street in Brixton? Do you know where it is?'

'I sure do, man. Just like many other West Indian immigrants, I live in Brixton.'

'I've just left the Windrush and I'm going to stay with my Uncle William Hodge in Brixton.'

'Is William Hodge your uncle?'

'Yes, Sir. He came to live here a few years ago.'

'He's a really well-respected man. He's just been elected to the local council making him the first black councillor in London.'

'It's great to hear that.'

'You sure do come from good stock. It would be a real pleasure to drop you at William's place.'

'I'm glad to hear he's carrying on the excellent work he started in St Kitts. He was always helping poor people to obtain better living conditions.'

'By the way I'm Algernon. What's your name?'

'My name is Ronald but my eldest son is also called Algernon.'

'You're sure gonna see a different way of life in this country. I had a shock when I came from Jamaica.'

'In what way do you mean?'

'Your uncle is continually fighting to get better conditions for black people. What you experienced with the white taxi driver is not unusual in Britain.'

'That's going to make life difficult.'

'There are a significant number of white people who feel threatened because we're supposed to be taking their jobs.'

'That's sad because the British government wanted us here.'

'The thing is there are plenty of jobs for everyone. These people are just racist.'

The incident with a white taxi driver had opened Ronald's eyes to the difficulties he might encounter in Britain. Dejectedly Ronald proclaimed, 'I don't get it, Algernon. This is our mother country and we're entitled to be here. Men from the Caribbean fought side by side in World War II with British soldiers and were fully prepared to give their lives for freedom. We were wanted then so why not now? Britain is our country and Queen Elizabeth our Queen.'

'It doesn't work like that. We're seen as a threat to their way of life. Some people led by Arthur Chesterton have founded the League of Empire Loyalists. They're right wing and make life difficult for us.'

'I'm struggling with this because we're led to believe Britain is a democracy where all should be valued. At the end of the day, we're all flesh and blood.'

'Quite right but since the Windrush first came in 1948, animosity against people of colour has intensified. Some politicians have started to speak against us.'

Flabbergasted at what he'd just been told, Ronald wanted to probe further.

'Politicians are supposed to fight for every citizen not just those who are white.'

'Some in the Conservative Party want us repatriated. Thankfully, it's not the stance of the leadership.'

'I'm really beginning to wonder if it's a good idea to stay here. I was hoping to get a good job and a top education for my children.'

'Where are they?'

'My wife and kids are at home in St Kitts. I came to get myself established and the plan is to bring them over when I am.'

'Remember not all whites are the same. There are some who see our integration into British society as a good thing.'

Ronald had paramount concerns for the family's future making it difficult for him to conceal his indignation at what he'd just been told. Determined to adopt a positive attitude, he declared, 'We'll just have to prove these people wrong. I'm going to prove myself an exemplary citizen, ready to make a positive contribution to life in Britain.'

'Many of these whites who discriminate are pompous using discriminatory language, which is so far removed from the truth.'

'I agree with you, Algernon. These people are creating a melodrama. They're probably just drawing people into their xenophobic web.'

'Well, Ronald, I'm astounded at how intelligent you are.'

'Thank you for your kind words. I won a scholarship to attend the University of the West Indies. Trouble is, there was no way I could get to Jamaica. How could I afford that? But I do want better for my kids. That's why I'm here.'

'I've got a similar story because I was one of the first of the Windrush Generation to come here in 1948 when I was a lad. I took the Eleven Plus Exam and passed. The problem was my parents couldn't afford the money for the school uniform to attend the grammar school. This was a barrier, so I went to the secondary school. At fifteen, I left school to get a job. I'm only twenty now but I set up my own taxi company in Brixton.'

'Good Lord, you've done brilliantly, Algernon. You must have an excellent business acumen to have set up a business at such a young age.'

'Just make sure your youngsters get the best chance possible when they arrive.'

'Unfortunately, from what you've said, the spread of right-wing fascism might hinder their progress.'

'Remember, Ronald, there's lots of good people in Britain of all ethnicities. Keep positive.'

'Yeah, you're definitely an old head on young shoulders and I'll bear it in mind.'

'We're here. This is your Uncle William's house.'

'How much do I owe you?'

'Nothing this one's on the house. Welcome to Britain.'

Chapter 12

Brixton during the 1950s was a sanctuary for people of Afro Caribbean and Irish descent. Many lodging houses in London would have signs stating "Vacancies, but no coloureds or Irish". Devoid of racism, people treated each other as equals making this area of London a pleasure to live in. Brixton market was central to the people's lives and was such a colourful place.

Walking through the arches, a person was confronted by all manner of traders, hawkers and stalls selling all types of goods. Colourful clothing which would only be worn by Brixton residents were on sale. All varieties of vegetables and fruit were sold by Caribbean barrow boys who'd developed the gift of the gab.

People from all corners of Brixton would come to be entertained by their constant chatter and banter. Caribbean inspired music resonated through the streets as buskers performed for the crowds. Ronald's Uncle William had helped to develop this inclusive community where all were welcomed and racism was frowned upon.

Ronald had settled well in this community and his time spent in Brixton was always going to be a transitional period before he settled somewhere outside London. In February 1959, Ronald spotted an advertisement in the *Evening Standard* newspaper for Caribbean peoples to settle in Cardiff. New council estates had been developed in the city, giving Ronald the opportunity to move away from the perpetual hustle and bustle of London.

He would have his own place ready to resettle his wife and children. Ronald contacted Isabelle by phone.

'I've got good news, darling. There's places in Cardiff for Caribbean peoples to work and there's also new housing estates.'

'Where's Cardiff, Ronald?'

'Well, it's the capital of Wales and I know it's much smaller than London.'

'Have you got a job?'

'I've applied for a job at a company called Super Oil Seals.'

'What do they do?

'They make oil seals for cars.'

'But you were a newspaper editor in St Kitts.'

'Yes, but I didn't earn much money and this company pays really well.'

' What do we do now?'

'When everything is confirmed, I will get you all a berth on a ship and bring you over.'

'That'll be good because we've been apart nearly two years and the kids need their father.'

'I'll ring as soon as I hear anything.'

A few days later, two letters Ronald had been waiting for arrived in Brixton. Tentatively opening the one envelope he looked at the contents. Ronald letting out a yelp brought his Uncle William running into the passage and he shouted, 'What's up?'

'Uncle, I've got the job in Cardiff at the Oil Seals Factory.'

'Open the other one.'

The postmark showed this letter had also come from the Welsh capital. Normally steady, Ronald's hand began to falter as he opened the second letter. He took the folded letter and cautiously opened it out. To his delight, he'd been successful in his application for a council house in the Caecoed area of the city.

Such unbridled excitement caused Ronald to do an on-the-spot jig, much to his uncle's amusement. Hopefully, his reasons for emigrating had finally come to fruition.

'Uncle William, I'll soon be out of your hair. I can't wait to tell Isabelle.'

'She won't be very happy because it's only 4 in the morning in St Kitts.'

'Oh I forgot the time difference. I'll wait.'

Barely able to contain his excitement, Ronald phoned Isabelle to convey the good news. Immediately, Ronald put a plan in place to bring his family to Wales. In May 1959, the Foster family were reunited and moved into a brand-new Council House in Steer Avenue on the Caecoed estate in the east of the city.

Chapter 13

In May 1959, Isabelle, Algernon, Perry and Lynne arrived at Uncle William's place in Brixton to be reunited with Ronald. Barely able to contain his excitement, Ronald had tears in his eyes as he firstly hugged Isabelle and in turn each of the children. His outpouring of emotion was a joy after spending so long separated from the family.

Ronald declared, 'I couldn't wait for this day to arrive but at least I've been able to establish myself in a job in London, and thanks to Uncle William's generosity, I've been able to save enough money to buy furniture for the new house.'

'It was really good that you got a job as a bus driver, Ronald.'

'Isabelle, many Afro Caribbean men are employed by London Transport and they have good work conditions.'

'Although, Algy was able to get some schooling in St Kitts, we're going to have to arrange a school for him. He's just like you, Ronald, academically very able.'

'That's heartening to hear, Isabelle. We need to make sure we get a good school for him. Hopefully, when he's eleven, he'll do the Eleven Plus Exam.'

'What's that, Ronald?'

'It's an exam done by children to decide whether they go to a grammar or secondary school.'

'Is there any difference?'

'They are very different. Grammar schools are very academic and many of the pupils go on to higher education.'

Algy was mature for his age and proclaimed, 'I want to be a teacher because Mrs Williams who taught me to read in St Kitts was lovely.'

'Teaching's a great job, Algy, but you might change your mind. You're only six and eighteen's a long way off.'

'Dad's right, Algy, let's get you into one of those grammar schools and the world's your oyster.'

Just as Isabelle finished speaking, Uncle William came into the room declaring, 'Being a local councillor, I know all the tradesmen and I've done a deal with one to move your belongings to Cardiff.'

'How much do I owe you?' Ronald exclaimed.

'Look, Ronald, I've sorted this out. It's a gift because we people from the Caribbean need to support each other.'

'Uncle William, I'm totally indebted to you. What would I have done without you?'

'I've also put feelers out in Brixton for some second-hand furniture.'

'I'm adamant I'll pay for that.'

'That's fine, Ronald. The furniture is nearly new because the lady who owned it had only just bought it and she suddenly passed on. Rest assured, it's really good quality and a very reasonable price.'

'No worry. I'll get the money out of the building society. Who do I pay?'

'Her son and he's a top bloke.'

'You've been so helpful, Uncle William.'

27 May 1959, a removal van arrived in Steer Avenue on the Caecoed council estate. Ronald, Isabelle and the family followed the van in their family car. Leaving their vehicle, they could see faces in the windows peering at them. Ronald wondered what sort of response they'd get from neighbours.

At the end of the day, Brixton had been a sanctuary for Afro Caribbean people but his family might be forced to confront the harsh reality of life in 1950s Britain, where blacks could be victimised because of their colour. Their next-door neighbour opened the door and walked towards the Foster family. She declared, 'Pleased to meet you. I'm Mary McColl and this is my ten year old son, David.'

Ronald recognised her Irish accent, and replied, 'It looks like we're going to be next door neighbours. I'm Ronald and this is my wife, Isabelle, and children Algy, Perry and Lynne. Which part of Ireland do you come from?'

'I'm a Catholic and lived in Belfast but left the city because there were some family issues making it better for me to leave.'

'Well, I've read about these problems,' proclaimed Isabelle.

Ronald and Isabelle realised that Mary was a really lovely lady and they were pleased that she was their next-door neighbour. They hoped that other local people would be as welcoming as this Irish lady.

'Which Caribbean Island did you come from?'

'We come from St Kitts but I've been staying in London saving money to bring Isabelle and the kids over. It's been a long two years but my Uncle William's been brilliant.'

'What job did you do in St Kitts?'

'I was a newspaper reporter and then the editor of *The Democrat* newspaper in Basseterre.'

'Did you work as a reporter in London?'

'No, I was a bus driver which was well paid and I've got a job here working in an oil seals factory. I'll be making oil seals for cars.'

'Well, I can't wait to meet your husband, Mary,' said Isabelle.

'There is no husband. I became pregnant outside marriage and that was frowned upon by the Catholic community. I understand intolerance and discrimination because I've experienced it myself.'

'I'm really sorry to hear that, Mary,' said Isabelle sympathetically.

'I brought David to Wales, otherwise he would have had a torrid time. It looks like David is about the same age as your son, Algy.'

'Algy's six,' said Ronald.

'That's the same age as David.'

Ronald was obsessed with the idea that he needed to ensure a good education for his kids and he asked, 'Where does David go to school?'

'He goes to St Ignatius Primary which is a Catholic school run by nuns. Mind you, I haven't told them I'm a single parent.'

'Don't worry. We'll keep quiet.'

'Thanks a lot.'

'It could be a good thing for Algy to go to this St Ignatius school. Hopefully, being a church school there'd be no colour discrimination.'

'It would be nice for David to have some company.'

'In Brixton, we were sheltered from racism. There were so many black people so it was comfortable living in the community.'

Mary's personal experience enabled her to empathise with Ronald and she declared, 'There's an area of Cardiff called Tiger Bay where the community comprises many different nationalities living in harmony with each other.'

'That's really interesting, Mary, but I'm hoping that by going to a largely white school, Algy will win the respect of everyone and eventually benefit.'

Just as Ronald finished speaking, the heavens opened, leading Isabelle to say, 'Let's get our stuff inside. It's been great to meet you, Mary.'

Chapter 14

Ronald, Isabelle and the Foster children settled into their new home. Caecoed was a council estate which had been well planned with numerous green spaces for children to play. This leafy suburb of Cardiff could potentially be a good place to bring up children, offering Ronald, Isabelle and their young family the opportunity to have a pleasant work-life balance.

Having moved the furniture provided by Uncle William's contacts into the house, Ronald and the family decided to go for a walk to explore their new surroundings. These were so completely different from the built-up congested streets in Brixton. First impressions were that Caecoed gave the family space. By contrast green areas in Brixton were limited but it had been an excellent place to acclimatise to the British way of life.

However, Ronald's experience with the racist taxi driver meant that he was perceptive enough to realise that Brixton was not typical of 1950s Britain. Ronald and the family were unfortunately going to get another taste of what he'd been dreading. Walking a short distance along the road, Ronald's eyes were drawn to a poster in a neighbour's window.

The children were too young to understand the problem of discrimination in post-war Britain but Ronald and Isabelle were distraught at what they saw. In the window was a despicable placard stating, "Coloureds and Irish Out". Brixton had been devoid of anything of this nature but Ronald was well aware that blacks and Irish were not welcome in some lodging houses throughout London.

In Ronald and Isabelle's opinion, such hurtful words demeaned those who were prepared to display discriminatory material of this nature.

This unpalatable message struck a chord with the young couple striking fear into their hearts. Ronald wondered if they had done the right thing leaving Brixton where life would have been comfortable. Having such a reprehensible neighbour terrified Ronald and Isabelle. Shattered by what they'd just witnessed the family decided to return home.

Having met Mary their next-door neighbour when they arrived in Caecoed they decided to knock her door. Before she could fully open it, a distressed Ronald blurted out, 'There's a poster in the window along the street with "Coloureds and Irish Out". I've seen those in London but I didn't expect to see one here.'

'Ronald, this type of discrimination is not just confined to London. Some people in all areas of Britain discriminate against minority groups. Lacking understanding they are ignorant, causing them to behave in this way.'

'I came across colour discrimination in London. Fortunately, I was lucky to live at my uncle's place in Brixton. Many whites who discriminate try to say blacks are taking jobs from whites. It's blatantly not true. There's plenty of jobs for those who want to work.'

'What I don't understand is why you Irish people are discriminated against. At the end of the day, you're the same colour as the perpetrators of this discrimination.'

'Unfortunately, there's a long history of discrimination against Irish people called hibernophobia.'

Isabelle was fascinated by what Mary said and joined the conversation.

'What does that mean?'

'Hibernia is an old name for Ireland. This type of anti-Irish sentiment can be traced back hundreds of years when the English used to think of us as filthy and ignorant. This ill feeling towards the Irish is older than bigotry against black people. We've got something in common,' Mary proclaimed.

'Isn't it scandalous that one group of people see themselves as superior to another, making them think it's right that they can control them. This was the case with the slave traders and owners who wanted to control Africans by putting them into slavery,' said Ronald exasperatedly.

'Ireland was systematically colonised by the English from the reign of Elizabeth I when they called the Irish ignorant people. This perception became common among the English population. Such an attitude gave the English the excuse to discriminate against Irish people by promoting the idea that they could benefit from English rule.'

'Making people subordinate to another country just puts them under another nation's authority, reducing them to subservience. Compliant people eventually become angry making them long for freedom.'

Isabelle re-joined the conversation. 'Living in the Caribbean, we were obviously never taught about Irish history. Listening to you, Mary, I can see there are similarities in the way we've suffered.'

A highly intelligent well-read woman, Mary added in an exasperated voice, 'Even renowned philosophers have put the boot into the Irish. David Hume, a famous Scottish philosopher taught that the Irish were profoundly barbaric and ignorant. Unfortunately, it didn't stop with one eminent philosopher.'

'During the 1830s, a Parliamentary inquiry stated that Irish immigration was an example of a less civilised population spreading into a more civilised society. Parliament producing such a demeaning idea meant discrimination against Irish people was inevitable.'

Ronald quickly pointed out, 'It's no wonder there are posters like this in windows when people don't see other races as their equals. We need to knock the door and demand the poster is taken down.'

Walking uneasily along the road, the Fosters and Mary McColl decided to confront their racist neighbour. Ronald took the lead in knocking the door. The noise produced by the heavy plodding footsteps intensified as the occupant approached the door. Suddenly, the door opened. Standing in front of them was an unshaven, villainous, demoniacal looking bully boy in the doorway.

Surely, it was impossible for this brute to have any sensitivity in his voice and he gruffly said, 'I don't want a nigger or a mick knocking my door. Now bugger off.'

'We want you to take that discriminatory poster down.'

'I don't take orders from immigrants.'

'If you don't take it down, we'll go to the police.'

'You see who you like. We don't want people like you living here. You lot don't belong in this country. You need to go back to Bongo land. That's where you belong. Same for you, Paddy, but they probably won't have you back because your child is a little bastard.'

Mary's fiery Celtic temperament came to the fore and she seethed with anger. At that point, Mary could have committed murder. However, Ronald's equable Caribbean disposition calmed the situation. He said, 'Treat him with disdain. Well, it's the police then.'

'Go where you like immigrants.'

The ogre slammed the door in their faces, prompting Ronald to declare, 'Unfortunately, Mary, we seem to have walked into another community who are hostile. That horror is nothing but a belligerent, pugnacious, individual. We've got to go to the police.'

Deciding to visit the police, they walked half a mile to Caecoed police headquarters. A blue light outside the building was supposed to represent a nonpartisan organisation prepared to defend the rights of every member of the community. Unfortunately, the sergeant gave the impression this complaint was being made by a West Indian and Irish family and was not deserving of his attention.

No doubt it would have been a different story if the complainant had been a white British person. Ronald was normally placid but he became incensed.

'That man has broken the law and what are you going to do about it?'

Sounding like some southern United States far right activist, the sergeant said, 'Boy, who are you talking to? Carry on and you'll be locked up.'

'We only want fair play and there's no way such a discriminatory poster should be in the window. We're the ones who've been sinned against and we all respect the law.'

'Blacks are renowned for lawbreaking.'

'Oh, by the way my son, Algernon, is a boy. I'm a man.'

'I want no more lip from you. We'll speak to him.'

Chapter 15

Unsettled by the racism he'd encountered on their first day in Caecoed, Ronald and the family settled into their new home. Yesterday Ronald and Isabelle became aware that discrimination was not just restricted to people of colour. Mary McColl was an Irish lady who'd also been subjected to the taunts of the individual living along the street. Although, disappointed by this prejudice, the Foster family adopted the attitude that such behaviour was restricted to a minority.

The following day as Ronald rummaged in the outhouse, his attention was drawn to a police car stopping along the road. Maybe his initial thoughts about the sergeant's attitude had been erroneous. Possibly he'd been too hasty in his judgement but there again the sergeant's form of address towards him was belittling and unworthy of somebody in a position of authority.

As the officer reached the door, it was opened by the man they'd confronted yesterday. When Ronald had spoken to him on the previous day adrenaline had coursed through his veins, wondering whether the ogre would become aggressive. Thankfully, there had been no physical violence but Ronald's heightened hypersensitivity to protecting his family prevented him from fully appreciating what a grotesque specimen this man was.

Ronald could see his head was shaved to the bone, appearing to be stuck on his shoulders like a block of stone. More neanderthal than human, this was a truly frightening looking person. Ronald's initial thoughts about the integrity of the police sergeant came to fruition when he hugged the man. This custodian of the law and the loutish looking human being appeared well acquainted with one another.

Following the initial greeting, the police officer went in and the door closed. Ronald decided to walk towards the house and he could see the poster had been removed. He thought to himself was this a smokescreen to their real intentions.

Ronald returned home anxious to tell Isabelle what had happened but before doing so he called at Mary's.

Mary answered the door.

'Hi, Ronald.'

'The police made the guy along the road take the poster down.'

'That's excellent news. There's only one thing. It might have been removed but his attitude will remain the same. Discrimination is ingrained in him and taking the poster down won't change it.'

'Quite right. We'll have to be vigilant.'

'We need to remember there are lots of good people living around here as well.'

'I'll be going to the shop in a minute. Is there anything you want?'

'That's kind of you, Ronald. I could do with a pint of milk and a loaf please.'

'I'm just popping in the house to tell Isabelle what's happened and then I'll go to the shop.'

Isabelle was thrilled to learn that the poster had been taken down and Ronald set off to the shop. His mind was awash with a myriad of thoughts and he couldn't help wondering how many other discriminatory characters lived in this area. As he approached the shop, a woman came out and spoke to him, 'Hi, I'm Alice and what's your name?'

'I'm Ronald and I've just moved in from Brixton in London. I originally lived in St Kitts.'

'You're really brave moving here because there are some very nasty types living in the area.'

'I've already met one.'

'Yes, and I know who you are talking about. He's the worst but rest assured, there are also some very nice, supportive people living here who are prepared to help others.'

'I'm really glad to hear that because we've had a derogatory poster taken down from his window.'

'His type are ruthless, giving the area a bad name. The police have allowed him to get away with murder and they seem to sympathise with him.'

'Why did you use the word brave?'

'Well, you could have gone to live in the Docks. Many of the Windrush Generation who came to Cardiff have settled there. So many different nationalities live there that racism is unheard of in that community.'

'Well that's like Brixton in London. That's the same.'

'Listen, Ronald, if you want to mix with some nice members of the community, you need to come to the Church of Wales on the estate.'

'Trouble is we're Anglicans.'

'Well, it's an Anglican Church with the Archbishop of Canterbury as the spiritual head and the Queen as the overall leader.'

'That's exactly the same as the church in Basseterre. Thanks, Alice, we'll see you there.'

After seeing a disparaging poster in the window, meeting someone like Alice was a real stroke of good fortune. Ronald appreciated that Alice's proposal was an excellent idea to help the family settle in the area. He picked up shopping and dropped Mary's off at the house before returning home to Isabelle and the family. Isabelle came into the kitchen.

'Thanks, Ronald, for getting the shopping.'

'I've just had a bit of luck. A lovely woman called Alice came out of the shop and told me that the best place to meet nice people is to go to the Anglican church on the estate.'

'That's good news because it'll be just like home.'

'Well, it's Sunday tomorrow, Isabelle. Let's worship there.'

Ronald and the family went to bed content in the knowledge that there were good people on Caecoed with an inclusive ideal for society. Unfortunately, the right-wing activist further along the road was not prepared to let the matter of the poster being removed from his window stop his intimidatory behaviour. His piece de resistance would involve leaving unwanted messages for the Foster and McColl families.

During the early hours of Sunday morning, he disgustingly defecated into two envelopes which he intended to deposit through their letter boxes. He hoped this intimidation would result in them feeling pressurised to leave the Caecoed estate. He had no need to worry about any police investigation because his relationship with the authorities would ensure that they just went through the motions.

This right-wing individual left his house in the early hours to walk down the road. Initially, he went to Mary McColl's house and emptied the contents of the envelope through the letterbox into the hallway. He swiftly moved next door repeating his odious behaviour. Deep rooted hatred of immigrants resulted in further obnoxious behaviour when he urinated through the Foster's letterbox.

Such repugnant behaviour was designed to show his intense hatred of immigrants. Leaving the crime scene, he hastily returned home. Isabelle heard the sound of running water and shouted, 'Wake up, Ronald. I think we've got a leak. I heard water running.'

Groggily, Ronald stirred himself and exclaimed, 'I'll check it out now.'

Stupefied through being half asleep, Ronald carefully negotiated the stairs. What he saw immediately brought him to his senses. His eyes were drawn to some sort of befouling by the door. Drawing closer a foul odour was a tell-tale sign as to what had happened. Angrily he shouted, 'It's unbelievable! Someone's had a poo and urinated through the letterbox. It's disgusting.'

'Ronald, keep calm. You'll wake the kids.'

Recovering his normal poise, Ronald exclaimed, 'What animal would think of doing this?'

'Well, you won't need two guesses. It's obviously the savage from up the road.'

Mary McColl had been disturbed by the commotion next door. Assuming there was a problem, she went downstairs to be greeted by a pile of faeces directly below the letterbox. The noise had woken her son, David.

'I'm feeling sick to the pit of my stomach,' she proclaimed.

'David, somebody has tried to threaten us.'

'What do you mean, Mam?'

'I think our house and the Foster's has been targeted by that right wing monster. Anyone who poos in somebody's hallway has to be a psycho. Nobody in their right mind would do this.'

Simultaneously, opening their front doors, the two families were flabbergasted at what had happened.

'We need to inform the police, Mary,' declared Ronald.

'But the sergeant has right wing leanings and he'll just cover for that horror.'

'We need to phone in the morning. He can't just get away with it.'

'We need to photograph both hallways. I've got a new Polaroid camera, Ronald.'

'In the meantime, let's clean it up.'

Chapter 16

Ronald phoned the police to report the hate crime perpetrated by an individual who detested people from minority groups. Having taken his details at reception Ronald was told he'd have a phone call in the afternoon. Anxious to observe the Sabbath, the Fosters dressed for church. In keeping with West Indian tradition they all dressed in their best clothes. Walking along they had butterflies in their stomach caused by the uncertainty as to the type of welcome they'd receive. Any trepidation was replaced by euphoria at seeing Alice on the door distributing order of service leaflets. Seeing the Foster family produced a beatific expression on her face. She calmly said,

'What a pleasure to see you all at St Teilo's Church.'

'Well, I took your advice about the church being a good place to meet nice people. This is my wife Isabelle and my young family Algernon, Perry and Lynne.'

'It's fantastic to see you all and hopefully you'll stay for a cuppa once the service is over.'

Taking their seats near the back of the church the congregation sang 'Guide me O Thou Great Jehovah.' Participating in Holy Communion was a pleasurable experience for Ronald and Isabelle, bringing back memories of good times at the parish church in Basseterre. Both Ronald and Isabelle realised that being a part of a worshipping community would help them settle in Caecoed irrespective of the terrible start they'd had to life in Cardiff. Parishioners were anxious to talk with the Fosters and a middle-aged gentleman asked.

'How are you settling in?'

Swiftly replying Isabelle said.

'We've been made to feel welcome in church. However there was a derogatory poster in a neighbour's window.'

'In any community there are good people but there's always going to be a minority with right wing leanings.'

'During the night we received a visit and faeces was deposited through our letterbox.'

'Right wing thugs are trying to intimidate you. They've been allowed to get away with this insidious behaviour because of sympathisers in the local police, who are guilty of scandalous discriminatory behaviour.'

Returning home, the Fosters were ecstatic at having met some very supportive people. Any elation from the positive reaction at the church was replaced by despondency when the police phoned in the afternoon to tell them they'd be taking no further action, using the excuse that the evidence was not strong enough to prosecute. Dumbfounded by the police ineptitude, Ronald struggled to contain his emotions and blurted out,

'Surely the police must have an idea about who is responsible for this reprehensible behaviour. There's a bloke living up the road who'd put a pernicious poster in his window. Surely you need to question him.'

'Look, this is not the Caribbean. We need hard and fast evidence to prosecute.'

Astounded by this attitude Ronald put the phone down. At that moment he decided there's no way he would cower down to right wing pressure. On Monday he was starting work at the Oil Seals Factory and he was hoping that this would be a better experience than his first weekend in Caecoed.

Chapter 17

Having encountered difficulties with racism when the family moved into Caecoed, Ronald didn't know whether to be excited or dispirited as he walked to work. It was inevitable that he'd be apprehensive about his future promotion prospects following the confrontation with his racist neighbour and the subsequent police attitudes when he reported the incident. The Oil Seals Factory was situated in Tremorfa and as he walked towards it, Ronald could see that a good percentage of the men going into work were Afro Caribbean.

Seeing this his spirits lifted, realising he would not be on his own. Ronald found his card and clocked in. As the time stamped onto the card, a voice behind him said, 'You're the new chap, aren't you?'

'I am and my name's Ronald Foster. I've just moved to Cardiff from Brixton. By the way what's your name?'

'I'm Stephen West. I've been working here for two years.'

'What's it like to work here?'

'It's the best job I've ever had. We're really well paid but more importantly, the management are really respectful. The owner is committed to equality for all.'

'That's great news because I was worried about starting after my experiences at the weekend.'

'What happened, Ronald?'

'A neighbour living just up the road put a poster in his window with "Coloureds and Irish out".'

'You'll find this everywhere, Ronald. There are characters who try to intimidate us. Fortunately, there are a good number of people who believe that inclusivity is important.'

'Unfortunately, I've heard racist comments on the telly and radio since I've been in the country.'

'That's very true but I don't think the programme makers realise how demeaning this is. At the end of the day we all belong to one human race.'

'What was pleasing at the weekend was that we were invited to a church and the people were very supportive.'

'You'll find that support here. It's a really happy and welcoming place to work.'

It was just as Stephen had said, the management were committed to equality for all. Excellent wages were paid and as Ronald settled in, he enjoyed working with his mates. Any disparaging comments aimed at the Afro Caribbean men were forbidden, ensuring the Oil Seals Factory was a harmonious place to work.

Following an eventful weekend, Isabelle prepared Algernon for school. She accompanied him to St Ignatius Catholic School, hoping he'd be in the same class as David, their next-door neighbour. Mary had no concerns about anti-Irish sentiment as there were so many Irish in the school.

Any anxiety she had revolved around her being an unmarried mother. Hopefully, this would never come to light because of the Catholic Church's stance in Ireland on this matter. Most of the nuns working at the school were Irish. Consequently, their approach to Mary's status as a single mother would be to treat her with disdain.

Fortunately, Mary had received help from her family in Ireland who helped conceal the pregnancy. Her mother's liberal approach to her daughter's situation saved her from the ire of the Catholic Church. After David was born, she was then helped to leave the country and came to Wales. Most Irish parents were not like Mary's.

Most conspired with the church to treat these young women as evil doers. Mother and baby homes had been set up in Ireland run by nuns. Mary knew about the nun's behaviour in the homes where little kindness was shown to the women. Even as the children were being born the mothers were abused by these women of God, instead of showing the intrinsic kindness demanded from someone who was a servant of God.

Abuse would be both physical and verbal. Being treated as sinners was an insult to a loving God who would have frowned upon this appalling behaviour. These homes received state funding and many of the babies were taken from their mothers and sent to the United States for adoption.

Ronald and Isabelle considered a church school the best option for Algernon. Hopefully, the school would respect biblical teaching "that all men were created in God's image". Even though he was the only black child in the school Algernon settled well. Being a gregarious youngster, he made friends easily.

His enquiring mind ensured that his academic progress was excellent and an added bonus was that he was the fastest runner in his class. His physical prowess certainly impressed his contemporaries who always wanted him on their side in any game.

The Foster family were able to put the bad start to life in Caecoed behind them. Being members of a faith community meant that steadfast, uncomplicated friendships were made in Saint Teilo's Church. Ronald had hit the jackpot in work because of his fair-minded employer.

At this point, Algernon was happy in school. Isabelle and Mary had become good friends and her status as an unmarried, single parent would never be disclosed by the discreet Foster family.

Chapter 18

Cuba, one of the Caribbean islands, was governed by a military dictatorship with President Fulgencio Baptista as president. This changed on 26 July 1953, when the Cuban Revolution began, led by Fidel Castro. This insurrection finally succeeded on 31 December 1958, allowing Castro to assume full control in the country. Cuba adopted Communism as their political philosophy leading to a decline in relations with the United States.

Castro began a programme of nationalisation, centralisation of the press and the transformation of Cuba's economy. Cuba actively sought the support of the Soviet Union, who at first had little interest in the affairs of a Caribbean Island. Unfortunately, for world affairs this changed after an American led invasion came to grief in Cuba.

On Monday, 9 April 1961, Ronald went to work as usual. It was a lovely spring morning and he was unprepared for what was going to happen. He sat with the other men enjoying a coffee when one of the foremen came to the table and announced that the boss wanted to see him.

Being a worrier, Ronald couldn't help thinking that he might have stepped out of line. This would have been done unwittingly because he couldn't think he'd done anything untoward. Knocking the door, Ronald's mind was engulfed with a myriad of thoughts.

A booming voice bellowed, 'Come in, Ronald.'

Ronald opened the door to see his boss, Jimmy Jones, and another man sat at the table. Ronald was a bag of nerves and exclaimed, 'I hope I haven't done anything wrong.'

'To the contrary, Ronald. This is Mr Terence Williams, the editor of *The Times* newspaper.'

'That's interesting, Mr Jones. You mean *The Times* in London.'

'That's right, Ronald. I'm going to leave you now with Mr Williams who's going to make you a proposition which I think you should give serious consideration to. By the way, I didn't realise you were a newspaper editor in St Kitts.'

'Well, I never thought to mention it, Mr Jones. I just didn't think it was relevant.'

Ronald's boss left the room, leaving the two men alone. Mr Williams began the conversation by saying, 'It's nice to meet you, Ronald. You must call me Terry.'

'Thanks very much. I'm intrigued to know what you're doing here?'

'I had the pleasure of going to the Council offices in Brixton to report on work they're doing integrating immigrants into the community. It was there I met your Uncle William who's become quite a celebrity in London. I told him we were looking for someone from the Caribbean to go to Guatemala where an army of Cuban exiles is being trained, backed by the American government.'

'What are they training for?'

'It's pretty hush hush but they're training to overthrow Castro and retake Cuba from Communist control. Sadly, we have no reporters born in the Caribbean working for us. But when William told me you were a newspaper editor in St Kitts, I thought you might like to cover the story for *The Times*.'

Ronald's eyes lit up at this prospect but he was perturbed.

'What about my work here?'

'Mr Jones is fine with it. We're going to look after the company financially. I will personally ensure that they'll be handsomely compensated for letting you go to Cuba. Once the assignment is over, your boss has guaranteed that you'll return to your job.'

'What about paying me?'

'All I can say at the moment is you'll be well remunerated for your work. Your report will be a world exclusive.'

'I just need to phone my wife to let her know about your proposition. Hopefully, she'll agree to me doing it.'

Ronald realised he would have to be economical with the truth if Isabelle was to agree with him going to the Caribbean. This was almost certainly bound to be a dangerous assignment. Tentatively picking up the phone Ronald dialled their home number. Isabelle answered the phone and to her surprise Ronald was on the other end. He'd never phoned her from work before.

'What's the matter?'

'Nothing, Isabelle. You'll never guess I've been offered a reporting job in Guatemala.'

'We haven't got to move out there, have we?'

'No, it's a one off. *The Times* newspaper has asked me to report on some American led operation in Guatemala. By all accounts the rest is secret.'

'Knowing your love of press work, nothing I say is going to stop you. I just hope it's not dangerous. There's just one thing, Ronald, why don't they use one of their own reporters?'

'It's probably a sad indictment of the time we live in when a highly regarded newspaper hasn't got a black reporter. It's important that the person is black so they can mingle unobtrusively with the local population.'

'You go with my blessing but please be careful. We all love you. Are you coming home first?'

'I'll have to ask Mr Williams.'

'No, Ronald, we're going straight to London. Don't worry we'll provide you with everything you need,' promised Mr Williams.

'I hope you heard that, Isabelle.'

'Yes, I did. We all love you and be careful.'

'You worry too much but I can understand why, being that I'm such a lovable character.'

'I wish you good luck, Ronald. Love and kisses.'

Ronald and Mr Williams left the Oil Seals Factory and travelled to Cardiff Central train station to catch the train to London. This was the first time in his life Ronald had travelled first class. He was treated to a silver service breakfast which he demolished. Arriving in Paddington just before midday, a taxi was waiting to whisk the two men to Fleet Street.

Ronald's first job was to attend a briefing about the reporting task he was to undertake. In the newsroom were the great and good of the newspaper industry. All were eager to meet Ronald and instruct him about what they wanted him to do. Immediately, Ronald was made aware by those present that he would be embarking on a very important mission. *The Times* owner introduced himself as Mr Phillips and spoke to the group.

'We have brought Ronald Foster here to go to Guatemala to report on a group of American backed Cuban exiles intending to invade Cuba. They have been given the task of recapturing it from Fidel Castro and his men following the revolution. Communists are now in charge and the United States want it out of their hands.

'Everyone here's been sworn to secrecy and under no circumstances must there be a leak. If this information falls into the wrong hands it will cost people their lives. Ronald's an experienced Caribbean journalist having worked in St Kitts and he'll integrate quite easily into the local population. Our people on the ground in the United States have accessed a report that President Dwight Eisenhower has given 13.1 million dollars to establish a Cuban exile army.

'These are Cuban patriots now living in the States. We want this newspaper to be able to say we've got a worldwide exclusive story. Plans are being made by the CIA (Central Intelligence Agency) to recapture Cuba because of its strategic importance to the United States. This army will be called Brigade 2506 and will be a counter revolutionary unit.

'Training for this brigade is taking place in Guatemala. The reason being is that conditions there resemble the terrain and climate in Cuba. It's the American Government's aim to retake the island. There's no way they want the Soviets involved in Cuba.'

'So where do I come in, Sir?' Ronald exclaimed.

'You're going to Guatemala and our readers will want up to date news about what's happening. The plan is to invade Cuba. However, no news is to be released until the invasion begins.'

'I understand why you want me to go. But will I be going to Cuba.'

'Obviously, Ronald, and that's when you release the information.'

'This is a first for me. I've never been a war correspondent before.'

'Let me tell you we are adamant you'll be financially well rewarded.'

'When do I fly to Guatemala?'

'You're going on 12 April and we will provide you with combat clothing but you'll be unarmed. However, you'll be displaying on the front and back of your bullet proof clothing that you're a member of the press.'

'Thank you, Sir. I'll do my very best.'

'I'm sure you will, Ronald. Start your preparations for flying to the Caribbean.'

That evening, Ronald stayed in the Mayfair Hilton. He'd never before enjoyed such luxury. Better still it was all paid for by *The Times* newspaper. Seafood and prime steak were the order of the day at the evening meal. Ronald felt like royalty but he was realistic enough to understand that he was potentially embarking on a very dangerous mission.

He passionately believed that war reporters had a duty to put themselves in harm's way to bring news to the public. If there was a war it was important that people were told the truth about events.

On the morning of 12 April 1961, a cab arrived at the hotel to transport Ronald to Heathrow. His flight to Guatemala City, the capital was at midday. Mixed emotions ranging from euphoria to trepidation swirled in Ronald's brain. Nevertheless he really wanted this assignment.

Following the 10-hour flight, the aircraft landed in the Caribbean and was met by a Cuban exile captain from 2506 brigade. He introduced himself, 'Good day, I'm Capt. Cortez.'

'Same to you, Sir. I'm Ronald Foster, *The Times* war correspondent. I'm really pleased to meet you.'

'I've come to take you to our training camp. We began our training in the Florida Everglades. Once we'd done the basic training there, we moved to secret locations in Guatemala because the climate is similar to Cuba.'

'How long have you left in training here?'

'Our departure date is imminent but write nothing until we've fulfilled our objective.'

'I fully understand that.'

Ronald was taken to the Sierra Madre training camp. First impressions told him that mobilisation of this brigade was looming. Ronald became aware that on 15 April 1961, two American B52 bombers took off from Nicaragua and bombed Cuban military aircraft on the ground hoping to wipe out Castro's Air Force before the planned invasion. Later that day, two other bombers landed in Miami with the pilots claiming to be Cuban defectors who'd participated in the air raid.

Ronald realised this was fake news and the Americans were attempting to cover up their involvement in Cuban events. It was being presented by the Americans that Cuban defectors to the United States had participated in the raids. Ronald appreciated that a ground invasion was only a matter of days away and he needed to prepare for the most important reporting assignment of his life. It seemed to him that the Americans were trying to make a fool of Castro causing him to wonder if their strategy would backfire.

In the early hours of 17 April 1961, Ronald was woken to be told that the military operation was about to begin. He checked his equipment, including his bulletproof vest and most importantly the signs with "press" emblazoned on it. Refusing to carry arms was an important facet of being a member of the press corps. Each side would hopefully realise that being a non-combatant these media people were not to be targeted.

Their responsibility was to bring the news to the world's attention and Ronald hoped that this would be respected by the combatants. Travelling by boat with the invasion force, Ronald came to recognise the commitment of this group of Cuban exiles to remove Castro from power. On 17 April 1961, the invasion force landed by night at Playa Giron in the Bay of Pigs.

Leaving the landing craft, the brigade made their way up the beach. Ronald brought up the rear with a rucksack strapped to his back. Inside were the tools of his trade—pens, paper, books and maps—all essential if he was to produce an accurate account of this invasion. Having studied a map of the region, Ronald knew there were coral reefs bordering the Zapata Swamp.

He knew the brigade would have to avoid this part of the bay. To succeed it was essential they took the eastern route. Staying on firm ground bordering the beach 1,400 men took this less hazardous course. Negotiating this solid ground, the group managed to avoid the mangrove swamps.

Journeying an hour inland, the paramilitaries came across a local militia. A confrontation followed and the brigade easily overwhelmed this small group. Such a straightforward victory gave rise to the brigade presuming what lay in front of them was going to be just as uncomplicated. Unfortunately, the unit developed a swagger which would be their undoing.

Ronald counted about twenty dead militia bodies. He was fully aware that these Cubans had little chance of success. This one-sided engagement was a complete mismatch in favour of the American backed Cuban exiles. Entering the incident into his notebook this was his first experience of war and he was determined to ensure the facts were accurate.

Experiencing this action, Ronald quickly appreciated the folly of armed hostilities. In his opinion, there could never be winners in any conflict. Always a razor-sharp thinker, he thought to himself there was no way the Cuban military would take this lying down. How right he was. A counter offensive was launched by the Cuban army led by Capt. Jose Ramon Fernandez.

Incensed by the audacity of the United States backed paramilitaries, Castro then decided to take control himself. Ronald was compelled to report the truth that this aggressive incursion onto Cuban soil was totally misguided and in the context of world affairs had the potential to ignite a problem the world could do without.

This United States Cuban exile paramilitary invading force was made up of five infantry battalions and one paratrooper battalion. Ronald discerned that the Americans were supposed to provide air cover but there were time difference difficulties, disastrously preventing any aircraft from arriving. Castro assumed full control of his forces and the Cubans easily defeated the invaders.

The Bay of Pigs was an unmitigated disaster causing the invading force to surrender on 20 April 1961. Ronald would have to report in *The Times* that the paramilitaries were so badly prepared that the invasion became a farce. Running out of ammunition was the ultimate humiliation for an American backed invasion, dooming the expedition to be no more than a damp squib. Castro had given the Americans a bloody nose through their poor planning, arrogance and underestimating his resolve.

More than a hundred of the paramilitaries were killed and the remainder imprisoned. Castro might have lost a large number of soldiers but he managed to secure his country. American contempt for the Cubans had created a war, resulting in avoidable deaths. The Cubans saw Ronald's presence as an opportunity to show that their country had been invaded by an aggressor.

Reporting the truth, he produced a world exclusive for *The Times*. His account would be picked up by every press and news agency around the world. Ronald was just glad to be alive and the Cubans knew press freedom in Britain meant that he would report the truth in his story. Thankfully, his status as a British press man and non-combatant was respected by the Cubans.

The Bay of Pigs was a United States led military disaster and his innate honesty meant the Cuban Government trusted him to report this. It was difficult for Ronald to fathom how the most powerful country on the planet could allow the invaders they were backing to run out of ammunition. United States desperation had led them to bite off more than they could chew. The defeat at the Bay of Pigs was the culmination of a catalogue of disasters.

Cuban concern about getting positive publicity ensured that Ronald was escorted to Havana airport to be flown by private plane the 228 miles to Miami. Reporting the truth about the events of the Bay of Pigs was also of paramount importance to *The Times* owner because he knew they'd increase their circulation thanks to Ronald's world exclusive. More importantly, they'd make a fortune by selling the rights to other news agencies throughout the world.

Ronald was anxious to get back to London following this disastrous invasion attempt. Flying into Heathrow on 24 April, he was met by the owner of *The Times.* He was immediately transferred to their newsroom, where he used his notes to write an unbiased report that the Americans had initiated a disaster by invading Cuba.

Perceptively, he finished his report by stating that originally, the Soviets had no interest in a Caribbean Island. However, this military blunder would almost certainly open up a can of worms in the area, giving the Soviets a foothold in this region of the world. On handing over his world exclusive, the owner gave Ronald a cheque for £2,000.

His eyes came out on stalks when he saw the amount he'd been paid. Finally, they handed him his expenses and he travelled home to Cardiff.

The Bay of Pigs was an unmitigated disaster for the Americans and as Ronald had predicted the invasion opened a pandora's box of world problems. In October 1962, Nikita Khrushchev, the Soviet leader, installed nuclear armed Soviet missiles in Cuba. This was only 90 miles from American territory. John F Kennedy, the American president, created a naval blockade around Cuba, making it clear that the United States was prepared to use military force if necessary.

Khrushchev's response threatened their national security. American action at the Bay of Pigs had instigated this problem and brought the world to the brink of nuclear war.

Disaster was avoided when Khrushchev, the Soviet Union leader, agreed to remove the weapons in exchange for the Americans agreeing not to invade Cuba. Secretly, Kennedy also agreed to remove American missiles from Turkey which were close to the Soviet border. After Senator Robert Kennedy had personally delivered the message to the Soviet ambassador in Washington the crisis concluded on 28 October 1962.

In November, Ronald received a letter of commendation from the editor of *The Times* for the quality of his journalism but in particular it highlighted his perception in outlining the problems that the American action at the Bay of Pigs would cause.

Following this Cuban invasion, the Soviet Union drew up a plan to develop inter-continental ballistic missiles. Soviet action taken in response to American aggression in the Caribbean created an unprecedented threat to world peace. Ronald's perception had precipitated him reporting that this American action would take the Cold War into a new and more serious phase.

Chapter 19

It was September 1962 when Algernon and his next-door neighbour, David, were about to begin their last year at St Ignatius Catholic Primary School. Ronald and Isabelle considered all options when deciding on Algernon's school, believing a church school to be the best option to avoid exposing him to racism. Up to this point, Algernon thought school was okay but he had difficulty dealing with the intensely authoritarian approach of some staff.

Nevertheless, up to the present time he'd managed to "keep his nose clean" and avoid confrontation with a member of staff. Despite this, a sixth sense gave Algernon the impression that the nuns thought of him as having an inferior intelligence to the other kids in his class. Hitherto none of them had been openly racist but his intuition informed him that their attitude towards him was wrong. On other occasions he thought to himself, 'Am I being hypersensitive about my colour.'

Most of the teachers at Saint Ignatius were nuns, including the Head teacher, Sister Frances. Although, small, she possessed a stern, severe, unsmiling face making her an imposing figure for any young child. Dressed in a black and white habit, she prided herself in ruling with a rod of iron. Woe betide any child who crossed her.

Hanging in the folds of her habit was a cane which was crooked at the top. She seemed to relish the idea that she could wield it like some modern day D'Artagnan. Although, he'd never admit it, there were occasions when Algernon's thoughts ran amok and he thought Sister Frances looked like an underfed penguin. At other times, these naughty thoughts brought a smile to Algy's face.

Isabelle, Algernon's mum, was invited to St Ignatius for a parents' evening and was spoken to by Sister Frances who exclaimed, 'Your son spends a lot of time smirking to himself.'

Isabelle was quietly annoyed that Sister Frances had not used Algernon's name and thought to herself that this nun's holy orders had given her an inflated idea of her position in society.

'You mean Algernon. He's got a great imagination and thinks a lot. It sometimes brings a smile to his face.'

'I don't like children who smirk because I think they're sneering at me. We have ways of curing that type of bad manners.'

Isabelle's eyebrows raised as she took on board what Sister Frances had said. This eyebrow waggle coincided with her thinking how different this woman was to the smiling people in the Caribbean who invariably had a grin from ear to ear. Dour and stony faced this nun spoke with an unpleasant voice which sounded like it had passed through a grater.

'Well I've met you, now what's your husband's name?'

Isabelle thought this nun might be trying to glean whether she was a single parent or not. Knowing this would have been frowned upon, she replied, 'My husband's name is Ronald and he works in the Oil Seals Factory. Mind you when he was in St Kitts, he was a newspaper editor.'

'You don't need a great command of the Queen's English to work in newspapers out there because very few people can read,' she replied in a detrimental manner.

Inside Isabelle was seething but thought it better to hold her counsel. She knew how academically gifted Ronald was and this nun in front of her couldn't hold a candle to him. Growing more belligerent, Isabelle declared, 'In St Kitts, he won a scholarship to the University of the West Indies in Jamaica.'

'What do they learn there? How to cut sugar cane I suppose. A black man's lucky to have a job here at all.'

'Ronald has always worked really hard and he's an excellent father.'

Isabelle thought it better to keep her mouth shut about his work in Cuba but added, 'We thought this school would be the best choice for Algernon because we'd hoped there'd be no racism. Unfortunately, your words seemed to indicate that black people are unworthy of employment.'

Sister Frances grew incandescent with rage. Unused to being challenged, she became infuriated by Isabelle's defiance. This was something nobody ever did. Holding holy orders gave her an air of superiority and she expected people to respect her position in society.

Struggling to contain her emotions, Isabelle had succeeded in deservedly getting under Sister Frances's skin, causing her blood to boil. She'd instantly loathed Isabelle through her willingness to stand her ground in the face of undignified questioning.

Up to this point, Algernon had not encountered any major difficulties with his class teachers but he was now going into Sister Bridget's class who was another nun with a fearsome reputation for intolerance and an horrific temper. Algernon was dreading joining her class and his initial concerns proved to be right.

Sister Bridget was obsessed with children learning the Catholic Catechism. Unfortunately, Algernon thought this approach to teaching was compatible with reciting Mein Kampf. Algernon had been brought up in a family devoted to the church but to him this approach was a form of indoctrination. He found it totally mind numbing.

Taking out a little blue book, Sister Bridget screeched, 'Who made you?'

In unison, the class recited, 'God made me.'

Bellowing again, this woman in black and white shouted, 'Why did God make you?'

'To love, honour and serve Him,' recited the class.

Looking up, Sister Bridget screamed, 'You've made a deplorable start, Algernon Foster. Your lips haven't moved. Are you a ventriloquist?'

'I'm not a Catholic. I went to the Anglican church in Basseterre.'

'You can speak English so you shouldn't have a problem. Did you live in the jungle or a tree house? Not only are you coloured but you're not a Catholic either.'

Such horrific words resonated with Algernon causing tears to well up in his eyes. He'd just received a superfluous public humiliation from a woman who should have set great store on the equality of all human beings. Algernon was incensed and being academically able, he exclaimed, 'We are all created in God's image. There is no distinction between people of different colours. We're all equal.'

Being well versed in biblical teaching because of his love for the church in Basseterre, he said, 'Saint Paul reinforced Jesus's teaching when he said there is neither slave nor free, there is neither male nor female, you are all one in Jesus Christ.'

Grinding her teeth together made Sister Bridget look like a wild animal who was about to pounce on its prey. Bright red in the face with bulging eyes caused by her being deservedly humiliated by a ten year old, made her look maniacal. Her classic error had been underestimating Algernon's intellect. Trying to make Algernon look foolish in front of his class resulted in the tables being turned.

She screamed, 'Face the wall. We don't want to see your face and those thoughts can be kept to yourself. No Catholic child would ever defy or question a nun. The only place you're going is Hell.'

Algernon thought to himself, 'She just found out that I'm not naive and didn't grow up in some jungle village.'

Algernon stayed in the corner for an hour until Sister Bridget let him return to his seat. David, his next-door neighbour, gave a wink and consoled him with a friendly tap. Algernon was worried about how Sister Bridget would react when he put up his hand and asked, 'Could I have a maths book please, Sister.'

Still smarting from Algernon's challenge to her authority, she petulantly flung the exercise book at him in an unnecessarily aggressive manner. This was followed by a barrage of shouting, 'Name on the top line. Second line write the subject. It's maths. My name on the third line and your work better be immaculately set out or you'll be punished.'

'She's like one of those nasty people you read about in the Bible. I'm sure she'd have no problem putting all the babies in Egypt to death,' whispered David.

'We'll call her Pharaoh Bridget,' said Algernon under his breath.

One of the class snitches took the opportunity to get in Sister Bridget's good books by proclaiming, 'Algernon was mocking you, Sister.'

'Stand up you insolent thing.'

Algernon realised he'd touched a nerve. Unfalteringly, he stood up. As he did, this supposedly holy individual pulled him forward putting him against the blackboard. Having enraged this woman of the cloth Algernon wondered what punishment he might face. Within a split second, he had the answer.

Confined in the folds of her habit hanging on the cord around her waist was a bamboo cane. Before Algernon had time to think, the cane was in her hand. She had the look in her eye of someone who would enjoy inflicting pain on anyone who crossed her.

In a frustrated voice, Sister Bridget screamed, 'Left hand out.'

Travelling at full tilt downwards, the cane swished through the air swiftly contacting Algernon's hand. Not content with impacting the palm of his hand, she hit him on the fingers leaving him in excruciating pain. Totally disgruntled with Algernon, she cried out, 'Right hand as well.'

Sister Bridget repeated the punishment. Algernon defiant to the end tried not to flinch but he raised his hands to his mouth to blow on them in the hope of alleviating the pain. Determined to have the last word, Sister Bridget displaying her feline like teeth proclaimed, 'Don't ever defy me again. Sit down, you impertinent individual.'

Algernon did not want to upset his parents and decided to keep the incident from them. He knew that racism in Britain was always going to be a problem for the foreseeable future and his family would have to come to terms with it. His parents had enough worries of their own, and although he was young, Algernon thought he could cope with this issue himself.

Algernon was a talented sportsman. He could run like the wind and developed into a really skilful football player. Games were played in the school yard and as is the case with youngsters they often became over-physical. Such a robust approach could lead to confrontation and on one occasion, Algernon became involved with another boy.

It seemed he was singled out for a reprimand making him think that some of the teachers were innately racist, scapegoating him when other boys were also involved. In one such incident, Algernon tackled Michael Dwyer, whose uncle was a priest in Cardiff. The boys began tussling with each other and both were guilty of boisterous boyish behaviour.

Sister Frances spotted the altercation and pulled the two boys apart. She exclaimed, 'Both of you go to the hall.'

Michael Dwyer was allowed to walk under his own steam, whereas Sister Frances, the Headteacher, pulled Algernon along by the ear. She continued to pull leading Algernon to think that his "lughole" might come off in her hand. Arriving upstairs in the hall she put both boys in front of the Christmas crib.

'Kneel in front of the crib and make sure you pray to the Virgin Mary for my forgiveness.'

Michael Dwyer bowed his head and prayed out loud reciting the Hail Mary a number of times. Being a non-Catholic, Algernon wasn't sure of the words so he reverently bowed his head. Sister Frances appeared proclaiming, 'Michael Dwyer, you're a good Catholic boy and your prayers have been heard. You can go. I've been told it was Algernon Foster's fault.'

Algernon thought to himself, 'If your uncle's a priest you can do what you like but being black makes you fair game.'

Sister Frances shrieked, 'Get to my room. Your behaviour is no better than that of a wild animal. Do you think you're still living in the jungle? Will you ever be civilised?'

'But, Sister, it was just a game.'

'Don't give me that nonsense. Any wild animal must be tamed. Hold out your hand.'

Reluctantly, pushing his hand forward Algernon heard the bamboo cane make a swishing noise, closely followed by a stinging pain.

'And the other one.'

'Now get back to class,' instructed Sister Frances after inflicting the punishment.

Walking disconsolately, Algernon thought to himself, 'What was the point in praying because I was going to get it whatever. So much for equality in creation. It doesn't seem to exist if you're black.'

Months passed without Algernon falling foul of Sister Bridget or Sister Frances's prejudicial attitude. One afternoon, he was again victimised by Sister Bridget's intransigence when she began speaking about Catholic missionaries in Africa. Michael Dwyer, the boy who had had a disagreement with Algernon, spoke, 'My other uncle's a missionary priest in Ghana.'

'You come from a good family. You're so lucky. Catholic missionaries have done such good work in Africa. They've set up schools for children to be educated, helping to make them civilised. These angels of mercy also brought medicines improving the African's quality of life.'

On many occasions, Algernon had discussed his heritage with his dad and he knew his ancestors had come from West Africa. He felt compelled to address the point Sister Bridget had made about Africans becoming more civilised.

'Sister Bridget, Catholic missionaries have also been guilty of thinking Africans were savages living in misery. African tribal beliefs and practices were condemned by the church. I agree with you that missionaries brought medicines but people also forget tribespeople used the rainforest as their own chemist shop. Trying to wipe-out African culture and customs was a big mistake.'

'I don't mean to be cheeky but I can't see the difference between the Great Forest Spirit and God. Both are ways of finding an answer to what people don't understand. Missionaries failed to understand that African tribespeople had a rich way of life and some of their work led to their tribal beliefs being ruined.'

For a young boy, Algernon had produced an adept argument but it was too much for Sister Bridget, who suddenly blew a gasket.

'Foster, you're a savage. This is blasphemy and a mortal sin. May God strike you down.'

Shaking uncontrollably, she reached into the folds of her tunic, exposing the cane. Taking it in her hand, she began to swing it in an unrestrained way. She actually totally lost it randomly hitting Algernon. Her lunacy forced him out of the classroom into the hall causing her to scream, 'Heathen, you're the work of the devil. You'll end in hell.'

She then kicked him forcefully in the leg. Grabbing a handrail, Algernon managed to save himself. In a final ignominious act she screamed, 'Savage, get out and don't come back.'

Algernon returned home with David that afternoon to be greeted by his parents. David verified what had happened with Sister Bridget adding that Algernon had made really good points in his argument. Ronald remained quiet for a few seconds, then exclaimed, 'That's it I've had enough. We've got £2,000 from my press work in Cuba and I've seen a house in Maria Street in the docks. That's where we're going because I've had enough of this racism.'

Part 4
Injustice Anywhere is a Threat to Justice Everywhere Martin Luther King

Chapter 20

27 February 1964, The Packet Public House Tiger Bay

Joey Murrell had just finished work at the docks and decided to call into the Packet public house. This famous watering hole was Joey's favourite haunt. They always kept an excellent pint of the locally brewed Brains beer. Having completed his shift at the dock, he was ready to cut his thirst with his favourite tipple.

Joey's throat was as dry as an old bone. Standing at the bar was a new client who was also enjoying a pint. Joey was a sociable individual and there's no way he would ever ignore anybody.

'Hi, mate. I'm Joey Murrell. What's your name?'

'I'm Ronald Foster and I've just moved into the area.'

'I work on the docks, but where do you work?'

'I've got a job in the Oil Seals Factory in Tremorfa. We mostly make oil seals for cars.'

'You've chosen a great pub to have a pint.'

'It's very quiet at the moment.'

'Make the most of it because it's often rammed with people.'

'I expect the weekends are busy.'

'Every evening is busy here. Men finish work on the docks and come straight in to socialise.'

'Where do you live, Joey?'

'Adelaide Street and what about you?'

'Maria Street but we've only just moved in.'

'Where did you live before?'

'In Caecoed but it was time to move because of racism.'

'You won't have a problem down here. Everyone integrates well in Tiger Bay.'

'The final straw was my son was discriminated against by two nuns in school.'

'What! In a Catholic school?'

'Unfortunately, yes.'

'How many children are in your family?'

'My eldest son is Algernon, who's nearly eleven years old. He was discriminated against. Then there's Perry and Lynne. What about you?'

'I've got seven kids.'

'You've been busy.'

'Graham's my fourth child and he's about your son's age. No doubt they'll be in school together.'

'Algernon was a pupil at Saint Ignatius Catholic School but he'll be finishing primary school in South Church Street.'

'That's where Graham goes and if Algernon is good at sport, the school's got a great reputation for excellence.'

'I'm not really a rugby fan but I'm a cricket nut. I've heard that a young Tiger Bay rugby player called Billy Boston who went to the school is fantastic, but Cardiff Rugby Club refused to select him because of his ethnicity.'

'You're quite right. He's been forced to go to the north of England to play Rugby League. It's disgraceful when somebody with such amazing talent can't get picked because of their colour.'

'Well, racism's a big problem but at least living here we're lucky that everyone is considered equal.'

'It's definitely a model for the rest of society.'

Joey and Ronald related well to each other and as they continued speaking the Packet gradually filled up. Two days earlier, a young black man in the United States had taken the sporting world by storm. Regarded by commentators as a young upstart he beat Sonny Liston, who was world heavyweight champion.

Joey wondered if Ronald was interested in boxing and he asked, 'Did you watch the fight the other night?'

'Couldn't take my eyes off it. Clay was eight to one against.'

'Many thought the fight was fixed. Liston went down so easily at the beginning of the seventh. It didn't look to be much of a punch.'

'His fearsome reputation went before Liston and even our own Henry Cooper said he'd never go in the ring with him.'

'I saw the way he demolished the great Floyd Patterson. That would put anyone off fighting him.'

'Mind you that Cassius can talk.'

'Yeh but his fists seem to back his gob up.'

'Well, anyone who's got the nickname the "Louisville Lip" has to be a good talker.'

'I saw a programme on the telly the other evening about him. After winning a boxing gold medal at the Rome Olympics, his potential for the professional ranks was obvious because he was only eighteen.'

'What's more, he won his medal at light heavyweight.'

'In the four years since, he's filled out a lot, allowing him to fight in the professional ranks at heavyweight.'

'It's not just that he's big but he's got quick hands and fast feet.'

'And when he was asked how he was going to beat Sonny Liston, he told reporters I'm going to float like a butterfly and sting like a bee.'

'It's great entertainment; they didn't know what to make of it. So different from the dour Liston.'

'Yes, he's also become a Muslim.'

'He converted in 1961.'

'Even such a successful sportsman as Cassius encountered racism. It's not just ordinary people who are discriminated against.'

'I didn't know about that, Ronald. What happened?'

'When Cassius returned from the Rome Olympics, he went into a Louisville diner. This young boxer had been feted as a future world champion but the diner manager refused to serve him because he was black.'

'What happened then? Did he punch a few of them?'

'No, the police would have nicked him. He went outside and threw his Olympic medal in the Mississippi River.'

'I didn't know that. I can understand how upset he was after representing his country with such distinction.'

'Some white people just don't get that we're all equal. Blacks can excel in anything just like whites can.'

'Racism's bad in Britain but it's worse in the United States. I've heard there's an organisation called the Ku Klux Klan there.'

'It's a white supremacist organisation who have close ties with the police forces in the Southern United States, giving them immunity from prosecution.'

'I've heard they dress in white with a cross on their outfits.'

'What's more, they have hoods to cover their faces. It's impossible to identify them.'

'Most sickening of all is the idea of them using a cross as their symbol.'

'It's called the "blood drop cross", Joey, and is a symbol of these white supremacists shedding blood to protect the white race. They're totally misguided and think Jesus only died for white people.'

'It's a total farce. Recently, they've killed a civil rights activist in Mississippi and have blown up a church in Birmingham Alabama.'

'They're racist murderers and need to be stopped. Police corruption is a problem which needs to be dealt with in the States and it's bad here. In Caecoed, a white supremacist neighbour had a derogatory poster in his window but he was in league with the police. Although, he took it down, they didn't do anything to him.'

'Police misconduct has to be stopped but we're not helped by racist attitudes to black sportsmen and television programmes portraying racism as acceptable.'

Having enjoyed each other's company, the two men drank their beer and made their way home. Ronald headed north along Bute Street and Joey south to Adelaide Street.

'Goodnight, Ronald,' exclaimed Joey.

'Looking forward to seeing you again. I enjoyed our chat.'

'Well, the Packet gives us a chance to put the world to rights.'

Chapter 21

It was the end of the February half term and Graham Murrell, Joey's fourth child, made his way to South Church Street School. He was an academically able boy and was also the star pupil when it came to sport. He seemed able to turn his hand to any ball game. He'd already represented Cardiff Schools at rugby and baseball.

Although, baseball is a leading sport in the United States, British baseball has its own distinct rules. The ball is always bowled underarm, unlike the American sport where the ball is thrown. Cardiff is only one of three cities and towns where the game is played. Newport and Liverpool are the other two places where this sport is popular.

Graham was an accomplished batsman making him a favourite with classmates who when asked to pick a team always chose him first. His proficiency on the rugby field gave him the street cred that all kids crave.

Algernon Foster made his way from Maria Street as this was to be his first day at his new school. Whereas he'd been the only black boy in St Ignatius this was not the case in South Church Street. Cardiff Docks was inhabited by people from numerous countries making this Dock's school a complete dichotomy of Saint Ignatius. There'd be no racism here, hopefully allowing Algernon's learning to thrive.

He was also a really accomplished sportsman and differed from Graham as his sporting strengths were in athletics and football. And he was lightening fast. His best distance being the one hundred yards sprint. Combining speed with stamina, he'd already won the Cardiff Schools one hundred yards by a country mile and in the right environment, Algernon had the potential to possibly excel at the highest level.

Nervously entering the classroom, Algernon was greeted by a young teacher with a kind disposition who went out of her way to make him feel welcome. His class teacher was Miss Smith who addressed him, 'You must be Algernon.'

'Yes, Miss.'

'What are you interested in?'

'I like my schoolwork but I really love sport.'

'We've another sportsman in the class, so I think I'll sit you by Graham Murrell.'

'Where do I sit, Miss?'

'Graham's in the second row, third desk down. Go and sit by him.'

Algernon was hesitant at first but Miss Smith told him not to be nervous. Graham would show him the ropes. As he sat down Graham announced, 'My name's Graham but everyone calls me Gray.'

'Hi, I'm Algernon.'

'We can't call you Algernon, we're going to have to call you Algy.'

'My mother doesn't like my name shortened, so I've always been known as Algernon.'

'She's not here now, so we're re-christening you Algy.'

Miss Smith was a delightful teacher who treated every member of the class with total respect. This was in complete contrast to the bullying Algy had encountered at Saint Ignatius. Although, she was a stickler for ensuring the class were taught maths and English every day, she was also very aware of the countless different ethnicities in her class.

She was an inspirational educator whose teaching was innovative. Many of the children were youngsters of colour. Miss Smith was ahead of her time and talked to the class about black history. She informed the children about the slave trade and how their grandfathers and fathers had arrived from the Caribbean.

Although, young children they appreciated the relevance of what Miss Smith was doing. Her aim was to give them a grasp of how and why their relatives had come to Britain.

Today, Miss Smith wanted to let the class know about some of the race issues in other countries in the world. She asked the class, 'Has anyone here heard of Nelson Mandela?'

Algy and Graham's hands immediately went up. Miss Smith pointed at Graham saying, 'What do you know about him?'

'I know he's South African and he hasn't long gone to prison.'

Algy added, 'He belongs to an organisation called the ANC (African National Congress) which is opposed to apartheid.'

'Can one of you explain the meaning of the word apartheid to the class.'

'I will, Miss. It's the segregation of the races in South Africa,' exclaimed Graham excitedly.

'Well done, Graham. It's unusual for someone of your age to be so well up on current affairs.'

'Miss, the men in the Packet pub are always talking about these things and my dad tells me about it when he gets home.'

'It's really good that you youngsters are taking an interest in world affairs.'

'Apartheid started in South Africa in 1948,' added Graham who was anxious to impress Miss Smith.

'Excellent, Graham. Can you add anything else, Algy?'

'Yes, Miss, there's a white government in the country and they've got all the power.'

One of the girls, named Daisy put her hand up. She was far more reticent than the two boys. Nevertheless, she was keen to join in the discussion.

'Yes, Daisy, what can you tell us about apartheid?'

'My dad was from Jamaica and my mum is Welsh. That wouldn't have been allowed in South Africa. Mixed marriages are not allowed.'

'Excellent, Daisy. Never be afraid to answer. Where did you pick up that information?'

'My dad also drinks in the Packet and all the men talk about these things.'

Graham was desperate to speak again. His hand was up and down like a yoyo.

'Go on, Graham, I can see you can't wait to tell us something.'

'There's millions of black people in South Africa but they don't have a vote in the elections. This means the white people are always in power.'

'Do you know I'm really impressed that such young people are so well informed about this racist policy in South Africa.'

A girl named Mary was keen to add her tuppence worth to the conversation that had so engaged the class.

'Although, there are far more blacks in South Africa than whites, they're treated like second class citizens. What's more, they can't own houses, use the same beaches as whites and worst of all the children can't go to school together.'

Algy was agitated by what he was hearing and was decidedly anxious to get involved again. After his previous school had tried to undermine him, Miss Smith was helping him find his confidence.

'It was the all-white National Party who started apartheid. This is why Nelson Mandela was imprisoned because he fought against it,' explained Algy.

'I'm overwhelmed with what you've told me. The Packet pub must be a really good place for the local men to be discussing these issues.'

Bold as brass, Graham added, 'Miss, the beer loosens their tongues.'

'Tut, tut Graham you mischievous child. Your dad will have your guts for garters.'

Miss Smith had a great sense of humour and the class descended into fits of giggles because of Graham's remark. She was anxious to impress upon the class how erroneous racism is. Speaking from the heart, she emotionally exclaimed, 'It's the 1960s and society is slowly starting to change. Some people in this country are beginning to support black South Africans.'

'They're claiming Nelson Mandela has been wrongly imprisoned because he was only standing up for the equality of his people. We call this a miscarriage of justice. Then there's Martin Luther King in the United States who founded the Civil Rights Movement. He's beginning to get support from American politicians, musicians and sports stars.'

'This change is happening but it's all too slow for some people. We've got to accept it's going to take many years. There's no doubt you will be part of that change. Remember never cower down to people who try to dominate you just because your skin is a different colour. Please appreciate we are all equal created in God's image. I don't want any of you to forget what we have spoken about today.'

Miss Smith had inspired Algy and Graham. She'd lit a fire in their souls, and her words would resonate within them for the rest of their days. Would her words that society was changing come to fruition? For many people from ethnic minorities, this change was painfully slow, meaning there'd be much bloodletting before the majority of the white population realised that the equality of all mankind was a central tenet within God's Divine Plan.

Chapter 22

Graham and Algy had both been inspired by Miss Smith's innovative teaching. She certainly had the knack of pressing the right buttons with the Dock's children. Algy's short time in South Church Street School was a transformative experience when he contrasted it with his previous school where pupil learning was shackled and constrained by the fundamentalist religious teachings expounded by the nuns.

Petrifying the children with extreme religious beliefs about heaven for the virtuous and hell for the disobedient did not meet with Algy's approval. He thrived on Miss Smith's visionary approach to her job. This had been the catalyst both boys' education needed. Her ingenuity in allowing them to express their opinions, particularly regarding race issues stretched their thinking, bringing out the very best in them.

Both were visibly upset as they said goodbye to this creative teacher who'd fascinated them with her innovative approach to their learning. She had enthralled and spellbound the class ensuring that Algy and Graham's minds had been beguiled, giving her in their eyes, guru status. Although, upset at leaving South Church Street Primary, both boys realised that they were now ready to embark on the next stage of their education.

Along with the other children in their class, Algy and Graham sat and subsequently passed the eleven plus exam. Algy won a place at Howardian High School and Graham at Fitzalan High School. Being black and mixed race, Algy and Graham would face challenges over the coming years which would develop their fortitude and on other occasions try their patience. Although, Miss Smith was a white teacher, her willingness to discuss race issues had helped prepare all of her pupils for these future obstacles.

Secondary school provided an opportunity for both boys to consolidate their learning allocating them with the tools to achieve well in society. Although, in different schools both participated in sport. Graham's early promise as a rugby player marked him out as "one to watch for the future". Algy's speed and stamina led to him excelling in the 400 Metres making both boys highly respected among their peers.

This was not just because of their physical prowess but their Tiger Bay upbringing had helped cement in them an excellent sense of justice. Whereas Algy was the only black pupil at St Ignatius School, he was one of a number attending Howardian High School. Although, Graham was mixed race, black and Filipino, his skin colour was such that the ordinary man on the street would think he was white and not a person of colour.

Fitzalan School had many mixed-race children from the Tiger Bay area making school a pleasurable, inclusive experience. Living in adjacent streets, Algy and Graham spent countless hours together maturing and developing a close friendship.

It was 1968 and Graham and Algy, like many boys of their age, were just keeping their heads above water with their academic work. Most of their time was spent thinking about sport. Graham represented Cardiff Schools and Glamorgan County at rugby. Meanwhile, Algy had won the Welsh Schools Under 15s 400 Metres. As they matured, they were gaining a greater awareness of racism in society.

This was exemplified when one Saturday afternoon on a visit to Cardiff City Centre, they strolled along Queen Street. A police officer walking in the opposite direction stood in a threatening way in front of the boys. Approaching Graham, this custodian of the law set about intimidating him by asking, 'Why are you hanging about with this coloured bloke. They all cause trouble.'

Algy was visibly upset because he'd never been in any trouble in his life. What's more, he'd experienced racism in one junior school when he had done nothing wrong and now he was being stopped in the street by the police when he was minding his own business. He knew why this question had been levelled at him because the policeman thought Graham was a white youngster mixing with a black boy.

'My father's the same colour as Algy's dad,' replied Graham swiftly.

'Less of the lip, Son, or I'll arrest you. Your mouth's too big which is another problem with you lot.'

Fortunately, Father Stephen, the Anglican priest from St Mary's Church, Bute Street saw the policeman unjustly challenge the boys and he intervened.

'I know these boys from Tiger Bay. Like many of the youngsters living there they're honest and upright. There's never been a moment's trouble with them and they're always willing to help other people.'

Having a man of the cloth stick up for them caused this agitator in uniform to change his tune. His word against the priest would be a no contest and he backed off saying, 'You two get on your way.'

The priest's intervention was greatly appreciated. With gratitude in their voices, both boys exclaimed, 'Thanks a lot, Father.'

As the boys turned and walked away, Graham and Algy were incensed at what had just happened. Graham couldn't contain his feelings and said, 'It's no wonder we're having to confront racism in our everyday lives.'

'Why's that, Gray.'

'Well, did you hear that Conservative politician from Wolverhampton.'

'You mean Enoch Powell the Member of Parliament.'

'That's the one. He gave that **Rivers of Blood** speech at the Conservative Political Centre meeting in Birmingham. During the speech, he criticised mass immigration and the proposed Race Relations Bill put forward by the Labour Government.'

'By all accounts he didn't actually mention **Rivers of Blood** in the speech but he was alluding to the Roman Virgil's Aeneid which he quoted, *As I look ahead, I am filled with foreboding, like the Roman, I seem to see the River Tiber foaming with much blood.*'

'You did well to remember and quote that, Algy. I just wonder how much of an effect his words had on the ordinary man on the street. Powell said that one of his constituents told him that he was hoping his children would move overseas because in fifteen or twenty years the black man would have the whip hand over the white man.'

'It was absolutely ridiculous when Powell said that if Labour passed the Race Relations Bill it would bring about discrimination against the white population. Who's he trying to kid.'

'Mind you, good on Edward Heath the Conservative leader who sacked Enoch Powell.'

'Luckily, he had ample support from members of the shadow cabinet who were upset with the racist material in the speech.'

'Unfortunately, many members of the public thought that Powell had made good points consequently supporting his discriminatory stance on immigration.'

The encounter with the policeman and then recalling Enoch Powell's speech further enlightened the boys about the problem of racism in 1960s Britain. As they walked down Bute Street, Miss Smith's words were ringing in their ears. She had said the world would change and they would be part of that transformation.

When politicians who are supposed to treat all ethnic groups equitably and then those who enforce the Law act in such a discriminatory way, it made Algy and Graham wonder if she had misjudged society.

16 October 1968 was a day that would endorse what Miss Smith had said about humanity changing its attitude to race matters. That autumn, the boys were really excited because the Olympic Games were in Mexico City. Algy was incredibly hyped up as he walked towards Graham's house.

These were the first Olympics where there was extensive television coverage and an American athlete named Tommy Smith was expected to break the world 200 Metres record. Algy arrived at Graham's place eager to put his knowledge of his favourite sport on display.

'Gray, the world record's going to go tonight.'

'How do you know that?'

'Mexico City is at altitude meaning the air's thinner. There's less resistance as the sprinters run and they can go faster.'

'What about the long-distance runners?'

'That's a different matter, Gray. There's less oxygen for the runners to breathe meaning that their lungs will feel like they are burning. Long-distance races are made more challenging because of the thin air.'

Graham's dad, Joey, was in the room listening to the conversation and he declared, 'Algy's right about that, Graham. It should be a great race. The Americans are top class sprinters.'

Algy was really pleased with himself because the race ended just as he predicted with Tommy Smith breaking the world record. Peter Newman an Australian was awarded the silver medal and John Carlos, another American, the bronze.

Later that evening, the 200 Metres medal ceremony took place. Seeing the podium brought out and the Olympic flame burning created a real sense that the medal ceremony was a significant occasion. Algy and Graham appreciated that for an athlete this was the culmination of years of hard training. Their emotions welled up when they saw the flags of the two different countries being raised and the national anthems played.

They were watching the world's foremost sporting competition, including athletes from around the world. It was these occasions which gave the boys a lump in their throats. It produced within them the motivation to succeed at their chosen sport. Algy was probably dreaming that one day it would be him having that gold medal placed around his neck.

Graham remarked, 'You never know what might happen if you train hard, Algy.'

In his usual self-effacing manner, Algy replied, 'I'm not that good, Gray.'

Just as Algy finished speaking, the three athletes climbed onto the podium. What the boys were witnessing on the television reverberated around the world. Television cameras focused on badges the athletes were wearing on their jackets.

'Look, Algy, they've got special badges on their jackets.'

'What's on them?' Graham exclaimed.

Graham's dad, Joey, joined the conversation and explained the symbolism to the boys.

'They're human rights badges and the Australian's wearing one as well.'

'Algy, the United States athletes aren't wearing any shoes,' remarked a surprised Graham.

'That's really unusual because they're wearing black socks,' observed Algy.

'Boys, that's a sign of black poverty in America,' explained Joey.

'Tommy Smith is also wearing a black scarf,' added Graham.

'Boys, that's a symbol of black pride.'

Algy picked up on the fact that John Carlos had his shirt open to display beads he was wearing.

'What's the symbolism of him wearing those beads?'

'Boys, it's very sad but these beads represent all the blacks in the States who have been lynched, tarred and feathered and killed. The Ku Klux Klan have committed terrible atrocities against blacks in America.'

'Look, Dad, the American athletes are making a black fist salute as the Star-Spangled Banner is being played.'

'I don't know whether that's a black power salute or a human rights salute. The scarf, beads and black socks seem to indicate it is a black power salute,' said Joey in an amazed voice.

'This has never happened at the Olympics before. What will happen to these two athletes, Dad?'

'There's no doubt they're going to be ostracised by the United States authorities. Really they've been very brave. The United States has serious problems with racism. I'm sure in time these athletes will be proved to be right. American society has very slowly started to change with bus boycotts, freedom marches and the expansion of the Civil Rights Movement. Martin Luther King's non-violent approach has helped change attitudes over there and hopefully in time it will spread here.'

'Miss Smith was right after all. Attitudes towards racism are very slowly starting to change,' declared Algy.

Chapter 23

Algy and Graham sat their "O" Levels in the summer of 1969. Both boys were academically able but their all-consuming passion was sport. However, they'd come to realise that if they were to fulfil their ambition to teach Physical Education, they would have to achieve reasonable "O" Level passes.

Betty Campbell, a Tiger Bay resident, had been the first black woman to be offered a place at Cardiff College of Education and having qualified, Betty was now teaching in the new Mount Stuart Primary School. Being a Tiger Bay resident, she thought it her duty to offer encouragement to any youngster from the locality with the ambition to achieve. Betty fully understood the difficulties that youngsters from ethnic minorities might encounter because she'd experienced these herself.

Algy and Graham fell into the category of young people who aspired to do well. When Betty visited Graham's mother and the boys were there, she would take the opportunity to give them the shot in the arm they needed.

'You're good at sport but it's very important that you pass your academic subjects or they won't accept you to train as teachers at Cardiff College of Education.'

The boys took her advice on board and worked hard for their "O" Levels. Their short-term diligence paid off with both achieving seven passes including English Language.

'I went to church so many times in the month before the exams I think God was doing them for me,' declared Graham.

'Don't underestimate yourself, Gray. We worked hard in the end.'

'Trouble is we've now got to do an "A" Level course.'

'Don't forget, Gray, we were told in school that to get into teacher training college you don't have to pass them. You've only got to follow the course.'

'The trouble is that could be a charter for me to take it easy in the Sixth Form.'

'There's always our sport. This could be a good time to concentrate on developing our sporting prowess.'

'That's a good word, Algy. Where did you get that from? Did you have a dictionary for breakfast?'

'I read an article about Lynn Davies. You know Lynn the Leap and it mentioned his prowess in the long jump.'

'He went to Cardiff College of Education so it must be good there because he won an Olympic Gold medal in 1964.'

'Gray, I want to use this year to try and get a Welsh Schools athletics vest. They like you to have a good sporting profile at the college.'

'I'd like to play for the Welsh Secondary Schools in rugby. We'd be guaranteed a place then.'

'As long as we follow that "A" Level course.'

Algy and Graham's "O" Level year had been an important period in the history of racism in the country. Whereas the boys had always listened to their dads speaking about this issue they were now old enough to discern the problem for themselves.

During their last year in primary school, Miss Smith had made them aware of South Africa's apartheid policy. Whites ruled the country even though blacks comprised the vast majority of the population. Blacks being treated as second class citizens in South Africa became an important issue for left wing political supporters in Britain.

This activist element wanted South African sports teams banned from competing on the world stage, rightly claiming that they were not truly representative of the country. Only whites were able to compete for South Africa, blacks being excluded on the basis of their colour.

This issue came to a head when the English cricket team were due to tour South Africa. England had a former South African mixed-race cricketer named Basil D'Oliveira who was a top all-rounder and likely to be selected to go on the tour. He'd arrived in Britain because South Africa would only select white cricketers and he wanted to play international cricket.

Graham visited Algy after seeing this item on the news. It was the BBC News lead story and became an important topic of conversation for the boys. Their interest in racist issues particularly those linked to sport meant they'd taken a great interest in this case.

'Let's hope that the tour to South Africa is off. If they don't select Basil D'Oliveira, it's a travesty of justice because he's a great all-rounder,' exclaimed Graham.

'I'd go even further, Gray. The tour should be called off in any case. South Africa's apartheid policy makes it an unsuitable place to visit by any fair-minded country. The main problem here is the M.C.C. (Marylebone Cricket Club) want to maintain their links with South African Cricket, and it's likely they'll side-line D'Oliveira so as not to upset their hosts.'

'The talk is that the South African president realises there's an element in Britain who would like to see the tour cancelled and he's using politics to fix things in South Africa's favour.'

'Some people are saying he's making it look like he's ready to appease international opinion but secretly he's working hard to prevent D'Oliveira taking part.'

'Early in 1968, his batting form wasn't good and the England selectors dropped him from the team.'

'That was the perfect reason not to pick him for the tour and it would give that double headed South African president the excuse he was looking for.'

'But it all backfired because Basil D'Oliveira hit 150 in the final Test against Australia.'

'All cricketers experience a dip in their form but they invariably bounce back.'

'It happens in all sport.'

'After hitting all those runs against Australia, they still didn't pick him.'

'It was only when Tom Cartwright dropped out, they decided to include D'Oliveira.'

'Yes, and what did the South African president do? He threw his toys out of the pram, saying that the selection was politically motivated.'

'Politically motivated be damned. They're the ones who are unfair with that racist policy they've got.'

'It was great that the tour was cancelled on 24 September 1968.'

'Power to the people, Algy.'

Once the boys had started their "A" Levels, problems with South African sport continued to dominate the news. Rugby was tantamount to a religion for white South African players and supporters. White South Africans saw it as the ultimate expression of their manhood.

Afrikaners the descendants of the original Dutch Boer settlers saw the game as a way of proving their physical superiority over all opponents. Depriving the Afrikaners of rugby would really hit South Africans hard.

The 1969 tour to the United Kingdom became a flashpoint for anti-apartheid supporters in this country. Algy and Graham were in the sixth form and because of their ethnicity, they could understand why feelings among some people in this country were running high. Nelson Mandela was a real hero for the boys because of his imprisonment for the belief that all men are equal.

They were determined to demonstrate their support for black South Africans who were being victimised by a minority white government. Although, Graham was obsessive about rugby, the South African government's policy was an anathema to him and he would definitely play his part in trying to change it.

Algy and Graham were both in school with other boys of colour and feelings would run high in their respective sixth forms. Both were now old enough to go to the Packet to play snooker. Here the tension was palpable because of the total opposition to the tour within the Tiger Bay community.

Obviously, this atmosphere had an effect on Algy and Graham and they were not afraid to give vent to their feelings. Both were angry at what was being allowed to happen in the name of sport and they would bristle with indignation.

'Can you believe that one of the two most important academic institutions in Britain is playing a game against the South Africans,' exclaimed Graham.

'Fancy Oxford University playing this racist country in their first game on tour,' replied Algy.

'They can't think anything of their black students who are bound to be upset by this tour going ahead.'

'The excuse is always used that politics and sport are different. How can it be? The rugby team represents South Africa.'

'They're not representing South Africa at all.'

'You're quite right, Gray, they're only representing white South Africa.'

'There's four million whites and eighteen million people of colour in South Africa. None of this black majority have a say in the way their country is run.'

'Apartheid is wicked and Britain should stop the tour.'

'There are whites here who want the tour stopped. Peter Hain is the young leader of the Anti-Apartheid Movement. I've read that he was born in Kenya to white South African parents. In South Africa, they became banned persons because of their anti-apartheid activities.'

'Being banned persons they endured severe restrictions on their movements, political activities and associating with people. They were constantly watched and could only be in a room with one person at a time. These are incredibly courageous white people who were prepared to make a stand against an evil policy.'

'There are some brave people who are prepared to put their bodies on the line so there can be justice for all people. These heroic individuals certainly need to be supported.'

'We need to join this movement. We know people can live in harmony if they put their mind to it.'

'Quite right, I love living down here because nobody is concerned about anyone's colour.'

'Changing the subject, I heard my dad say that there's new houses being built in Christina Street and we are going to move in there.'

'I see those houses are just off Bute Street and I won't have to go far to see you.'

'You won't because I heard your dad's buying one as well.'

'That's news to me, Gray.'

'Maybe I shouldn't have said anything. He might have wanted it to be a surprise for you.'

'It won't be a surprise at all. He always plays his cards close to his chest. Don't worry, I won't drop you in it. I'll just act surprised.'

Chapter 24

The Foster and Murrell families moved into Christina Street just as the South African Springbok Touring Party embarked on the Welsh leg of their rugby tour. Algy and Graham were determined to demonstrate their opposition to the tour. They were motivated through anger at a discriminatory political system which treated people of colour as second-class citizens with no vote, poor healthcare and limited education prospects.

Feelings among the anti-apartheid movement were running high, causing Algy and Graham to decide their protests would be peaceful. How could they ever get into teaching if they had a criminal record? Controlling their emotions was a prerequisite if they were to fulfil their ambition.

The Springbok rugby bandwagon rolled into Cardiff and feelings were at fever pitch among many in the Cardiff student population. One of Algy's "A" Level teachers had told him that the Cardiff University students were going to cancel a major contract for the supply of beer to the Cardiff Students Union unless certain conditions were met by the Cardiff Rugby Club players. They were one of the Welsh club sides who were due to play the Springboks.

Algy couldn't wait to get home to tell Graham. Knocking the Murrell's front door, he was eager to divulge what he'd found out that day. As usual, Graham invited him in for a cuppa and they sat in the front room.

'Gray, Cardiff University are going to cancel a big beer contract for the Cardiff University Students Union if the Cardiff players aren't given an opportunity to look at a petition signed by many of the students asking them to consider withdrawing from the game on Saturday.'

'What's a beer contract got to do with Cardiff Rugby club?'

'One of the Cardiff players is a brewery representative and he's negotiated the deal with the university. It's a contract worth an enormous amount of money to the company.'

'What have the committee in Cardiff said about it?'

'They've refused. They're not going to be railroaded by a bunch of students who they see as young upstarts.'

'That's the end of it then.'

'It's not because the contract is so big, the Cardiff player is worried that his job will be affected if the company loses it.'

'What can he do about it? Surely, it would be harsh if he lost his job.'

'To be fair to the students, they've been very reasonable because they just want the petition presented to the Cardiff players. It'll then be up to their consciences whether they play or not. To present the petition, the brewery rep has agreed to meet the students outside the ground at the Gwyn Nicholls Gates. It's off the premises and he will present it to his teammates.'

'That seems a very fair approach by the university students but have the Cardiff committee agreed to that.'

'It seems so.'

'I bet that made no difference at all. The players will have already made up their minds.'

'It didn't but the students only wanted the Cardiff players to see the petition. None of the players withdrew from the team and the game will just go ahead. I can see how fair the Cardiff Students Union have been and this reflects well on their attitude. However, there's going to be a demonstration in Cardiff on Saturday.'

'We'll be there.'

'There's going to be a number of Cardiff churches involved in the demonstration, so there should be a lot of people. Hopefully, the protest will go off peacefully.'

Algy and Graham joined a peaceful march organised by the Anti-Apartheid Movement, the Church in Wales and the Communist Party. It passed off peacefully and there were no unsavoury incidents. On the Friday prior to the march, Algy and Graham made two banners. The first stated *Nelson Mandela is innocent* and the second one proclaimed *Set him free.*

Other members of the Tiger Bay community had joined the demonstration to express their sentiments to a system they saw as blatantly inequitable. Older residents of the area were delighted that two young sixth formers had made a stance against a tour which was totally unrepresentative of the South African people.

The following morning, Algy and Graham were incensed when they read the contents of the Cardiff Chairman's after dinner speech.

'You must be heartily sick of demonstrators and it's a matter of regret that the tour is full of incidents. Please do not be misled by the minority of militant demonstrators.'

'You know the problem, Algy. These people don't have to live in a country where the law treats them as second-class citizens. They seem to be lacking in empathy towards a majority of citizens in a country who are being treated in a prejudicial way.'

'I agree, Gray. We've got our own problems here but like Miss Smith told us, attitudes are changing slowly.'

'This tour is going to get more and more difficult for the Springboks. The word is that senior religious leaders are starting to get involved and they are being joined by lots of university students and sixth formers.'

Graham was perceptive for somebody so young and he was quite right, the tour encountered major difficulties. Anti-apartheid demonstrators became so infuriated that the tour was going ahead that there were bomb hoaxes and threats made against players. Algy and Graham were so committed to entering the teaching profession that they were determined to keep their activities peaceful.

Their allegiances lay with following the teachings of Mahatma Gandhi and Martin Luther King who expounded the idea of peaceful protest if a cause was to succeed. They wholeheartedly disagreed with people's lives being threatened.

Returning from a trip to his sister's place, Graham went to visit Algy to have their usual cup of tea together. As they were chatting, the news came over the radio that there had been a serious disturbance at the Western Counties game against the Springboks in Bristol. It was reported that the demonstrators were chanting "Sharpeville, Sharpeville".

'Graham, they're referring to the Sharpeville Massacre when the black population in South Africa were demonstrating against the pass laws.'

'I think sixty-nine black people were shot dead by the police but there were hundreds wounded. Only black South Africans are forced to carry passbooks as a means of controlling their movements and employment opportunities. Many thought it a cause worth dying for. Black and mixed-race South Africans were regularly stopped by the police and humiliated by having to recite aloud which tribe they came from.'

'They've just said on the radio that a demonstrator who was a teacher has run onto the playing area at half time and thrown upholstery tacks onto the field.'

'Listen, I sympathise with the cause. The trouble is he's gone over the top because the anti-apartheid leaders are against violence. Those tacks will be classed as an offensive weapon. He'll probably be prosecuted and lose his job. If a player has one of those in his leg it could do some damage.'

'It goes against the instruction given by all the most inspirational leaders in history who have always advocated peaceful, non-violent protest because that is the only way to sway public opinion and win any cause.'

'There are great examples to copy. Jesus, Martin Luther King, Nelson Mandela and Mahatma Gandhi to name a few.'

'Although, he's only young I've read this Peter Hain is against violent protest and any intimidatory behaviour because he wants to attract people to the cause not drive them away. The religious leaders who support the Anti-Apartheid movement are committed to pacifism as well.'

'On 24 January, Wales are playing South Africa and we'll have to go to the demonstration.'

'I read in the paper that the Anti-Apartheid movement have written to the Welsh players asking them to consider dropping out of the game.'

'One Welsh player has said he'd never play against South Africa again.'

'Which one, Gray?'

'John Taylor who plays for London Welsh.'

'I know he's the one who went to South Africa with the British Lions in 1968.'

'What he saw out there convinced him he'd never play against South Africa again. People who support the tour are trying to say he went there in 1968 and played then, so why not now?'

'He experienced apartheid at first hand and realised it was morally wrong.'

'He's the one who's got the courage of his convictions and is prepared to stand up for justice.'

Algy and Graham joined the anti-apartheid march prior to the Wales South Africa game. Many courageous, uncompromising people possessing an iron will were prepared to demonstrate in Cardiff. Although, taunted by some rugby fans, the demonstration went off peacefully with protesters ignoring the catcalling and verbal barbs being hurled at them by rugby supporters.

Algy commented, 'They don't appreciate what their fellow human beings have to go through in some countries. If they were treated like the blacks in South Africa, they'd soon come to realise how unfair life is for millions of people.'

'To put a game of rugby before the lives of millions of South African blacks means they can't see any further than their noses,' exclaimed Graham. 'Spot on, Gray.'

Chapter 25

October 1970 was to be a significant milestone in Algy and Graham's lives. They had a decision to make about their futures. Both had achieved well in their "O" Levels but their minds were in a quandary over what to do when they finished school. Sport was an obsession, and like many boys of their age, they would often prioritise sport over their schoolwork.

Algy had represented the Welsh Schools Athletics team and Graham the Welsh Schools Rugby team. Their aptitude for sport was never in question but their dilemma revolved around whether they were academically good enough to teach.

A regular visitor to Graham's house in Christina Street was Mrs Betty Campbell who was best friends with Graham's mother, Beattie. In 1960, Betty was one of the first six women to be offered a place at Cardiff Training College. More importantly she was the first black woman to train as a teacher at the college.

Having started her teaching career in Llanrumney Primary School, she had now returned to Butetown. In the past, the area had been universally referred to as Tiger Bay. As this former coal port had changed, the region's name had been replaced by Butetown.

Betty Campbell continued to live in the area and was employed as Headteacher at Mount Stuart Primary School. Well respected within the local community, Betty held the Butetown people close to her heart.

Algy and Graham met as usual on the way home from school and popped into Graham's house for a cuppa. Entering the kitchen, Algy and Graham saw Mrs Campbell deep in conversation with his mother, Beattie.

'Hiya, Mrs Campbell,' said Graham politely.

'It's good to see you boys. What have you two been up to.'

'I've been concentrating on my rugby,' explained Graham.

'I hear you've been selected for the Welsh Schools. Well done, Son.'

'Thanks, Mrs Campbell.'

'What about you, Algy? I understand you could be a prospective Olympian.'

'I don't know about that but I've won a Welsh Schools Athletics vest.'

'You never know, Algy. Just keep thinking big.'

'I live in hope.'

Sensing the boys had side-lined their academic work because of their sport, Betty enquired, 'What are you pair going to do next year because you can't stay in school forever.'

'I thought I'd like to teach Physical Education,' said Graham.

'And me,' agreed Algy.

'Come on now. Isn't it time that the pair of you did something about it?'

'What do you mean, Mrs Campbell?' Graham remarked sheepishly.

Betty Campbell emitted an aura and could be a daunting, determined character if you didn't know her. Nevertheless, she always had a heart of gold. One thing she appreciated was how difficult it was for anyone from the Butetown community to break into a profession like teaching. Straight to the point, she exclaimed, 'Apply, you pair of nitwits. Don't think somebody from the college is going to walk down here and offer you a place.'

'How do we do that?' Algy asked.

'Get the application forms from school and bring them home. I'll give you a hand to fill them in, particularly the personal statement you'll need to write.'

Answering for the two of them, Graham said, 'We'll do it tomorrow.'

'Oh, and by the way, some advice for the two of you. You'd better finish your "A" Levels. It's easier now for people of colour to be offered a place than when I applied. I am indebted to the college because they gave me the chance to fulfil my ambition.'

'Thank you, Mrs Campbell,' remarked Algy.

'Just get those forms, boys.'

Betty Campbell's advice might have been direct but she always kept her word. Algy and Graham gained confidence from being helped by this Butetown icon. Her help paid off and they were both offered a place at Cardiff College of Education to study Physical Education. Qualifying as teachers was now in their hands but knowing the boys could sometimes get their priorities wrong, Betty offered some crucial advice.

'Don't forget, it's not all sport in college. There's academic work to do as well. By the way you've been given an unconditional offer based on your "O"

Levels but you need to work hard at your "A" Levels. It'll be beneficial if you pass them.'

Cardiff Training College was an exceptional three-year experience for both Algy and Graham. They were the only students in their year from ethnic minority groups and integrated well with aspiring young teachers from all parts of the United Kingdom. Being a Welsh teacher training college, there were many young adults from predominantly Welsh speaking areas of Wales. This gave Algy and Graham a totally different perspective on life.

Coming into contact with Welsh speakers was an indispensable learning experience for two young trainee teachers whose previous experience was primarily confined to the Docks area of the city. Determined to make an effort at a new language, Algy and Graham were able to acquire some Welsh words, pleasing the native speakers. Many were from homes where Welsh was the first language, and to have two boys from the Butetown area of the city giving it a whirl with their predominant language was gratifying.

The college environment was mutually beneficial for prospective young teachers from rural Wales. Coming into contact with Algy and Graham assisted them by boosting and strengthening their understanding of people from a different community to their own. Many would eventually secure teaching posts in large cities with expanding diverse communities.

Having Algy and Graham in their year group was a worthwhile introduction to the different cultures they would experience in their teaching careers. Having a connection with Butetown residents helped their fellow students to appreciate how difficult it had been for the boys to overcome prejudicial behaviour and to achieve within society as well as they did. Their peer group started to understand that the discriminatory language on television and the racist abuse meted out to ethnic minority sports stars was appalling and unwarranted.

By having Algy and Graham in the year group, they were receiving tutorials from an important hidden curriculum. For teachers, the equality of all human beings was mandatory. In the future, these young trainees would realise that these college life lessons were a vitally important part of their development.

Teacher Training College gave Algy and Graham an opportunity that few people from their background experienced. Betty Campbell had started the ball rolling in 1960 but during the intervening eleven years, very few people of colour had trained in Cardiff. Nevertheless, the college had displayed a willingness to give people from ethnic minorities an opportunity to enter the teaching profession.

Algy and Graham both represented Cardiff College in their favoured sports. College was an exceptional and unforgettable experience for them. However, one incident in their three years put a dampener on what was otherwise a first-rate time in their lives. They were disillusioned with the college authorities when they invited Natal University from South Africa to play rugby against the College First XV.

South Africa gave very few blacks the opportunity to attend university and in 1974 apartheid was a heinous government policy, one that Algy and Graham had protested against during their time in the sixth form. The college that had been a pioneering institution by giving Betty Campbell, Algy Foster and Graham Murrell the opportunity to enter the teaching profession was now embracing an all-white rugby team, compromising the British value that education was an entitlement for all people.

Graham was perturbed that the college had decided to accommodate a rugby team selected on the basis of race. At the conclusion of lectures, he went home to Christina Street, distraught that a grave miscalculation had been made by the college authorities. Algy appreciated this misjudgement had really affected both of them but Graham had always worn his heart on his sleeve and he called to see him.

He knocked the door and Graham answered. The anger on his face was obvious and Algy did wonder if anything he said would placate him.

'Graham, I feel the same as you about this rugby match.'

'There is no way I can play against an all-white South African team knowing that millions of blacks are living in poverty.'

'Believe it or not, there are other people in college who feel the same way as you do but nothing will be done about it.'

'The college is being quite devious about this match by not playing at the college ground.'

'What are they doing then?'

'The players are being taken to a secret venue. They've no idea where they're going to be playing.'

'That's all a bit cloak and dagger, isn't it?'

'It's to stop anti-apartheid demonstrators disrupting the game.'

'Our team should definitely refuse to play.'

'That won't happen because they're all desperate to play against a South African team.'

'I can sort of empathise with how the boys feel but the college should have taken it out of their hands. It's a grave miscalculation by the college authorities which is the real problem. The boys are all young and lack the necessary life experience to make a measured decision.'

'Those in charge of the college should realise that it's wrong for one man to think he's superior to another by virtue of his colour. At the end of the day, it's a teacher training college. Surely that means it should support equal opportunity for all.'

'I've spoken to one or two of the boys who are really good blokes but rugby is like a drug to them and it's fallen on deaf ears.'

'It's awful that this is going ahead. Imagine if one of them walked into a class and there was a black kid. Would they refuse to teach the child?'

'Of course not.'

'Then they should think about all the young black children in South Africa being excluded from education by apartheid.'

'I won't have anything to do with it.'

Covert planning led to the game being played at a secret location in Port Talbot. Cardiff Training College might have won the game but they certainly lost the moral high ground by playing against an all-white South African team. That evening, the Cardiff and the Natal teams attended a dinner at the college. Algy had a late lecture and when it concluded, he went to the toilet.

As he opened the door, he was confronted by three white South African rugby players in their university blazers. It crossed his mind that he should turn around and walk out. He hastily decided that this was his college and there was no way he was going to be intimidated by three people indoctrinated by a country with a legal racist policy.

Their only experience of black people was their parent's servants who looked after their every whim. As Algy walked towards the urinal, the tallest of the three remarked, 'Are you allowed in here, Kaffir?'

Algy knew the word kaffir was the most lamentable racial slur used by whites in South Africa. Bristling with indignation but remaining calm and retaining his dignity, he exclaimed, 'Just in case you don't realise it, my wee is the same as yours.'

For the first time in his life, this South African had been challenged by a black man, causing his face to contort. Clenching his teeth and glaring at Algy, his hostile stare could so easily have resulted in him lashing out. As the South African was a college guest, Algy had him over a barrel. Algy decided to turn the tables on him by using some of the Welsh Valley boys favourite form of address.

'Good evening, boyo,' and he walked out.

Chapter 26

All good things have to come to an end. Apart from the one aberration, Cardiff Training College was a fantastic three years, allowing Algy and Graham to make lifelong friends. Suddenly, reality was staring the boys in the face. There would be no more grants for study. It was now time for them to pay back the debt they owed society for giving them the opportunity to train as teachers.

Algy and Graham both needed a teaching post and competition for jobs was keen. Many of their peers left to teach in London and Essex, where there was an abundance of jobs. Being home birds, the boys wanted jobs in Cardiff as their girlfriends were from the local area.

Both were besotted with their partners and it wouldn't be long before their commitment was sealed through marriage. Attaining a teaching post would provide them with the financial security, which allowed them to take this step.

Algy and Graham met at the Packet pub where they began to discuss their futures. The frivolous behaviour of their youth had been replaced by a more mature attitude to life as they realised their heady student days were behind them.

'I'm being interviewed at Cardiff City Hall on Tuesday. Have you heard anything, Algy?' Graham asked.

'I'm going on the following Friday with a group of newly qualified teachers. The letter said there are six jobs going and they'll be choosing the best six from the group who are there.'

'They're doing the same thing on Tuesday so hopefully we'll have a bit of luck.'

Finishing their drinks, Graham was obviously taking this interview deadly seriously. He remarked, 'I'm going home to prepare for the interview.'

'Good idea. I'll be doing the same. These head honchos will probably want to know things like how we're going to engage all pupils in sport.'

'We need to be careful not to place too great an emphasis on elite team games. Making sure every kid is included in our programmes is the most important thing and I'm certain that's what they'll be looking for.'

'Good luck on Tuesday, Gray.'

'Same to you, Algy. We both need to get jobs.'

Algy started to prepare for his interview on the Monday so he had a few more evenings where he could fashion his answers. Tuesday was the night he always met his mates at the Top Rank nightclub on Queen Street. Although, Algy was facing an impending interview, he saw no reason not to have a night out. Always a great night, Algy danced until 2:00 am, only stopping when the lights came on and it was time to leave.

He left the club turning left, then sauntered along Queen Street. Approaching Marks and Spencer, he became aware of a strident sound. The noise was raucous and by the time he reached the store, Algy suddenly realised someone had put the front window through and stolen clothes. At this point, the ear-splitting sound from the alarms made his ears ring.

To relieve the noise, Algy put his fingers into his ears. He could see that the perpetrators had made off with hundreds of pounds worth of clothes. By now a group gathered on the pavement and stared into the empty window.

Travelling at a rate of knots, two police cars arrived on the scene. Instantly, the officers jumped out and began to move the assembled group of people away from the window. Clapping eyes on Algy and seeing he was black, the four officers made a beeline for him. One of the police put him in a wrist lock while another one removed handcuffs from his belt.

Algy was in significant pain from the officer's wrist hold. His hands were then forced behind his back and he was cuffed. Finding it difficult to maintain his balance, he felt helpless and vulnerable. He blurted out, 'What have I done?'

'Don't try denying that you broke into the shop.'

'I was just walking away from Top Rank.'

'All you coloureds are trouble and you don't want to work. You're just looking to make a quick pound.'

Frightened but remaining polite, Algy exclaimed, 'I've never been in any trouble in my life.'

'Don't give me that nonsense. What's your name?'

'Algernon Foster, officer.'

'You're coming into the station with us.'

'But I haven't done anything.'

'We want to know where you've put the clothes.'

'The only clothes I've got are the ones I'm wearing.'

'You've either stashed them or given them to someone.'

At that moment, two street pastors left a doorway opposite where they'd been helping a homeless man. They approached the police to support Algy's claim that he'd nothing to do with any robbery.

'This man has done nothing wrong. He was just walking along the street,' proclaimed one of the pastors.

'How do you know?'

'We watched him come from the Top Rank. I think you'd better let him go. He's innocent and we'll go to court to support him. It seems you picked on him because he's the only black man here. You've got no evidence against him. It's getting as bad here as the United States, if what you're doing is going to happen to any black man who's just walking along.'

Turning to Algy, the police officer asked, 'Have you got a job?'

'I've just qualified as a teacher and I'm being interviewed for a job on Friday at City Hall.'

'We want the handcuffs taken off this man immediately or we'll report you to your senior officer,' demanded the pastor.

Reluctantly, the police officer took out the key to release Algy from the handcuffs. He was ecstatic that the two street pastors had supported him. Being charged and found guilty of theft would mean his teaching career had ended before it had started. He was euphoric that these two caring members of the public had thrown their weight behind his dire situation.

Algy was indebted that these two were prepared to fight his corner. Their concern for the underdog was apparent in the work they were doing on the streets, and Algy was delighted that this seemed to extend to all aspects of their life.

'Thanks so much. No words can express my gratitude for what you've done.'

Having been caught displaying such a racist attitude left the police in an awkward position. Their thoughtless impetuosity made a mockery of the office they held but the officer in charge, wanting to have the last word exclaimed, 'You're lucky. Get home before we change our mind.'

Algy left the scene but he wondered if having told the police he was a newly qualified teacher who had an interview on Friday would come back to bite him.

The experiences he'd had throughout his life made him suspicious of the authorities. He was almost paranoid about the way he could be treated because of his colour.

Racism during the 1970s was rife and he pondered that the tentacles of these bent coppers would reach out and exact revenge on him by attempting to strangle his teaching career. Algy's past experiences resulted in him on occasions being overly suspicious. He thought that these police officers could report him to the education authorities in the hope that mud might stick. Common sense told him that surely people in education would ignore what was an attempt at a wrongful conviction.

Graham attended the interview at City Hall and managed to gain one of the available teaching posts. After telling his parents he'd secured the job, he telephoned his fiancée, Gill, blurting out, 'Now I've got a job, we can get married.'

'If you think you're asking me over the phone you've got another thing coming. You're getting down on one knee if you want me to say yes.'

'I'll come over later on to do obeisance to you.'

'Don't worry, I'm only winding you up. It's a foregone conclusion.'

'That's good. I thought you were serious for a moment. I just need to go to Algy's place to wish him all the best. He's got an interview tomorrow.'

'Don't forget to give him my best wishes, and by the way when are we getting married?'

'Next summer. Is that okay?'

'I'll tell you after you've gone down on one knee. So long, love.'

Desperate to get a teaching post, Algy was fretting over the interview. He'd been disconcerted by his altercation with the police and embedded in his mind was that their vindictive nature might extend to them reporting the incident to the City Education Department. Graham knocked the door and an agitated Algy answered.

'Come in, Gray. Did you get the job?'

'There were six jobs and I got one of them.'

'That's good. I had a problem on Tuesday night with the police.'

'They did their usual I suppose and blamed you for something you didn't do.'

'It was lucky, some street pastors stood up for me.'

'Although, I'm mixed race, most people don't realise my father's a Barbadian. In the eyes of the authorities, I look more white than black.'

Graham's colour was certainly an advantage when it came to getting a job or avoiding being stopped by the police. Be that as it may it didn't change his attitude towards discrimination. His blood would boil if he heard racist language and he seethed with anger when Algy or any other person of colour was the victim of racism.

Graham would not hold back on giving any bigoted individual a piece of his mind particularly if they used racist language and then claimed they were not racist. Graham quite rightly thought these two could never be disconnected from each other.

'At times I find it difficult having worked my socks off to achieve well in college and I'm praying I don't get discriminated against during tomorrow's interview,' muttered a disconsolate Algy.

'It would be scandalous if that happens, Algy. They need black teachers in Cardiff's schools.'

'We know diversity is important but do the people who run education think in the same way.'

'They should because there's been an increase in the number of kids from ethnic minority groups in the schools.'

'I'll give it my best shot.'

'I'm going because you're preparing for tomorrow. Good luck, Algy.'

Chapter 27

Friday, 14 June 1974, was a bright, balmy morning as Algy set off for City Hall. This was the day he hoped would set him on the path to a career in teaching. Hopefully, his prospects would be as radiant as the morning itself. Nevertheless, he was ambivalent about his expectations.

His college achievements filled Algy with a sense of pride and he was exhilarated by what he had accomplished. This ebullience could just as easily be replaced with the thought that his colour might prevent him from getting a job. Would the interviewing panel judge him on his achievements or would they discriminate against him?

Growing overly suspicious about the interview, Algy wondered if his brush with the law a few evenings earlier might come back to haunt him. He'd made a point of saying that he was a newly qualified teacher who was going for interview and this worried him.

Entering City Hall, Algy decided to push this foreboding to the back of his mind. He went to the reception desk and was shown to a waiting room where there were three other candidates. All were tense brought on by anxiety through wanting to secure their first teaching post. Three other candidates arrived and Algy wondered how many teaching jobs were on offer.

A City Hall clerk came into the room and announced that there were six teaching posts. Unfortunately, one candidate was going to be left high and dry. Algy was yearning for a job to give him the financial security needed to marry his fiancée, Sarah. One of the interviewing panel came into the waiting room and announced, 'The interviews will be done in alphabetical order Adams, Barnes, Davies, Foster, Hughes, Jones and finally Thomas.'

Algy would have liked to be first to get the ordeal over and done with. Notwithstanding he was grateful for not being last because the wait would seem endless.

Each candidate seemed to be given about 20 minutes and when Mr Davies's name was called, trepidation enveloped Algy. 20 minutes flew by and Algy was called into the interview room where three men and a woman seemed to be glaring at him.

'Take a seat, Mr Foster. Let me introduce you to the panel. On my far left is Mr Lewis, a head of a Physical Education department. Next to him is Mrs Barry, an adviser for girls Physical Education. I'm Mr Thomas Senior Adviser for Cardiff and on my right is Mr Davies, boys' Physical Education adviser,' said the senior adviser.

Politely, Algy replied, 'Good morning to you all.'

'I'm going to start the interview by asking why you want to teach,' announced Mr Thomas.

Algy had prepared what he thought was an appropriate answer and he began, 'I've always wanted to teach from a young age and that motivation has developed as I've matured. Having been taught by some excellent teachers who've stimulated my interest in education, I've always believed that education is the greatest gift that children can be given and nothing would give me greater pleasure than to participate in this process.'

Having completed his answer, Algy thought he'd made a good fist of it. Although, he'd entered the room as a bag of nerves, his response had helped to relax him. Mrs Barry then asked, 'In your opinion, what is the most important aspect of your subject and how will you make sure this is taught well?'

Algy was concerned to convey that teaching physical education was not about teaching a few top-drawer pupils to represent their country, and he explained, 'My philosophy is such that physical education has to cater for all pupils. It is so important that every student enjoys the subject because a fit body will produce a fit mind.'

'Physical Education is such an important part of any school curriculum because of the impact the subject has on a child's physical development. All pupils need to fulfil their potential and if that is achieved then the elite athletes will prosper as well.'

Algy was very pleased with the way he'd answered the two questions to date and was convinced his answers would have impressed the panel. Up to this point in the interview, the questions had elicited good responses from him. Unfortunately, the panel's line of questioning changed and became more of an interrogation. The chairman asked, 'Do you think you'll be able to cope with teaching in a Cardiff school where the overwhelming number of children are white?'

Algy was thrown by this prejudicial line of questioning. Alarm bells began to ring in his brain as he knew this must mean the panel had grave reservations about a person of colour being able to teach in a predominantly white school. For Algy, the chairman had shown his hand and he knew there was no way he would ever fit into their plans. However, he attempted to answer the question but knew he was not going to be able to acquit himself well and this made him fractious.

'This is a totally irrelevant question because I don't see how a person's skin colour relates to their teaching ability. A class should respect the teacher for their subject proficiency not the colour of their skin,' exclaimed Algy.

Having touched a nerve with him, the chairman decided to call a halt to the interview.

'That's all, Mr Foster. Wait with the others.'

Through no fault of his own, Algy knew he'd blown it. There was no way he'd get a teaching post. Did he really want to work for such a biased organisation? Surprise, surprise six candidates were awarded jobs but Algy was excluded.

It was time for a rethink. Algy wondered why he'd wasted three years in college because it seemed the overriding factor in whether he'd get a job was his colour.

That evening, Graham phoned a distraught Algy to ask how the interview had gone. He was convinced that he would have obtained one of the available posts. When Algy told him what had happened, Graham went quiet. Although, he hadn't personally been discriminated against his blood began to boil at the thought that a person of colour could be treated in such an appalling way.

Graham was always troubled by people in authority who would make a big outward show of saying they'd never discriminate against anyone but their prejudices were innate. They were ingrained into their psyche. After regaining his composure, Graham exclaimed, 'Algy, I'm so sorry and disappointed for you. I'm sure there will be other teaching jobs.'

'That's it for me. I don't want to be involved in such a discriminatory process again. The interviewing panel might not have inflicted any physical punishment on me, nevertheless the psychological damage they've done is just as bad. I feel demeaned and worthless as a result of their discrimination.'

'It seems the hard work I did for three years was a waste of time. Having achieved well in college that panel maltreated me because of the colour of my skin. Society needs to change its attitude and give people of colour a fair crack of the whip.'

Graham was able to empathise with Algy who was distraught at the treatment he had received at the hands of people who should have known better. Algy's pain was palpable and was upsetting for his soul mate. Realising that consoling his friend was futile, Graham decided to end the call. Algy would need time to lick his wounds.

Daunted by his experience, Algy decided a complete change of tack was mandatory if he wanted to marry Sarah. As a matter of urgency he needed employment. Fortunately, the following day a post as an accounts clerk became available at the Julian Hodge building and Algy applied for the job. At last, good fortune smiled on him and he was offered the job.

Although, the teaching interview had left a really sour taste in Algy's mouth, it seemed that one organisation at least had placed some value on him, irrespective of his colour.

Chapter 28

Algy and Graham's lives had taken them in different directions. They were both now married and no longer living in Butetown. Nevertheless, they remained bosom buddies even though they did not see each other as often as they once did. Graham had moved on in teaching and was now at his old school, Fitzalan High.

He was also playing rugby for Abertillery, a renowned Welsh valleys team, who during the 1960s had three British Lions in their squad. Algy moved on from the Julian Hodge building and in 1980 was working as a sports shop manager in James Howells, a big store in the centre of Cardiff. His experience at the teaching interview had left him dispirited and he'd decided not to put himself through such an intimidatory and discriminatory process again.

On Saturday, 17 May 1980, Graham flew to Miami, Florida on a British Airways flight. He'd been exhilarated for weeks at the thought of going on his first long overseas rugby tour. Having spent a fortnight in Miami, he gained an insight into the extent of racism in the Southern United States and what he witnessed nauseated him. There were many aspects of the tour he had enjoyed but on his return to Cardiff, some of the more disparaging experiences prompted him to pick up the phone to speak with Algy.

Algy answered, 'Who's speaking please?'

'Hiya, Algy.'

'How did the trip go?'

'It was an interesting experience but I was disgusted at the level of racism over there.'

'It's bad in this country, Gray.'

'I think it's worse in the States.'

'In what way?'

'When we arrived, we were driven from Miami Airport to our hotel. Remember we were supposed to be in the richest country in the world. Our bus took us on the Interstate Highway where we passed the black ghetto district. What an impoverished place!'

'It's an example of the extreme segregation that exists in the southern United States. Black people are living in tin shacks with appalling facilities. Crime and drugs are rife thanks to the poverty. It's no wonder there are so many murders in the city because black people are treated appallingly. It's bound to create disharmony in society.'

'There are some poor areas in Britain.'

'But nothing like this. We'd been at our hotel a few hours when all hell broke loose in Downtown Miami.'

'Is that the riot you're referring to. It was on the telly and I read about it in the papers. I've got to say it sounded pretty scary.'

'It was really frightening.'

'I wondered if you were anywhere near it.'

'Surprisingly only a few miles away.'

'Wasn't it something to do with a court case. What happened, Gray?'

'The trouble kicked off in the early hours of Sunday morning in the black ghetto areas of Overtown and Liberty City. It was only a few hours after we'd arrived in Miami. A black insurance salesman named Arthur McDuffie was killed through police brutality and the ensuing court case was a complete miscarriage of justice.'

'How was he killed?'

'On 17 December 1979, he was illegally riding a black and orange Kawasaki motorcycle. Arthur McDuffie had accumulated traffic offences and was driving with a suspended licence. The police also claimed he had jumped a red light. Following an 8-minute chase through residential streets, the victim was said to have come off his bike and attempted to run away.'

'The police caught up with him. A fight ensued and the man was badly hammered by four officers. In the process of the arrest, the victim's helmet was removed and he was thrown to the ground. McDuffie was then beaten by the police with flashlights and batons.'

'Disgracefully' the police beat him around the head and chest. In the end, he was taken to hospital where he died four days later. In an attempt to cover their brutality, the police drove the car over the bike to make it look like there'd been an accident. The all-white jury acquitted the police officers, even though the coroner was not fooled by what the police had done and he said it was no accident.

'Dr Wright, the coroner, stated that the injuries were not consistent with a motorcycle crash. Multiple skull fractures one of which was 10 inches long were proof of the brutal treatment meted out by the police. Absolute proof was provided by the gauges on the bike being smashed when the police drove over it which would not have happened if there had been a crash.'

'These were smashed by incorrigible racist law enforcement officers who were prepared to go to any lengths to cover up their villainy. Dr Ronald Wright decreed that Arthur McDuffie had been beaten to death.'

'What happened then, Gray?'

'Following the verdict, thousands of people attended a protest at the Miami Justice Building. There was a riot and the National Guard were brought in. Despite this, there were eighteen deaths, three hundred and fifty injuries and hundreds arrested.'

'There doesn't seem to be any justice in the American courts if a black person is tried. It's no wonder there was a riot. It seems a black man's life is less valuable than that of a white man. We've experienced racism here because people see us as inferior.'

'With the poverty and the court injustice, it's no wonder there's riots. The worrying thing is it could easily happen here. It'll get to the point where black people will have had enough of this mistreatment and they'll rebel.'

'You didn't get caught up in it, did you, Gray.'

'No, but we had an unscheduled visit to Orlando over 250 miles away until everything cooled down.'

'I bet the visit to Disney World was great.'

'It's a great place. Unfortunately, it was overshadowed by another racist incident.'

'What do you mean?'

'Our bus driver was black. What a cracking bloke. Nothing was too much trouble for him. He really went out of his way for us. Our team captain asked if we could buy some beer for the trip. His reply was "Man, leave it all to me. Just collect some money and I'll sort it".'

'Well, we had a kitty and he bought a dustbin, filled it with ice and bought cases of beer for us in the supermarket. We were sorted.'

'I bet all the boys were grateful, Gray.'

'They were, Algy. When we got to Orlando, he took us to Rosie O'Grady's which is a famous jazz club. When we went in, the management stopped the bus driver and told him coloureds were not allowed inside.'

'Surely that broke the equality laws that the Civil Rights Movement fought for.'

'That's right, Algy. There were fifty of us, including supporters and we told them if Clint didn't go in, then we wouldn't.'

'Did people power win the day?'

'It did but I reckon if they knew my dad was from Barbados, they'd have tried to stop me as well.'

'It would be interesting to know if the management had called the authorities, whether the police would decree the law had to be upheld.'

'I'm glad it wasn't put to the test. Disappointingly, so many of the police in this part of the States are racist. Knowing our lot, there'd have been uproar and I dread to think what might have happened.'

Graham and the team returned to Miami on 20 May, following the cessation of the riots. Florida newspapers carried only one story and the black population who rioted were taking the blame. This biased approach by the press disappointed Graham who thought they needed to look at the poverty and discrimination experienced by the black population.

The lack of social justice for black people was bound to create a pressure cooker atmosphere. Graham's upbringing and light colour enabled him to take a unique perspective of a dire racist issue.

Returning to their five star hotel on Miami Beach, Graham was well aware of the harrowing racism faced by black workers. Late May in Miami was swelteringly hot with high humidity. His time at the hotel gave him an insight into the appalling conditions experienced by black employees which Graham now tried to explain to Algy.

'The black staff at our hotel were maids and laundry workers but their conditions of employment were appalling.'

'Why's that, Gray?'

'It was a really oppressively hot, humid day and I was walking towards the swimming pool. The door to the laundry was open and being inquisitive, I looked in. To my amazement, there were at least twenty black people sitting around. Miami's high temperature and humidity meant the room was searingly hot and steamy.'

'Inside black laundry workers were sweating profusely. Beads of perspiration ran down their faces and they looked devoid of energy. I asked what they were doing. At first they ignored me, not realising that I was mixed race. They thought I was just being nosey and couldn't empathise with their dreadful conditions.'

'How did you manage to get them to talk?'

'I asked them if this was where they took their breaks. One of the older members of the group said it was the only place they were allowed to take a breather. I could sense the exasperation in the group as this was the only room without air conditioning in the hotel. The hotel management wanted them out of view of the guests.'

'Definitely a case of out of sight, therefore out of mind. Obviously, they were reticent about talking to me until I told them my father's family was from Barbados. To prove this, I showed the workers a photo of my clan which fortunately broke the ice. They understood that my family history was the same as their own.'

'We shared a common heritage as the descendants of slaves. They began speaking freely to me about the difficulties faced by black people in that part of America. It gave me the chance to explain that racism was also a problem in Britain.'

'I wanted them to know how fortunate I'd been to train as a teacher and had a job in a school. Knowing they earned little money, I went to a store and bought bottles of coke and crisps for everyone in the room.'

'I bet they really appreciated that, Gray.'

'They did and I spent a lot of time speaking to them about the problems they faced.'

'It makes me realise that society throughout the world has to drastically change if there's to be equality.'

'What I witnessed in restaurants made me wonder if Martin Luther King's dream would ever be realised.'

'What does happen?'

'Waiters and waitresses are always white?'

'Were there no blacks doing the job, Gray.'

'I didn't see any. All the blacks worked in the kitchens washing up. They are paid low wages but people serving in the restaurants carn far superior money. In the States, diners are expected to donate a big tip to waiting staff. It helps explain why blacks are frozen out of that type of work.'

'Society has to change in many countries if people are going to live in harmony.'

'It was a fantastic trip filled with positive and very negative experiences, but there's no way I could shut my eyes to the race problems in the States.'

'The problem's everywhere, Gray. A lot of people have blood on their hands.'

Chapter 29

Sadly, Algy's experience during the teaching interview at Cardiff City Hall had dented his confidence to such an extent that the desire he once had for the profession had diminished. Although, Algy always considered himself a determined character he was convinced racism was a battle he couldn't win. There needed to be a transformation in society.

Institutions which should have been treating every citizen equally needed to dispense with the systemic racism which had infiltrated them. Having been sports shop manager at the prestigious James Howell store, he applied for a managerial post in another large store. A wage increase would be advantageous at this critical juncture in his life.

His wife, Sarah, had given birth to three children. Algy was now at a crossroads in his life. He enjoyed the work at James Howell but he needed a job paying higher wages if their children were to be appropriately catered for.

It was the run up to Christmas 1981 and stores were working flat out maximising sales. At the best time of the year for making a profit, Algy's department had been particularly busy and as he left late one evening, he told the doorman he was shattered. Turning right out of the store, he headed towards Cardiff Castle to catch the bus home.

Cardiff City Council spent generously on Christmas decorations. A myriad of different lights gleamed against the winter sky creating a warm ambience at this coldest time of the year. As Algy reached the entrance to Cardiff Market, two policemen stepped out of the shadows and stood in front of him. Algy was completely taken aback to see these two officers of the law blocking his path.

The bigger of the two policemen ordered, 'Turn around we're going to search you.'

Stunned, Algy replied, 'On what grounds are you doing this?'

'We suspect you're carrying a weapon because a lot of blacks do.'

'I'm twenty-eight years of age and I've just come from work.'

'That's unusual because a lot of you people don't work. Most of you are involved in criminal activity.'

Trying to hold his temper and be polite Algy declared, 'You can't stereotype black people, as there are good and bad in all ethnic groups.'

Algy touched a nerve with these prejudicial custodians of the law. They had no idea what the word stereotype meant.

'You've got too much to say for a black boy.'

'I'll have you know I'm a man, not a boy.'

'Shut it and put your hands on your head.'

Reluctantly, Algy raised his hands, waiting for one of them to put his paws on him. Starting at his ankles, the officer began to feel his way up his legs, paying particular attention to his lower leg with the expectation of finding a knife stashed in his sock. This process was a source of great embarrassment to Algy. He was made to feel worthless and degraded by this despicable police behaviour.

Many passers-by shopped at Howells and knew him. To be stopped and searched in the middle of St Mary's Street in Cardiff was belittling for a man who prided himself on providing his customers with excellent service. As the policeman finished searching his jacket pockets, Algy's voice quivered with anger, 'You just stopped me for no reason. There's no way I'd ever carry a weapon.'

'Shut it or we'll cuff you.'

Just as the officer finished threatening Algy, a Howell's doorman came by and spotted the commotion. People were stopping or turning around to look at this totally unnecessary altercation in the street.

Immediately recognising Algy, the doorman proclaimed, 'This is Mr Foster, one of our managers. He's incredibly popular with senior management, customers and other staff. I've no problem vouching for him. He's just left work and has definitely not done anything wrong.'

Hearing these supportive words, the police realised they'd have to let Algy go.

'You're lucky this time. Get yourself home.'

'I'm not lucky. You had no reason to stop me,' said Algy.

He was determined to have the last word. This was the second time he'd been stopped by the police and their discrimination daunted him. Algy couldn't help feeling victimised because of his colour. He was a citizen with an exemplary record being treated as a common criminal in the full gaze of the Cardiff public.

The police skulked off with their tails between their legs knowing they'd stopped a man of colour for no reason other than racism. Algy thanked the doorman and headed for home.

Lovingly greeting Sarah and the children, he sat down to his evening meal. This stop and search had traumatised him and he decided to phone Graham. Gone were the days when the friends could just pop across the road to each other's houses. Most of their conversations were now carried out on the phone. Algy rang and Graham answered, 'Hello. Who is it?'

'It's Algy, Gray.'

'Hiya, mate. What's up?'

'I'm twenty-eight and I've just been stopped and searched by the police on my way home from work.'

'Good God, there's no end to the discrimination we have to face. It's got to stop. How can the police think that a black man is more likely to be carrying a weapon than someone who's white?'

'It's just racism.'

'It's not going to stop anytime soon unless politicians are prepared to do something about it.'

'The police need to realise that Britain's population is becoming more diverse and their attitude to this needs to change.'

'A more diverse police force serving the public is needed to reflect this change.'

'Appointing police from ethnic minorities would certainly be a step in the right direction. This would be essential in the areas where a large percentage of the population are from minority groups.'

'There were serious riots in Brixton in April.'

'That's where my dad lived for a while when he came to the country.'

'The Metropolitan Police were going out of their way to stop black youths and search them. White police officers were openly racist to the black youths. Tensions became so bad over this issue, it was more of an uprising than a riot. On 11 April 1981, two hundred and seventy-nine police were injured along with forty-five members of the public.'

'I had seen it on the news but I've become so fed up with seeing racism on the telly so often that it just washes over you and you disregard it. Many white people think, "There's those blacks kicking off again and it's a pity they don't go back to their own countries",' sighed Algy.

'A lot of white people will blame the black kids but some good might eventually come out of it.'

'What do you mean?'

'I don't like the violence but it might eventually help to change people's attitudes. Youngsters today are showing they're not prepared to tolerate it.'

'You could be right. If black people just accept racism, then nothing will change. In time I suppose, a more tolerant society might eventually grow out of this disorder.'

'Fifty-six police vehicles were burned and many buildings damaged. Civil disorder spread to other cities like Toxteth in Liverpool and St Paul's in Bristol. It led to William Whitelaw, the Home Secretary, commissioning the Scarman Report which was published less than a month ago.'

'I should have been aware of that but mistakenly I paid no attention to it.'

'The riots were bad but Lord Scarman's report stated that there was disproportionate and indiscriminate use of stop and search powers by the police against the black population.'

'Other factors definitely need to change. I think the main one is raising education standards among black kids. That's it. I definitely need to take my life in a different direction,' exclaimed a determined Algy.

'What are you going to do?'

'I'm going to apply to be a supply teacher. That's what I trained to do and now's the time to change. I want to play a part in transforming society.'

'Well said, Algy, and by the way, report those police that stopped you. We don't want riots in Cardiff because of rogue cops.'

Chapter 30

Graham continued to work at Fitzalan High School which had been the establishment where he'd received his secondary education. By the early 1980s, Graham had become a valued member of staff. His devotion to Physical Education and his willingness to run teams and after school clubs gave children the opportunity to experience different sports.

Fitzalan was a unique educational institution thanks to the diverse nature of the pupils who attended the school. Many came from the Butetown area of the city giving Graham an advantage in being able to solve problems other staff members might have difficulty with. He'd been brought up in the area and knowing many of the families gave him valuable first-hand experience and an in-depth knowledge of the pupils' backgrounds.

This equipped him with the tools to solve disputes before they escalated. The head teacher was grateful to have such a competent member of staff who added real value to the school environment.

Algy continued to work in retail but in late July, he applied to join the supply list of Cardiff teachers. He was determined to put behind him the bad experience he'd encountered at the interview when he left college. There was no contact with the Education Department for four months but his luck was about to change.

On Friday, 3 December 1982, Algy returned home late from work. He'd had a busy day and went into the kitchen to be handed a brown envelope by Sarah. Thinking it was probably a utility bill, he reluctantly opened it. Inside was a letter from Cardiff City Education Department. An exhausted Algy was immediately invigorated as he read the contents.

'I've got a two-term supply teaching placement,' shouted an excited Algy.
'Where, love?'
'I can't believe it. I'm going to be in Mount Stuart Primary school.'
'Isn't that where Betty Campbell's head?'
'Yes, love. I've hit the jackpot.'

'What happens after the two terms?'

'It's a start, Sarah. Once you're in, hopefully there'll be other jobs.'

Algy realised he'd done it. This might only be a start but he'd fulfilled a fervently held ambition to teach. He was elated and losing all his inhibitions, Algy began dancing on the spot. Such was his excitement, his frenzied dancing was a joy to behold.

Exhausted by the physical effort, he stopped jigging around and cleared his mind. This was a touching moment as he realised what he'd achieved. Overwhelmed with emotion, Algy began to sob uncontrollably. These tears of joy were the culmination of years of struggle against racist attitudes. Thankfully, the first black head teacher in Wales had given him the opportunity he'd craved when he left college.

God willing his days in retail were behind him. Tomorrow he'd hand in, then work his notice ready to start in January.

'I'll have to give Graham a ring and let him know,' exclaimed Algy.

His hand was shaking as he picked up the phone and before Graham could ask who was on the other end, Algy screeched, 'I've got a teaching job.'

'Where?'

'Mount Stuart Primary School.'

'Wow, you're lucky. Betty Campbell will look after you. Mind you, you'll have to work hard.'

'There's no worry about that. It's taken me eight years to get into teaching. I won't be blowing this opportunity.'

'Betty demands high standards but she's fair and rewards those who work hard.'

'That's all I want is fair play. My life has been blighted by unwarranted racism. I've encountered problems with the police and even discrimination by the Education Department.'

'Unfortunately, Algy, racism has become an integral part of society.'

'It's institutional racism and has to change.'

'I'm teaching so many children of colour in Fitzalan, I'd hate to think of them facing a society tolerating discrimination.'

'I wanted you to be the first to know because we've been friends a long time and gone through such a lot together.'

'Algy, sit down and drink in what you've achieved. No, better still pour a glass of wine for Sarah and yourself and have a drink. No doubt you'll sleep well tonight.'

'I will. Thanks for the encouragement and your support through a difficult period of my life.'

Prior to the Christmas holidays, Algy visited Mount Stuart Primary to see Betty Campbell. He was so eager to impress in his first teaching post that he couldn't wait to find out who and what he'd be teaching. This imposing black woman who was revered in Cardiff Bay, stood at the door to her office waiting for a nervous Algy who was strolling towards her along the corridor. He was determined not to disappoint Betty, so in Algy's eyes a good first impression was essential.

'You look petrified, Algy,' exclaimed Betty.

'Well, I don't want to mess up, Mrs Campbell.'

'I've known you for a number of years and you'll be fine here.'

'I appreciate what you did for me when I applied to college, and I'm so grateful for this opportunity.'

'We work hard here. Educational and disciplinary standards are high among the children. We want to give them the best opportunity to achieve in a changing world. Mind you, there's still a long way to go to eliminate racism.'

'I appreciate that having experienced it myself. I want to be part of that change.'

'I experienced it as well when I was in school. A teacher told me I'd never be able to get into teaching because of my colour. This attitude deflated me but like a good boxer who has been knocked down, I eventually climbed up off the mat and was determined to prove that woman who tried to undermine me wrong.'

'What it makes me realise is that many people of colour have been discriminated against. Changing attitudes in society is important to me.'

'You will be part of the change and I'm pleased to hear your mate, Graham, is doing well in Fitzalan High School. His mother and father are really proud of what he's achieved.'

'We don't see as much of each other as we used to because we're both married but we regularly talk on the phone.'

'You were both good boys; a little mischievous but you always had a good sense of justice and I knew you'd do well. That's why I gave you the leg up that you needed.'

'Listen, we'll never forget what you did for us when we were young.'

'You'll be teaching children who are nine and ten. We've introduced an innovative approach to the youngsters' education. We're teaching black history so the children will learn about their roots. A trip to the United States inspired me when I learnt about some of the female anti-slavery activists like Harriet Tubman and the Civil Rights Movement.

'Martin Luther King and his non-violent approach in the face of horrific injustice inspired me to orchestrate change in school. We're teaching the children about slavery, black history and apartheid. I feel this is really important and innovative.'

'I'm with you on that, Mrs Campbell. When I was with Graham in South Church Street Primary, we had a teacher called Miss Smith who told us about apartheid in South Africa. This roused our interest in Nelson Mandela and we demonstrated against the South African rugby tour when we were in the sixth form.'

'That was an inspirational subject for a white teacher to deliver at that time. It's pleasing to hear you demonstrated because that rugby tour should have never gone ahead. I hope you demonstrated peacefully.'

'Of course, we did, Mrs Campbell.'

'We're making every effort to raise the children's self-esteem. I've told the staff that I want our children to embrace their ethnicity and be proud of it. Our history has been one of a fight against adversity. Although, some people create barriers for people of colour, change is slowly taking place.'

'It'll take time but I want Mount Stuart School to be at the forefront of this change. Bute town children have much to offer the modern world.'

'I haven't really given it a lot of thought but I suppose Graham and myself have been part of this change.'

'You need to be proud of what you've done. By the way, Algy, you're only here for two terms because of a teacher secondment. I'm going to insist that the Education Department counts this towards your probationary year, which you have to pass.'

'That's really good news, Mrs Campbell.'

Two terms at Mount Stuart Primary provided Algy with an invaluable learning experience. What a bonus it was working with this inspirational black headteacher who taught him so much about having high expectations for the children in their care. Being such an enjoyable experience, the time flew by. Algy began to wonder whether he'd have a job to go to in September 1983.

Just before the end of term, Mrs Campbell asked to see Algy. He tentatively walked towards her office and was greeted with the words he wanted to hear.

'Algy, Howardian High School phoned because they need an EAL teacher on supply and it's right up your street.'

'You'll have to excuse my ignorance, Mrs Campbell, but I don't know what EAL means.'

'Well, I wouldn't expect you to. It means English as an additional language. You'll be teaching immigrant children. This is spot on for you, Algy.'

'Will I need a reference?'

'It's already done, Algy. Your work here has been first class and I appreciate what you've achieved with the children. If I had a job available, I'd keep you here. But what you're going into is a wonderful opportunity. By the way, I've told them that your work is exemplary.'

'It's my old school, Mrs Campbell.'

'I know and some staff still remember you and were effusive in their praise. You certainly made a good impression when you were there.'

'I'll never be able to thank you for what you've done.'

'You already have by working so diligently with the kids.'

Algy began at Howardian in September 1983 and within a fortnight, he had hit the jackpot. There was unbridled joy in the Foster household. The Head had made his post full time, so Algy was now a fully-fledged teacher. Eight years of angst had come to an end allowing him to fulfil his boyhood dream.

There were many good people in this world and in the last year Algy had experienced the justice he'd craved in 1974 when he was first interviewed for a teaching post. It was time to put past disappointments behind him and build a productive career.

Part 5
They Don't Care. Anybody Will Do.
Tony Paris (One of the Cardiff Three)

Chapter 31

Graham woke early on Sunday, 14 February 1988, knowing he'd have to present his wife, Gill, with a Valentine's card. Failure to do this would almost certainly lead to an awkward silence, rendering Gill unamused by such thoughtlessness. Rummaging in his bedside cabinet, Graham found the card he'd bought just over a week ago. He'd been neurotic about purchasing it early, in the realisation that his life wouldn't be worth living if he'd forgotten.

He knew that Gill would never forget his card. Buying one for her was the prerequisite to having a peaceful day. Removing the card from the drawer, he gently tapped Gill on the shoulder. Drowsily, she turned towards him and with slumberous eyes, she caught sight of the card.

Although, heavy eyed, she'd suddenly remembered it was Valentine's Day. Graham handed her the card and exclaimed, 'Love you.'

'Let me get yours,' Gill replied.

Having placed Graham's card under a pile of books, she located it easily and handed it to him. Simultaneously opening their cards, they both smiled when they read the verses inside, causing Gill to declare, 'I wonder who makes these verses up. They must be a real romantic.'

'People will write anything if they're paid to do it,' exclaimed Graham cynically.

'You know what I think of you. I don't need verses, Gill. Turn the radio on, please, love.'

Gill stretched over and switched on the radio. The national news headlines had just started. The first item involved the murder of a prostitute in Butetown who had been stabbed numerous times. No name was given but Graham pronounced, 'There's no doubt I'll know the woman who's been killed if she's a local.'

'It sounds like it was a frenzied attack, Graham.'

'Poor girl, I'll phone Algy later on. No doubt he'll have his ear to the ground.'

Algy liked his beauty sleep, so Graham decided to phone him after 11.00 am. Finishing breakfast Graham spoke to some of his pals, who told him the woman's name was Lynette White, a well-known Butetown lady of the night. Graham was visibly upset when he heard the name. He'd been her form teacher at school. Lynette's attendance record was atrocious, causing her to drop off the school's radar.

She was a little girl lost, just one of a number of school children who have a difficult time as a youngster leaving them vulnerable to unscrupulous characters. Unfortunately, vulnerable children had suffered abuse in bastions of society where they should have been safe. Regrettably some children's homes, schools and the church which should have been safe sanctuaries for the young had a minority of evil people who were prepared to engage in deviant criminal behaviour to satisfy their sexual cravings.

On hearing the woman's name, instead of waiting, Graham decided to promptly phone Algy. Having already heard the gruesome news, Algy had made a few calls of his own. He'd just finished a call to one of his mates when Graham rang.

'Hiya, Algy, it's Graham.'

'I can guess why you're ringing.'

'It's really grim news. I knew Lynette very well.'

'Gray, I've been told she was stabbed over fifty times.'

'She was a really stunning looking girl with a lovely nature but through no fault of her own, she fell in with a bad lot when she was an adolescent. When she was very young, Lynette's mother split with her father and left to go to Essex. Her father insisted Lynette stayed in Cardiff. Fortunately, Lynette's beloved Nanna was her rock and loved her with all her heart.'

'Sadly, Lynette's grandmother died, creating within her a terrible emotional trauma. Her world began to implode, leaving a young teenager at the mercy of disgusting creatures who prey on underage girls.'

'I saw the interview she gave to a BBC journalist about life on the streets for child prostitutes.'

'It was revealing and definitely spoken from the heart.'

'It's really sad to be drugged and kidnapped at fourteen years of age, then taken to Bristol to work as a prostitute.'

'She escaped and returned to Cardiff and began working the streets here.'

'Unfortunately, the die was cast. It's difficult to know how the authorities can allow this to happen.'

'We saw Lynette so little in school because of the breakdown in her family life. She was young and impressionable which was the crucial element in her demise. A poor domestic situation makes it easy for such a young person to go off the rails. Take it from me, she was a really lovely girl. When she was present in school, Lynette was no trouble at all.'

'It's easy for people to be judgmental about girls like Lynette. But it's like being caught in a spider's web. She was young, susceptible and prone to mistakes, like all young people are. In no time at all she found herself in a situation which was bound to escalate leading to a way of life that no child should ever be enticed into.'

'You have to feel sorry for youngsters who find themselves in such a bad place.'

'Recently, she'd been living with her boyfriend, Stephen Miller, in Dorset Street in Grangetown.'

'She was besotted with him and a lot of her earnings went to feed his drug habit.'

'We've known him a long time and again I've always found him okay.'

'People can be judgmental about someone with a drug problem. What they don't appreciate is that people can have difficulties in their life. Problems like that can happen to anyone. Being human none of us are exempt from the complexities of life.'

'Prior to her death, Lynette had disappeared but it seems not even Stephen Miller knew where she was.'

'Lynette had to give evidence at two trials. The talk in the city was that she was keeping out of the way to avoid going to court.'

'They were both very serious cases. The one was an attempted murder by Francine Cordle. The second was to give evidence in a trial where a thirteen year old girl had been acquired to be used as a prostitute.'

'I bet Lynette was scared to death because plenty of people in the underworld would be prepared to murder her if she blabbed.'

'Nobody knew where she was lying low. Stephen Miller was even at a loss to know where she was holed up.'

'She must have had a key from another prostitute to carry on as a sex worker while she was keeping out of the way.'

'7, James Street, the flat where she was murdered was owned by Leanne Vilday.'

'She's another sex worker and must have been the only one who knew where Lynette had gone.'

'By all accounts she couldn't get into her flat and had to go to the police. Lynette had the key and the cops had to break in. The police were going to take Lynette into custody for trying to avoid giving evidence in court.'

'Sadly, when they found Lynette's body, it was absolutely mutilated by some monstrous predator.'

'Let's hope the police get him.'

'Somebody who's prepared to cut a girl's throat, then disfigure her in such a way deserves to spend the rest of their time in prison.'

'Let's just hope they get the right man.'

'The word is that a white man with blood on him was seen near James Street.'

'Sounds like he's the one the police should be looking for. He was probably a regular client.'

'Knowing how some police behave, they'll probably try to blame a black man like they did with Mahmood Mattan.'

'I know it was just before we were born but he was a soft target after Lily Volpert had been murdered.'

'There was no evidence against him but they still hung him. People still talk about it today because he was the last man to be hung at Cardiff prison. This was another example of the racism pervading society.'

'This case was certainly a miscarriage of justice because Mahmood could speak no English and today solicitors are working to get the guilty verdict overturned.'

'Lily Volpert was a shopkeeper murdered for money, whereas it sounds like the man who murdered Lynette might have had perverted sexual motives.'

'Possibly, let's just hope they get this madman.'

'I'm taking Sarah out for a Valentine's Day lunch but what's happened to Lynette is enough to turn you off food. Such a frenzied attack must have been carried out by a monstrous human being. An assault of this nature is totally inhuman. I'll speak to you again, Gray.'

'Enjoy your meal. I just hope justice is done.'

Lynette White's murder left Butetown residents aghast at the level of violence meted out to the victim. People were uneasy at the thought that there

184

could be a brutal murderer living in the locality. This was such an odious crime causing a normally vibrant community to become spooked and panicky overnight.

People who were normally confident about life in their community, grew paranoid at the thought that a pernicious individual was on the loose. These normally self-assured inhabitants metamorphosed into faint hearted individuals, cowering in their homes daunted by the prospect that they could be the next victim.

Chapter 32

When the police had opened the door, Leanne Vilday, the owner of the flat at 7, James Street was traumatised by the scene that greeted her. It was difficult for her to comprehend that a human being had behaved in such a depraved way. The room resembled an abattoir with blood spattered onto walls where major blood vessels had been severed. How could anyone act in such an animalistic way?

There and then, Leanne thought that the person who'd carried out this attack was subhuman. Their basic instincts were those of a psychopath. Unfortunately, Leanne had entered a world of commercial sex where the very business she was working in left her vulnerable to abuse, particularly physical violence. She was not somebody who had much time for the police but she fervently hoped they would quickly catch whoever was responsible in order that normality could return to Butetown.

Having somebody as perverted as the individual who'd carried out the crime in James Street on the loose was unsettling for everyone in the area. Most of the punters who used prostitutes were looking to satisfy their carnal needs but there was a minority of men who resorted to physical violence. Many of the prostitutes were resilient women who could look after themselves because some of their clients could be dangerous, debased members of society. This client was truly warped to furnish this type of attack.

Butetown residents were quickly made aware of the brutality doled out to Lynette leaving many cold at the thought that some subverted individual in Butetown could be stalking prostitutes. Through their countless contacts in the area, Graham and Algy were kept informed about the direction taken by the police investigation.

On 27 February, Algy and Graham met for a drink at the Claude Hotel situated in the Roath area of the city. Both were traumatised by the inhumanity of Lynette's murder. All their sporting and other interests were put aside as the only topic of conversation revolved around the James Street murder. Algy and

Graham's past experiences with the police made them sceptical about whether they would ever arrest the right person.

Having bought Graham a pint, Algy exclaimed, 'There have been several witnesses who saw a white man in the James Street area.'

'People have said he was scruffy looking and about 30 years old.'

'Some of the regulars from the Packet pub I've spoken to have said he had a cut hand and blood on his clothing.'

'Whoever committed the murder would almost certainly be covered in blood, having cut Lynette's throat from ear to ear.'

'The police have put together an e-fit of the person they are looking for and it's going to be shown to the public on Crimewatch.'

'The cops have already arrested one man with a similar appearance to the character in the e-fit but they had to let him go.'

'Lynette was due to give evidence against Francine Cordle in the attempted murder case and the police detained Cordle as a suspect.'

'They had to let her go because the murderer's blood was on Lynette's clothing and it didn't match Francine Cordle's.'

'Everything points to this white man who was seen in the vicinity of James Street.'

'That's the waster they need to be looking for.'

'Bizarrely on 15 February, they even pulled in Stephen Miller who is black.'

'I know he's Lynette's boyfriend and most murders are committed by a person who knows the victim but in this case the police need to be going after the white man who was seen near the house.'

'I suppose they need to rule people out. The boys who drink in the Packet were saying that during his interview the police made fun of Stephen Miller.'

'Why's that?'

'He was wearing the same clothes as he'd worn on the 14. Disgustingly, he was made to sit in the opposite corner of the room.'

'Why did they make him do that?'

'They were saying his clothes stank.'

'That's typical of some police. Thick as a truncheon and no class at all.'

'The thing is they didn't find any blood on Stephen's clothing and had to let him go.'

'I don't suppose his blood type was the same as what was found on Lynette's clothing.'

'Quite right.'

'They just need to look for a white man, not someone who is black.'

'They claim everyone has to be ruled out.'

'Unfortunately, not until a number of innocent people have been traumatised in the process.'

'As for making fun of the smell on Stephen Miller's clothes, it was a disgusting thing to do.'

'I wonder if they're ever going to catch the murderer.'

'More worrying is that they're going to charge the wrong person?'

'It'll probably be a black man due to the institutional racism in the police.'

'They've tried to arrest me in the past and I've never broken the law.'

'You're a goody two shoes, Algy,' joked Graham. 'You're definitely excessively virtuous but you are right.'

'I've never even had a parking ticket.'

'We know a lot of boys living in Butetown involved in petty crime.'

'They are a soft target.'

'It doesn't make them a murderer.'

'I'd better drink up. It's time to go home.'

'And me.'

Algy and Graham finished their beers. Just like everyone else who had anything to do with Butetown, they were perturbed that there'd been such a harrowing crime in an area of the city they both loved. Making their way home, they wondered if the police would nail the right person or would they try to set up some innocent individual by using tenuous evidence to pin a macabre murder on them, in an attempt to get a result.

Negative past experiences informed them that prejudice had infiltrated some members of the police, whose sole purpose was enhancing their own status and making the South Wales Police Force look good.

Chapter 33

Two Months Later

Desperation to solve the James Street murder led to the police drawing up a list of twelve suspects. This was based on people who had a criminal history rather than any forensic evidence. At best, the police were taking a shot in the dark in the hope that this dreadful crime would be resolved. Without closure to this case, the community would remain unsettled at the thought that a maniac could be roaming Butetown's streets.

Was this nauseating individual someone with a warped mind who was sexually gratifying himself, then looked to terminate a prostitute's life because he saw them as sinful and worthless, or could he be a person who obtained thrills through a sexual game ending in the prostitute's death. On the other hand, there could easily have been an argument over how much money was changing hands. Whatever the reason, residents were frightened that the murderer would strike again.

Friends of Algy and Graham would continually surmise about who the culprit might be. Many of these suspects were regular customers of prostitutes working in Butetown. Algy, Graham and their friends were well aware of the behaviour of these men and their movements in the area. Having a crime of this magnitude committed in Butetown turned many locals into amateur sleuths.

Algy and Graham were not exempt from this real-life game of Cluedo. It seemed everyone living in the area had an opinion on who might have committed this iniquitous crime.

On 27 April, Graham couldn't wait to finish school because he'd some information for Algy. As soon as he arrived home, Graham picked up the phone to call Algy.

'Hiya, Algy.'

'Always good to hear from you, Gray. Any new info on the murder?'

'Oh yes.'

'Go on then. Hit me with it.'

'The police are saying they've arrested a prime suspect.'

'Have they released the name?'

'They're just calling him Mr X.'

'Has anybody got any idea of who he is?'

'He's supposed to be that convicted sex offender and paedophile, the one who's always hanging around James Street.'

'You mean that weirdo nutjob.'

'You've got the one.'

'The one nobody will talk to. Everybody gives him a wide berth.'

'It's no wonder with the crimes he's committed.'

'Who would want to associate themselves with a child sex offender.'

'By all accounts the boys at the Packet say the police are calling him Mr X.'

'Mr X is an appropriate name. He's definitely an X rated individual, one that got caught in the Devil's net.'

'In between his other perverted cravings, we know he uses Butetown prostitutes.'

'They're probably frightened to death of him and only have him as a client because they're desperate for his money.'

'The girls are taking a big risk having him as a client. By all accounts poor Lynette had him as one of her customers. One of our mates has said that he'd heard Mr X had no alibi for the night of Lynette's murder.'

'I suppose that makes him the prime suspect.'

'It did but the police took blood and he's in group AB. They also knew that Mr X was so bonkers that if pressed, he might just admit to the murder.'

'I can see that in his madness, he would see this as an opportunity to make a name for himself.'

'The police are keeping him under surveillance but they took DNA.'

'That'll conclusively prove whether he's done it or not.'

'The results have come in and they've eliminated him. We know he's a weirdo, but Mr X is not the murderer.'

'Basically, they're no further forward and the uncertainty created by this dreadful act continues.'

'I'm sorry that there's no conclusion to the case.'

'They've got to get the right one.'

'I agree, Algy. Speak to you again.'

'Have a nice evening.'

Chapter 34

9 December 1988

It had been ten months since the horrific James Street murder and the police were becoming increasingly desperate to solve the crime. To advance their case, they interviewed thousands of people. Some of the people involved in petty criminal activity living in Butetown were beginning to feel the pressure brought to bear by this unprecedented level of police inquiry. Fabricated stories began to take the law in a different direction.

It appeared that they were ignoring initial evidence given by witnesses at the time. These people had reported a 5 feet 10-inch white male with an unkempt appearance and blood on his hands. Going off at a tangent, the police were now focusing on Butetown residents and not the outsiders visiting the area to buy sex.

A run of the mill Wednesday at school for Algy and Graham was about to change. Arriving home, they both received phone calls from Butetown friends who conveyed astounding news. Arrests had been made but there was no white man amongst the group. They were all black or mixed race.

Algy phoned Graham and blurted out, 'No doubt you've heard the news.'

'I have. Let's meet for a pint in the Claude Hotel.'

'See you in an hour.'

Replacing their respective receivers both men were dumbstruck at what had happened. Travelling to their old college watering hole, which had been the venue for many a memorable night out. Algy and Graham were both saddened by the news they'd been given. Men they had known all their lives had been arrested. Graham arrived first and as Algy walked through the door, he found it difficult to contain his emotions.

His stomach was in knots and his hands trembled. He knew Algy's sentiments would be exactly the same as his own. Both men indulged in a warm embrace as a way of easing the pain they were feeling that men they'd known were now in police custody for the James Street murder.

Graham exclaimed, 'South Wales police have arrested Stephen and Tony Miller, Yusuf Abdullahi, Ronny Actie, Rashid Omar and Martin Tucker two days ago.'

'Today they've picked up John Actie and Tony Paris and released their names. The case has been handed over to the new team led by Detective Inspector Graham Mouncher, and it looks like they're determined to blame people of colour.'

'I've known these boys all my life and none of them are angels. One thing we do know though is that they're not murderers. Unfortunately, their past petty criminal activity has given the police the excuse they need to remove them from the streets.'

'It's unbelievable and callous because there's no forensic evidence to link the boys to the murder and don't forget we were no angels when we were younger. Unfortunately, mud sticks with the police and they're taking this opportunity to pin an horrendous crime on innocent men who in the past have had criminal records but not for this type of crime.'

'How can the police come up with these blokes as prime suspects because not one of them is white.'

'By all accounts, Violet Perriam who worked at the health centre and is secretary of Cardiff Yacht Club kicked these arrests off. She made a statement to the police alleging that as she drove home from the yacht club, she saw four black and mixed-race men outside the house in James Street on the night Lynette was murdered.'

'My mate, the one who phoned me said Violet Perriam had recognised John Actie and Rashid Omar. She identified them because they had been to the health centre on a number of occasions.'

'She doesn't even live in the area but that woman's tittle tattle has got those boys arrested without any conclusive evidence.'

'John Actie had told the police when they conducted the door-to-door enquiries that he'd gone to the Casablanca Club at midnight and left at 3:30 am.'

'From time to time, he hasn't helped himself but the police have always made John's life a misery and have been desperate to lock him up. This was the excuse they needed.'

'Fancy trying to pin a crime of this magnitude on him. John's no saint but once you know him you realise that he's a decent sort who's had a tough time. If he had the right support, John could have been a rugby superstar. His dad who was of paramount importance to his future prospects, unfortunately died at a time when John needed his counsel.'

'This tragedy was calamitous for John, causing a major upheaval in his life. He was his role model, delivering good advice which consequently kept him on the straight and narrow. Losing this tower of strength at a vital time in his life gave rise to confusion inducing him to stray from the straight path.'

'I saw him play for Cardiff schools and he was definitely the best player in the team.'

'He's a big old unit, that's for sure and his father's death hit him hard. His mother is lovely but she found it difficult bringing John up on her own.'

'There's no doubt these boys are being stitched up because of their colour. The main suspect should be a white man.'

'The one that people saw with blood on his hands and clothing.'

'I've experienced this type of discrimination myself and I feel sorry for these boys.'

'The cops will be looking for any shred of evidence they can get hold of to pin this on these boys.'

'That Perriam woman has given the cops the excuse they needed to make arrests. Anything to get a result and there are plenty of unscrupulous people who will talk in the hope that the police will leave them alone.'

'They've been taken into custody but I hope they can't detain them because there's no forensic evidence linking the group to the murder.'

'I hope that lady from the yacht club can sleep easy knowing that she's sent these boys hurtling towards the rocks.'

'I'm really perturbed by this. Drink up, Algy, I need to get home.'

18 November 1988

Desperate to convict somebody, the police used Violet Perriam's testimony to pressurise Leanne Vilday. Having initially raised the alarm by going to the police after lending Lynette White the key to her flat, they pulled her in for questioning. Lynette had been keeping a low profile to avoid being a witness at two court cases.

Leanne couldn't gain entry to her flat but the police now suspected she might be concealing information relating to the murder. Pressure was being applied and ramped up on a vulnerable prostitute, addicted to drugs. The police grew ever more unscrupulous by harassing Leanne on a daily basis. Constant visits to her home were threatening and would almost certainly lead to her eventual coercion with the police.

The police finally insisted Leanne left the flat she was sharing with another prostitute named Angela Psaila. In the interim, Leanne lodged with a couple. However daily visits by the police ensured that there was no end to the arm twisting she endured. Police duress continued and when Leanne was drunk, she named Stephen Miller and Yusuf Abdullahi as the killers. Later, Leanne retracted her accusation saying that she'd been inebriated at the time.

Violet Perriam's disclosure that she'd seen the men outside the property in James Street resulted in the police intimidating another witness with limited intellect. Angela Psaila was the most vulnerable woman soliciting as a prostitute in the Butetown area. Her flat was in St Clare's Court, Butetown, where she had an unrestricted view of 7, James Street.

Using Violet Perriam's earlier statement as a lever where she'd placed the four men outside the murder scene, the police questioned Psaila intimating that she was connected to the crime. Possessing limited intellect, she first provided a statement claiming Stephen Miller had visited her at about 1:00 am on 14 February, looking for Lynette.

Later, she gave another statement claiming she'd seen Miller, John and Ronnie Actie, Yusuf Abdullahi, Tony Paris and Tony Brace, a doorman from the North Star Club, outside 7, James Street. Further claims were made by an under-pressure Angela Psaila that she had heard screams from the flat and that Ronnie Actie had been let in.

The same day, Mark Grommek and Paul Atkins gave statements to the police. Grommek had a flat directly above Leanne Vilday's place where Lynette was staying and the two men had previously given accounts which had been disregarded due to the serious anomalies in their content. Angela Psaila claimed Ronnie Actie had been given access to Vilday's flat by Grommek.

Grommek and Atkins were both considered vulnerable because they'd been charged with petty crimes in the past and were homosexuals. This was the 1980s when many of the public had negative attitudes towards the gay community. In the men's eyes, making these initial statements would hopefully keep the police off their backs.

Giving these new accounts, Grommek and Atkins claimed they'd seen a group of men outside the flat including Ronnie Actie and Abdullahi. That afternoon, Grommek contrived to give a very detailed account of the circumstances surrounding the crime. Two claims made by Grommek were that he let Ronnie Actie into 7, James Street, then heard screams.

6 December 1988

Angela Psaila gave a new statement to the police, claiming that she had been in the flat at St Clare's Court with Leanne Vilday. After hearing screams, both women went to 7, James Street. Remarkably Vilday, Grommek and Atkins individually went to the police to give an account of the crime. Vilday claimed having heard screams, she'd gone to 7, James Street prior to turning up there with the police later in the evening.

White was dead and in the room were Miller, Abdullahi, Ronnie Actie and Tony Miller, Stephen Miller's brother and another unnamed mixed-race man. Grommek and Atkins gave statements corroborating Vilday and Psaila's version of events.

7 December 1988

Following the murder on 14 February, ten months passed before the police first arrested Stephen and Tony Miller, Yusuf Abdullahi, Ronnie Actie and Rashid Omar. Two days later, John Actie and Tony Paris were taken into police custody. Controversial arrests had been made on the basis of statements made by a group of at-risk witnesses. Trying to convict a group of men with this flimsy evidence and no forensic verification made the convictions unsafe from the beginning.

10 December 1988

This was the day forensics informed the police that Angela Psaila's blood group was AB. Lynette White's sock and trousers were spattered in blood belonging to this category. Angela Psaila was now brought back in for questioning.

A new version of events emerged during this interview that she and Vilday were present and participated in the killing. She now named Stephen and Tony Miller, Ronnie and John Actie, Tony Paris and Yusuf Abdullahi as the other killers. In a bizarre turn of events, Psaila named Leanne Vilday as the one who cut Lynette's throat.

Vilday was interviewed and gave a new statement naming Stephen Miller, Ronnie and John Actie, Abdullahi and Paris as the killers. In a flight of fancy, Vilday then claimed she and Angela Psaila had been forced to cut one of Lynette's wrists. This duplicitous action appeared to be the reason why the two prostitutes had initially clammed up.

Following these claims, Stephen Miller was interviewed nineteen times over four days. For the first two of these interviews, he was denied a solicitor. Miller had limited intellect but nevertheless he was interviewed for 13 hours in total and in anyone's books that was an inordinate length of time. During these interviews, he denied murdering Lynette White three hundred and seven times.

Eventually, his low intelligence quotient in relation to his chronological age combined with the pressure he was under led to him confessing to the murder. Sadly, he implicated both himself and the other men.

Algy and Graham found this an agonisingly difficult time. Having known the men and their families for many years left them inconsolable at what was definitely a travesty of justice. They'd both experienced racist attitudes by certain members of the police, convincing them that the men in custody had been "stitched up" because of their colour.

Possessing an in-depth knowledge of the characters of each man they knew these were not the murderers. Although, the group could be capable of criminal acts, they also possessed traits preventing them crossing the line needed to end a life. John Actie was renowned as a tough character but he was no bully and definitely not a murderer. Tony Paris was a Jack the lad but there again at no time in his life had he ever shown a hint of violence.

Everyone in Butetown knew him as the person you needed to know if you wanted a new item of clothing. He was adept at acquiring one for local people from city stores which proved an ideal hunting ground for a lovable rogue. As for the level of violence inflicted on Lynette White there was no chance, he'd ever stoop so low.

These arrests were a tragic development and cast a cloud over Christmas 1988 in Butetown. Algy and Graham always made a point of meeting in the

Packet pub at this time of the year where diverse conversation would normally be the order of the day. This year, a melancholy air hung like a pall of cloud over this historic public house.

Every punter would normally be ecstatic with Christmas just around the corner. An air of despondency pervaded the pub because a group of Butetown men were in custody. Algy and Graham dolefully sat down with a pint.

'They've got the wrong people and knowing them, they'll be traumatised by the injustice,' explained Graham.

'When you're "carrying the can" for something you've not done, it's the worst feeling in the world.'

'It's hard to believe that a group of black and mixed-race men have been arrested when a white man was seen with blood on him.'

'In my eyes it's not. It's an institutionally racist police force that's produced trumped up charges just to get a result.'

'You only have to look at the people they've interviewed to realise how biased and discriminatory their actions have been.'

'There's definitely a type of hidden apartheid in this country. Unfortunately, a police force which is supposed to be a bastion of justice are at the forefront of this corruption.'

'The way they fabricated evidence against these boys is disgusting.'

Algy, frustrated by this turn of events, took a larger than usual swig of his beer and proclaimed, 'Look at the people they've questioned. That secretary of the Yacht Club sowed the seeds in the minds of the police kicking off this chain of events, leading to these illicit arrests.'

'Then there's Leanne Vilday and Angela Psaila.'

'Leanne Vilday changed her story more times than she changes her knickers,' exclaimed an exasperated Algy. This was an unusually ungentlemanly statement from a normally courteous Algy.

'Poor old Angela Psaila has been treated appallingly. Academically, she wasn't the sharpest tool in the shed, yet the police took full advantage of this.'

'It seems these girls were making outrageous claims in their statements to keep themselves out of trouble.'

'The one where they said the men forced them to slit Lynette's wrist is outrageous.'

'Surely, the police could realise that these women were just saying they'd participated by cutting the corpse. By giving themselves a partial involvement, they were thinking that they could keep in the convicted men's good books, so nobody in Butetown would kill them. That's how dull they were.'

'Honestly, hearing what's happened sounds like the type of stories kids would make up in school to get themselves out of trouble.'

'Concocting these stories has led to both girls being given police protection. Local people are livid at what they perceive as devious claims.'

'I've got no doubt there'd be plenty of people looking to exact revenge for the lies they've told.'

'The problem is, Gray, these girls were put under so much pressure and being a pair of boneheads, they were bound to come up with something outrageous.'

'Limited intellect's the phrase you're looking for, Algy.'

'I'm so frustrated by what's happened; I'm sorry for the poor choice of words. That's not normally like me.'

'We're all human. I'm really livid at what they did to Stephen Miller.'

'They may as well have waterboarded him or put some thumbscrews on him. Interviewing him for the inordinate length of time they did was bound to crack him eventually.'

'What's happened to the "Cardiff Five" is an injustice. Let's drink up, Algy. Christmas won't be the same this year knowing these boys are locked up. They've been let down by South Wales Police's discrimination and their failure to unearth the truth.'

Chapter 35

Algy left Howardian High School to take up a new teaching post in September 1989. He'd been promoted and started in Cathays High School as Head of Department for immigrant pupils who needed to learn English as their second language. Seventy percent of the pupils in the school were newcomers to the United Kingdom which was a prime indicator as to the way the British population was evolving.

Regrettably, elements within communities remained stuck in the past and didn't appear ready to embrace change. The arrest of five black and mixed-race men on vague and untrustworthy evidence for the murder at James Street was a classic example of how some people needed to change their attitude towards racism. Meanwhile, Graham continued to forge a rewarding and worthwhile career at Fitzalan High School. Both were troubled by the thought that men they'd known for years were locked up for a crime they would never have committed.

Algy and Graham were filled with trepidation as the court case commenced in Swansea on 5 October 1989. Perversely, the trial was interrupted on 26 February 1990 when the judge suddenly died. Eighty-two days into the trial it had to be suspended, finally recommencing on 14 May 1990. In total, the trial lasted one hundred and ninety-seven days, and was the longest murder trial in British legal history.

On 22 November 1990, three of the five men were found guilty of Lynette White's murder. Tony Paris, Yusuf Abdullahi and Stephen Miller were given life sentences. Ronnie and John Actie were acquitted after spending two years in prison. The Cardiff Five now became the Cardiff Three.

Algy and Graham were in school when the verdicts were announced. Waiting by the radio to hear the news created an unbearable tension in both men. When the newsreader reported the result, Algy and Graham were deflated. They found it difficult to comprehend how a jury could find the three men guilty on such flimsy evidence.

This insubstantial proof had been extracted by a corrupt, callous investigation team from untrustworthy witnesses through oppressive interrogation. Any elation felt at the freeing of the Actie cousins was tempered by the thought that three innocent men were going into custody for a long time.

Graham waited for school to finish and phoned Algy who was still at work.

Algy answered in his courteous school voice, 'Who's speaking please?'

'It's Graham.'

'I've heard the result, Gray, and I'm mortified by it.'

'It's so unfair, Algy, and I'm sure it won't end there.'

'I can't see people accepting this. They know these boys too well. You wait, the Butetown spirit will come to the fore.'

'I'll be right there with them. It'll take us back to the days of the anti-apartheid marches.'

'This dire result will bring the residents together. You wait and see.'

'It's great to know Ronnie and John were released. They were obviously elated outside court but that elation could easily be replaced by guilt because three boys are still inside.'

'You're probably right but I don't understand how the jury didn't find in favour of the other three.'

'Some of these briefs are adept at creating a compulsive story from untrustworthy circumstantial evidence. They also presented Butetown in a negative way. There's no way we lived in a drug infested, crime ridden community which is what they tried to make out. We know it's not true. Something really significant is that it was an all-white jury.'

'All of the evidence presented is unbelievable. It just seems so wrong that convictions can be made without forensic evidence. I remember that case in Miami when I was on the rugby tour when an all-white jury found a white policeman innocent after he'd killed a black man. The riots were incredibly frightening.'

'You wait, they tried in court to present our former home in a negative light. They'll see that Butetown folks can make their point in a dignified but forceful way. We'll show them,' exclaimed a fired-up Graham.

'Something we need to bear in mind is the jury can only decide on the way the evidence was presented and in any case the judge guided them.'

'It's a travesty of justice. I'll have to go, Algy. I've got rugby training with the 1st XV.'

'Speak to you again, Gray.'

Chapter 36

Algy and Graham predicted the case of the Cardiff three would eventually begin to make headline news. There were so many anomalies in the evidence and the lack of any forensic verification cast doubt on the Swansea trial. Most people in Butetown were convinced of the accused's innocence and the size of the demonstration being planned would bear testimony to the case being a miscarriage of justice.

Algy and Graham felt strongly about the boys' innocence and a day wouldn't go by without them thinking about their three acquaintances. They were so disturbed by the case that the two friends met for coffee in the city centre, giving them an opportunity to talk through the difficulties they were having coming to terms with the case.

'Algy, it seems a number of journalists are starting to take an interest in this case,' exclaimed Graham.

'They're starting to question the safety of the convictions.'

'Channel 4 are broadcasting a programme where they are investigating the case.'

'Hopefully, this will really kick things off.'

'The word is that Tony and Yusuf are being allowed to appeal their case but they won't allow Stephen Miller to do the same.'

'You know why that is?'

'Because he was Lynette's boyfriend and the authorities still think he did it.'

'The pressure he was put under during interview would have cracked anyone.'

'There's an investigative journalist who's supporting Stephen's case.'

'I've heard he's tracked down two witnesses who were exempted from the trial. They can provide alibis for Stephen's whereabouts at the time of the crime.'

'By all accounts Stephen's managed to persuade this journalist to convince a solicitor to take on the case.'

'I've heard he's got a top silk to represent Stephen in court.'

'That's great news. What's his name?'

'Michael Mansfield QC.'

'Let's hope he's the business. These boys need a break.'

'Gray, according to what I've read there's none better. He's the tops when it comes to human rights.'

'We've known these boys all their lives and the injustice of the verdict makes it difficult to think about anything else.'

'Teaching helps take your mind off it but it's like a boomerang because it always comes back.'

November 1991

Algy and Graham were busy preparing their banner for the march in support of the Cardiff Three. Graham had studied art with his favourite teacher Mr George Thomas when he was a pupil at school and he took responsibility for designing and creating an impressive placard. Emblazoned on it were the words *Free the Cardiff Three* with hard hitting images relating to imprisonment.

Saturday, 23 November couldn't come quickly enough for the residents of Butetown who'd mobilised to protest against the unjustifiable decision of the Swansea Court. It was unfathomable how three Butetown residents were found guilty of a crime they obviously didn't commit. There was not one shred of genuine forensic evidence to link the boys to the crime.

The campaign had been initiated and led by two of the families of those who'd been imprisoned. Lloyd Paris, brother of Tony and Malik Abdullahi, Yusuf's brother were the two protagonists to initiate this movement. Algy and Graham put the finishing touches to their banner, and Graham exclaimed, 'This campaign has taken over Lloyd and Malik's life. It's all they ever think about.'

'It's understandable, Gray, blood is thicker than water. The thought of having your brother labelled as a murderer when he's innocent is awful.'

'They've pored over thousands of statements and it was strikingly obvious to the relatives that there were racist elements in the case.'

'You know there were 23,000 pages of material that were never used.'

'Lloyd told me there were twenty-two statements handed in after the case was over and nineteen were alibis for Tony.'

'It really stinks but the movement has gained recognition worldwide.'

'We've got the Reverend Al Sharpton from Brooklyn in the States coming to the demonstration. He's a renowned American Civil Rights activist and the founder of the National Action Network.'

'Al Sharpton has done a lot to raise funds for poor black kids. In America, it's called the National Youth Movement.'

'The National Action Network was founded to provide services to those living in poverty. He particularly focused on voter education.'

'If blacks didn't vote then nothing could change in American society. Initiating change through the ballot box is definitely the way forward.'

'Al Sharpton has been at the forefront of black people's rights in the States and he's going to give a press conference in Butetown.'

'He's going to call on the authorities to let the Cardiff Three go.'

'The March on Saturday starts in Butetown and ends at Cardiff Civic Centre.'

'On the way, the march is going to stop outside Cardiff prison where Tony Paris is being held.'

'Let's hope hundreds turn up. This case is such a travesty of justice that it needs people to act.'

'They will. See you on Saturday, Algy.'

Saturday arrived and Algy and Graham met in Butetown. Hundreds of people milled around as they waited for the organisers to start the protest. Activists gathered, each one eager to commence the demonstration. This was their opportunity for them to show their dissent at a justice system that had made a grave error. It would give the residents of Butetown an opportunity to showcase their community as peaceful and concerned about justice for all people.

Lloyd Paris and Malik Abdullahi used a loud hailer to bring the demonstrators to attention. They stood at the front of the multitude with Al Sharpton. The three men linked arms as a symbol of unity. People who had been excitedly raucous fell in behind the three men at the front in an orderly fashion. With a sense of purpose, this throng of humanity moved forward.

Algy and Graham were about 15 yards from the front with their striking banner held aloft. It had been twenty-one years ago that they'd demonstrated against the 1970 Springbok Rugby Tour. The significance of this procession was not lost on them. They personally knew the three men who had been scapegoated because of their colour and unethically incarcerated for a crime they didn't commit.

As the procession snaked its way along Bute Street, loud hailers were used to shout, 'What do we want?'

To which the throng shouted back, 'Justice.'

'When do we want it?'

'Now.'

As the march reached Cardiff Prison, Algy and Graham looked at the high stone wall surrounding this Victorian penitentiary. Bars on every window made escape virtually impossible. The grey stone of the building created an air of hopelessness for those interned there. Many years inside these walls could steadily dismantle even the strongest of human beings, particularly those who were wrongly confined.

Their thought processes would dwell on the unfairness of their sentence. Such injustice would play havoc with their mind where even those with the strongest will could succumb to the inequity of their sentence.

Near the gate, the Reverend Al Sharpton, a Baptist minister, raised his hand and the multitude fell silent. He began to offer prayers for the Cardiff Three. Sharpton had been ordained as a Pentecostal minister when he was only ten years old which could only happen in the States. However, during the late 1980s, Sharpton became a Baptist.

He was rebaptised into the Baptist Church and ordained as a Minister. This was a poignant moment for the activists. They were praying for deliverance of three of their own. Even atheists in the crowd had a tear in their eye as they reflected on the commitment of this American Baptist minister who invoked God to intercede on behalf of the three men.

Having completed the prayers, the demonstration made its way to the Civic Centre where Al Sharpton addressed the crowd. Speaking to the supporters of the Cardiff Three through a loud hailer, he said,

'I'm happy to be here today to join people of all races and colour to talk about the injustice that has happened to these three brothers. It is only because of their social, economic and racial status that they are in gaol.'

Reverend Al Sharpton had devoted his life to supporting the underdog. As well as racial injustice in the United States, he championed equal rights for gays and lesbians and same sex marriage. When asked to discuss same sex marriage, Sharpton was incensed by the question causing him to respond to his quizzers by telling them, 'they were inferring that these people were not like other human beings.'

Later in his ministry, Sharpton would lead a movement to eliminate homophobia which was prevalent in American black churches through their literal interpretation of the Bible. President Barack Obama would later say that, 'Al Sharpton was the voice of the voiceless and the champion of the downtrodden.'

Obama held Sharpton in such high esteem that during his presidency, he used him as an advisor on black racial issues. This heralded champion of innocent victims had come to Cardiff to add gravitas to the injustice inflicted on the Cardiff Three.

Graham was moved by his address to the crowd because of the commitment in Sharpton's voice and he whispered to Algy, 'He's hit the nail on the head.'

'Hopefully, his support will give the campaign the impetus needed to free the boys, Gray.'

'Gerry Conlon, one of the Guilford Four, has also visited Butetown to add his support. He knew what it was like to be wrongly accused of being an IRA bomber. His wrongful conviction meant he spent fifteen years in prison for the 1974 Guilford pub bombings. Let's hope these people make a significant difference.'

Gerry Conlon was born in Belfast in 1954, living in the Falls Road area of the city. In 1974, Conlon came to Britain to look for work and escape the everyday violence encountered by those living in Belfast. Arriving in London, he was homeless but moved in with a group of squatters.

On 5 October 1974, the Provisional Irish Republican Army detonated two bombs in Guilford pubs because they were frequented by British soldiers stationed at Pirbright Barracks. Four soldiers and one civilian were killed in the blasts. Many other people were badly injured. Conlon was arrested and on 22 October 1975 was convicted with two other men and a woman of the Guilford bombings.

The four were sentenced to life imprisonment by the judge who told them that if hanging were still an option in Britain, they would have been executed.

From his prison cell, Gerry Conlon continued to protest his innocence. He claimed that the police had tortured him into making a confession. Conlon was vindicated when the Guilford Four were set free in the London Court of Appeal because the police had fabricated the notes presented to the court from the interrogation.

At the trial, evidence that Conlon could not have carried out the bombings was withheld from the court. On 19 November 1989, Gerry Conlon was set free along with the three others who had been convicted with him.

'Some people have derided this march believing the police have a strong case. There are always going to be people who see Butetown as a hotbed of trouble. Problem is they lack understanding,' commented Algy.

'Don't worry, Algy, this day will have the desired effect and put the case on the world stage.'

'It deserves to be. It's so bad.'

A concerted effort by the Butetown residents, journalists and television reporters produced the desired effect. In 1992, a BBC current affairs programme produced a documentary entitled "Unsafe Convictions". Tenuous evidence led to an appeal being heard in December 1992 for the Cardiff Three. The Court of Appeal listened to Stephen Miller's police interview.

This interview was more of an interrogation, leading Michael Mansfield QC to argue that the officers' conduct in his interview displayed oppressive behaviour. The thrust of his argument was that the officers were by hook or by crook going to show that Stephen Miller's evidence aligned with Leanne Vilday's.

Algy and Graham had travelled to London and were in the public gallery listening to the evidence being presented. They had high hopes of justice being done.

'Gray, we're drinking in the last chance saloon,' exclaimed Algy.

'I'm pleased with what this silk has come up with.'

'We've got a chance here.'

'I really hope so. These boys have spent four years of their lives in custody for a crime they never committed.'

'Lord Taylor is about to pass judgement,' proclaimed a nervous Algy.

Lord Taylor addressed the court.

'Reviewing this case, it's obvious that the police had bullied and hectored Miller during a travesty of an interview and that short of physical violence, it's hard to conceive of a more hostile and intimidating approach by officers to a suspect.'

'My heart's in my mouth, Algy.'

'And mine.'

'Mind you, it sounds hopeful.'

'It's not over until the fat lady sings.'

Having attended the Court of Appeal, both men were hopeful that there would be a positive outcome for the three prisoners. Lord Taylor pointed out that the truthfulness of Miller's admission was irrelevant. The nature of his questioning was so brutally aggressive, it ensured that this grilling should be rejected as evidence. The police's bellicose behaviour during the interview was terrifying for Stephen Miller.

Lord Taylor ordered copies of the interview recording to be sent to the Director of Public Prosecutions and the chairman of the Royal Commission on Criminal Justice. The purpose of the instruction was that Stephen Miller's police interview would be an example of what would never be heard again in a British court. All three men had their convictions declared unsafe and unsatisfactory. At last, they were set free.

Supporters who travelled to London cheered as Lord Taylor gave his conclusion. People in the public gallery wept tears of joy for the three who had suffered torment at the hands of the British legal system.

'We've done it. Their release reminds me of the day Nelson Mandela was freed after twenty-seven years in prison, much of it spent on Robben Island,' proclaimed an ecstatic Algy.

'I'm over the moon that the boys are out but it's not over. There are the minority who still think that the five boys who were arrested killed Lynette.'

'I suppose you're right, Gray.'

'Unless the real killer's caught, then there will always be doubters.'

'Let's hope new evidence comes to light.'

'In the meantime, let's rejoice that the three are out.'

'Let's go to the press conference and listen to what they have to say.'

Stephen Miller spoke first by saying,

'In the police station they broke all the rules. I feel it in my heart that I now know what people feel when they've been wrongly accused.'

Yusuf Abdullahi spoke next,

'We were basically used as scapegoats for the police who couldn't find anyone else to put the crime on.'

Finally, Tony Paris spoke,

'It doesn't matter what you've been in, the police will find ways of getting convictions for the hierarchy who put pressure on them. They don't care. Anybody will do.'

'We know that's right, Gray. Look what's happened to us. We've suffered through racist attitudes but what these boys have suffered is intolerable.'

'Let's hope things change. They need to.'

'There are new techniques today used by the police for catching criminals.'

'Let's hope they bring the real killer to justice.'

'It's the only way these boys will find peace.'

Chapter 37

Graham continued to work at Fitzalan High School and was a well-respected pillar of that educational establishment. Algy had left his post at Cathays High School. Due to a restructure of the service that was responsible for scrutinising the education of immigrants who had entered the country, Algy was now based at County Hall in Cardiff. This new post involved providing vocational courses for young people whose parents had made their home in Britain.

Lynette White's murder continued to unnerve the Butetown community. Although, the Cardiff Three had been released from custody, complete exoneration could never be achieved without the real killer being apprehended. Lynette White's father, who was traumatised by the death of his daughter, continued to blame John Actie and even went to his home intending to end his life with a shotgun.

John saw him coming which fortunately prevented his life being terminated. Algy contacted Graham by phone blurting out, 'Have you heard John Actie nearly came a cropper.'

'Yes, Lynette's father took a shotgun to him.'

'It's time they caught the real killer. Lynette's death is a stain on the Butetown Community. This is a blemish which needs to be removed.'

'Well, I've got some good news on that front.'

'Have they caught someone?'

'No, but they're reopening the case following a cold case review. There's a new team investigating Lynette's murder.'

'Has there been a breakthrough?'

'A world-renowned forensic scientist has examined a tiny piece of cellophane found near Lynette's body.'

'What's the relevance of that to the case?'

'There was a speck of blood on it. They are calling the murderer Cellophane Man.'

'Do they know if it's the murderer's blood?'

'They now have the start of a DNA profile but they need more.'

'Have they managed to find anything else?'

'They've taken a skirting board off the wall and found drops of blood under all the layers of paint.'

'No doubt it's been painted numerous times since 1988.'

'The drops of blood matched the one on the cellophane paper. There was also matching blood on the door handle where he cut himself.'

'Well, let's hope there's a match on the DNA database because that's the only chance of catching him.'

'I'll keep my ear to the ground because I'm friendly with John Actie.'

'Let me know straight away if you get any info.'

'I will.'

'See you soon, Gray.'

Both friends replaced their respective receivers delighted to hear that some progress had been made in the quest to catch the killer.

Finding the blood was only a partial breakthrough. What was needed to be found now was a database match which would conclusively prove who the murderer was. A worldwide DNA screening search turned up no match with the killer. It seemed the case was at a dead end.

Some months later, Graham excitedly phoned Algy. 'I need to meet you tonight. It's good news.'

'See you in the Claude Hotel.'

That evening, the two friends met and sat in their usual seats. Graham in his most animated voice exclaimed, 'A police detective has noticed a similarity in the DNA of a youngster who was arrested for joy riding in Cardiff.'

'How much time must they have spent on that? The police have certainly been made more accountable and there's been a drive to employ more graduates.'

'That's a good thing and policing is certainly changing for the better. The days of clouting someone over the head with a truncheon and then asking questions are over. One thing I know is it won't go down well with some of those older coppers who feel threatened by this new recruitment policy.'

'You're right and greater diversity in the police has helped. Having more officers from ethnic minorities is a positive step forward. They understand the problems faced by people belonging to these groups, and hopefully it'll get rid of the xenophobes in the police.'

'I totally agree. Going back to this youngster, he had a partial DNA match to the killer. John Actie phoned me earlier and told me they've arrested a man today.'

'That's outstanding forensic police work and the officer deserves a commendation.'

'The partial match they found was the youngster's uncle. Algy, you've got one of those modern phones with the Internet. Have a look and see if they've named him yet.'

'Here it is on the BBC News website. His name is Jeffrey Gafoor and he lives in Llanharan. It says here that he's admitted to Lynette's murder as he was being arrested.'

'What a stroke of good fortune as well as excellent police work. If his nephew hadn't been arrested, he'd have never been caught.'

'Drink up, Gray, I'll get us another pint. Hopefully, this'll bring an end to the dark cloud hanging over Butetown.'

Chapter 38

4 July 2003

Jeffrey Gafoor pleaded guilty to Lynette's murder and in court he apologised to the Cardiff Five for their ordeal. To the five men who had been persecuted for the murder, this was an empty, meaningless statement. Not only did they serve prison sentences but they had been condemned to a lifetime of traumatisation. There could never be total justice for the five victims due to the way their lives had been changed.

A living hell could only be partially eased by Gafoor serving his sentence. Then there was the issue of the bent coppers who had imposed these charges without any forensic evidence. Holding these supposed custodians of the law to account could bring further relief to the five men's suffering.

During their trial in 2008, the people who had helped convict the men through their testimony at the original trial, admitted they had made the whole thing up through police coercion. Mark Grommek, Leanne Vilday and Angela Psaila were all given 18-month sentences. Paul Atkins the fourth man was deemed mentally unfit to stand trial. During proceedings, the judge considered the vulnerability of the three defendants.

Leanne Vilday had been threatened with having her baby son taken away from her. Angela Psaila's well below average IQ was a mitigating circumstance in her case. Andrew Grommek was considered vulnerable because of his sexuality. Societal intolerance to homosexuality in 1988 was taken into consideration by the judge.

One of the leading barristers in the country, Lord Carlile QC, who defended Leanne Vilday said,

'The sheer wickedness and dishonesty of the police and remorseless systemic corruption in this case is difficult to believe but it is true beyond

any doubt and is accepted by the prosecution. It would be an utter scandal if none of the police officers involved in the case were bought to trial themselves.'

Being accused of a murder they didn't commit had started to take its toll on the accused. Ronnie Actie struggled with the accusation levelled at him and slowly the false allegation chipped away at him. Eventually, the strain he was enduring led to his death from a deep vein thrombosis. In 2007, police reports stated there were no suspicious circumstances surrounding Ronnie's death.

At the time his life ended, Ronnie was reputedly living in a garden shed. Psychologically shredded, he succumbed to the stress of the situation he had been put through. Butetown residents were unequivocal about the reasons for his death. Acting as judge and jury, in their eyes unscrupulous police officers had blood on their hands.

Local people found it difficult to comprehend Gafoor's admission that he had changed his mind about having sex with Lynette and wanted the £30 he paid returned to him. A brutal, despicable crime was committed because Lynette White refused Gafoor's request. That refusal ruined the lives of many Butetown residents. Her client was a maladjusted psychopath who stayed free for years because of police prejudice.

Chapter 39

'The right man is now in prison but it's not really over,' exclaimed Graham.

'Five boys have been scarred for life and no amount of money can compensate for that,' remarked Algy.

'Then there's the psychological effect of the miscarriage of justice. Nobody likes being blamed for something they haven't done, let alone spending time in prison for it.'

'It's astounding that Jeffrey Gafoor was only sentenced to a minimum of thirteen years.'

'I doubt he'll be able to get out. The keyword is minimum. I'd never let a lunatic like Gafoor out.'

'You're quite right, Graham, but you also said it's not really over. What do you mean?'

'What I mean is the boys might have been exonerated from committing the crime but there are still bent coppers who have never been brought to justice.'

'I agree. Remember what the QC said at the trial.'

'I remember. He said there was systemic corruption in the case.'

'There have been improvements made in the way the police now operate but there's still a long way to go.'

'I still can't get over Gafoor reacting in such a way after Lynette failed to give back his £30.'

'Our initial thought was that it could have been some kind of sex game where Gafoor lost control.'

'The root cause of many crimes is money. The Bible says you can't serve God and money.'

'Nice to see you remember our Sunday school days. It certainly wasn't wasted on you, Gray.'

'Money's the root of all evil. Gafoor lost it over money.'

'Just like the bloke who murdered poor old Lily Volpert and Mahmood Mattan was unjustly executed for it.'

'Mattan was definitely innocent as well. The poor blighter couldn't even speak English.'

Mahmood Mattan was a Somali merchant seaman who was erroneously convicted of the murder of Lily Volpert on 6 March 1952. The crime took place in the Tiger Bay area of Cardiff when Mattan was convicted on the tenuous evidence of a single witness. Lily Volpert owned an outfitter shop in Tiger Bay. Having closed at 8.05 pm, she settled down to have supper with her family in the room behind the shop when someone rang the doorbell.

Lily's mother and sister saw a man outside the shop while she went to serve him. A few minutes later, another man was seen by her niece talking to Lily. A short time later, another customer who had come to the shop found Lily Volpert dead with her throat cut. The assailant's motive was money because £100 was missing from the till.

Cardiff City police investigated the murder and questioned a number of men. Mahmood Mattan was one of those questioned. Having searched the premises where he was living, the police found nothing that could link him to such a heinous crime. No blood-stained clothes, murder weapon or money were found at the property.

Later, some witnesses contradicted his alibi and he was questioned at length. An identification parade was organised which was attended by Lily Volpert's mother, sister and niece but they could not identify Mattan.

Two women, Mary Tolley and Margaret Bush, who were at the shop just before it closed were questioned. They gave statements but did not mention that anyone was in the shop. Following intensive questioning, Mary Tolley eventually claimed that Mattan had come into Lily Volpert's shop and then left.

Mattan was arrested on the basis of this tenuous evidence and charged with murder by the police. They claimed he had hidden in the shop and then murdered the victim. Ten days after the murder, Mattan was charged with the crime. Earlier statements made by the woman where she claimed no one was in the shop were suppressed by the police, along with statements made by Volpert's family.

Prior to committal proceedings at Cardiff Magistrates Court, the police confronted Mattan with another witness who was a twelve year old girl. She claimed she had seen a dark-skinned man near the shop but it was not Mattan.

During the hearing, Mary Tolley changed her story saying Mattan had not gone into the shop.

Nevertheless, an untrustworthy Jamaican man identified Mattan as one of two Somalis outside the shop. Mattan was committed for trial on the basis of this evidence.

The Jamaican man named Harold Cover was the main prosecution witness during the trial in Swansea. Another witness named May Gray stated that she had seen Mattan with a wad of bank notes. Mattan's counsel stated that she lied because the Volpert family offered a reward of £200 of which Harold Cover received part.

Evidence was presented to the court that microscopic drops of blood had been found on a pair of Mattan's shoes. These shoes had been reclaimed from a refuse dump and there was no scientific evidence linking these to the murder.

Mattan's barrister managed to have much of the prosecution's evidence ruled inadmissible. However, in his closing speech he described Mattan as "half child of nature and half semi civilised savage". These comments almost certainly prejudiced the jury undermining his defence.

Mattan was found guilty of Lily Volpert's murder and the death sentence passed. On 3 September 1952, Mahmood Mattan was hanged at Cardiff prison. He was the last person to be hanged there.

Algy exclaimed, 'His case was eventually quashed. Nothing had improved with the way the police investigated these crimes even though they were thirty years apart. Now the investigating police in the Cardiff Three's case need to be held to account for misrepresenting the evidence at their disposal.'

Graham and Algy were now well into their fifties and their minds turned towards retirement. Their lives had been tainted by the murder at 7, James Street and from time to time they would speak about the perpetrator of this horrible crime. Niggling away at them was the way the police had not been charged with the abuse of their position in society.

This was about to change. In 2009, following a lengthy investigation, eight retired police officers were charged with perverting the course of justice. Graham and Algy had waited a long time for this news.

'At last, the police are going to face trial and Violet Perriam with them,' exclaimed Graham.

'It was her initial statement that put John Actie at the crime scene.'

'She was the one whose statement helped the investigation to change direction.'

'The police definitely falsely incriminated the men on the back of her fairy tale.'

'They were corrupt and used Violet Perriam's concocted story against five innocent men.'

'I can't wait for their trial to start. I hope they are hung out to dry. Their behaviour ruined the lives of a number of people and they deserve it.'

'Unfortunately, it won't bring back the time or ease the stress endured by the five.'

'All the boys are struggling and poor old Ronnie's dead.'

'Hopefully, they'll get some satisfaction from it.'

During the trial of the policemen, the defence tried to allege that the Cardiff five were involved in the murder with Gafoor. Algy and Graham were following the case through the media and found it difficult to comprehend these outrageous claims made by the defence.

In an exasperated voice, Graham exclaimed, 'The defence is claiming that there were two attacks.'

'Who do you think they are trying to kid, saying that Gafoor stabbed Lynette but not fatally, and the five then took over to finish the job.'

'All I can say is that the defence must have been "on the booze", it's so outrageous.'

'It sounds like their trial was conducted in a kangaroo court. They're living in "Cloud Cuckoo Land". Gafoor admitted he'd killed Lynette on his own.'

'There's no forensic evidence to link the five men to the crime scene. What are they playing at?'

'What about the apologies from the two South Wales Police Chief Constables. They were convinced all the men were innocent and there had been a serious miscarriage of justice.'

'What's worse the four men left alive who were accused of killing Lynette are being called as witnesses.'

'Their suffering just goes on and on.'

It seemed that the four living members of the Cardiff Five were being tried again. They were in court for four days, yet they'd been acquitted of the crime. In a sudden twist, the trial against the police collapsed on 1 December 2011 after five months and £30 million being spent on it. The judge claimed that the eight police officers couldn't get a fair trial. Violet Perriam was also cleared of perjury.

Graham was incensed as he spoke to Algy. 'It's a complete stitch up.'

'I don't fully understand what's happened. To me, it was an open and shut case.'

'It's difficult if you don't have a legal background. As I read it, the prosecution don't have the material to nail down the case.'

'I think that's what they call disclosure. The prosecution have to provide information relevant to the case.'

'Four files proving the prosecution case, have been lost.'

'After five months of evidence, the judge has had to abandon the trial.'

'All the defendants have been found not guilty.'

'It's like a Brian Rix farce and retired policemen who were corrupt get away with it.'

'If it's any consolation, everyone knows what they did.'

'But we all wanted to see them banged to rights because you need to be able to trust the police.'

'It leaves a sour taste in the mouth.'

Seven weeks later, the missing files were found in a cardboard box with other documents relating to the case. Algy was first to hear this news and rang Graham. In an angry voice, he announced, 'The files were found in the offices of the police investigation team.'

'What a fortuitous coincidence. The Cardiff Five is one of the worst miscarriages of justice in British legal history and the boys have lost the chance of seeing the investigating police locked up.'

'At the time an institutionally racist police force framed five black and mixed-race men.'

'South Wales Police had been infected by racist behaviour and officers like this need to be weeded out. There have been changes in the police but there's still a long way to go,' exclaimed an irate Graham.

Part 6
The Pleasure Lies Not in Discovering Truth but in Searching for It. Leo Tolstoy (Russian writer)

Chapter 40

2017

This was a momentous time in Algy and Graham's lives. They had scheduled this year for their retirement. As July approached, the friends grew more apprehensive about what the future might hold. Mixed emotions were inevitable as Graham had taught for more than forty years. Although, circumstances had delayed Algy starting teaching when he left college, he still managed to work for nearly thirty-five years.

Trepidatious at the thought that this milestone in their life was nearly upon them, they wondered how they would adjust to change. For years, they both had to get up at "early o clock", and now they were going to be confronted with every day being a weekend. Routine is an important part of teaching, with Graham's life revolving around the bell ringing up to ten times a day.

On the other hand, Algy's job involved him constantly meeting deadlines by having to be in schools to speak with different groups of immigrant children.

Their work had been rewarding and both could look back at their careers with a sense of great pride. Having made a significant impact within their chosen fields of education, both would be sorely missed. The school where he'd attended as a youngster had a special place in Graham's heart. Fitzalan High School served the Butetown area giving Graham the advantage of knowing many of the families.

Having been raised in the area he knew many of the children's backgrounds, according him an invaluable insight into the lives of the pupils. This intimate understanding of the youngsters' home environment benefited the school, making Graham an invaluable member of staff.

Algy's experiences when he was younger provided him with the intuition needed to help young people who had come to settle in a foreign country. Although, attitudes towards immigrants had improved, prejudice could never be totally eradicated because of a small-minded white minority thinking they were a superior element of the human race. Algy was the ideal person to help young immigrant children integrate into British society.

The day they could never have envisaged at the start of their careers finally arrived. Children in Fitzalan High School were distraught that Mr Murrell was leaving. The despondency at losing an iconic teacher made Graham feel melancholy at the thought of his departure. He was leaving a big part of his life behind.

Nevertheless, his outstanding legacy was assured and he consoled himself with the thought that he had positively achieved throughout his career. Colleagues gave Graham a resounding send off at a local hotel.

The youngsters that Algy helped to integrate into British society were also saddened that their mentor would be embarking on a new phase of his life. As a mark of affection for Mr Foster, many of his students brought him gifts to remember him by. Their generosity moved Algy, triggering the thought that maybe he should have worked on.

On the other hand, he concluded that sixty-five was the right age to finish such a demanding job. He thought to himself, I'm ready for a bit of "me time". It was definitely the right juncture to rein back from what had been a hectic lifestyle. The Director of Education and other bureaucrats working in the Department of Education took Algy for a slap-up meal as a thank you for his commitment to the service.

The first six weeks of Graham and Algy's retirement were easy. This was the school summer holidays and it was normally the time when both would traditionally recharge their batteries. It was not until 3 September, when it suddenly dawned on them that they were now beginning the rest of their lives.

Graham followed in his father's footsteps by owning racing pigeons. This provided him with a time-consuming hobby, keeping him busy. Algy now had time to read, listen to music, meet friends and travel. There was no longer any need to jump out of bed when the alarm went.

Now they had the luxury of settling into a contented lifestyle giving them time to enjoy the pension they had accrued from their teaching service. Everything appeared blissful but would two men who had led such active lives eventually get itchy feet?

Chapter 41

April 2020

Algy and Graham would meet on a Thursday evening at the Claude Hotel. In the Spring of 2020, both were looking for a new challenge and while they were enjoying a pint Graham had a brain wave.

'Do you know I've often wondered whether I have any relatives left in Barbados.'

'It's also crossed my mind, Gray, that I must have family in St Kitts.'

'My grandfather was from such a big family, surely I must have relatives in Barbados.'

'Most families were big in those days and it's almost certain that there are other Fosters living in St Kitts.'

'Algy, we've got a lot of time on our hands. Why don't we go to the Caribbean and look for our relatives?'

'That's a great idea and you never know we might be able to find out where we came from in Africa.'

'I'll be able to get someone to look after the pigeons while we're away. I've done enough favours for people. They'll be anxious to pay me back.'

'It'll take a bit of organisation. We'll need to book plane tickets and accommodation.'

'What happens If we find out where we came from in Africa?'

'I think we should fly there. Our ancestors were obviously victims of the slave trade.'

'You never know what we might uncover about our past.'

'We'll book flights to Bridgetown first and stay there about five days. Then we'll take a flight to Basseterre.'

'That sounds like a French name. Is it the capital of St Kitts?'

'It is the capital. St Kitts was a French island for a while but later came into British hands.'

'We need to stay in Basseterre for five days as well.'

'We'll book it on bookings.com.'

'Good idea, Algy. What about a departure date?'

'Let's go on 20 May.'

'That's settled then. It should be a fantastic trip.'

'If we can find any of our relatives, it'll be a real bonus.'

'Are you sure Gill will be okay with it?'

'She's fed up seeing me around the house.'

'Sarah won't mind, she's always telling me to do something constructive.'

'All systems go then, Algy.'

'Let's drink up. By the way, you book the flights and I'll do the accommodation on both islands.'

Chapter 42

20 May

Algy and Graham set off from Cardiff Central Railway Station on the 9.40 am train to London. They had booked tickets to Reading where they would get the Heathrow link to transport them to Terminal Five for the British Airways flight to Barbados.

It was a pleasantly warm May morning when the friends met outside the station. Both wore shorts and T shirts anticipating that Barbados would be very warm. Algy and Graham were exhilarated at the thought of embarking on such an adventure. Excitement caused Algy's pupils to dilate and Graham's skin to tingle with excitement.

'We need to take our cases to platform 2. I'm going to use the lift,' exclaimed Graham.

'We're too old to be hauling cases up the steps.'

'With my bad knee, it's the last thing we need to do.'

'Knowing my luck, we'll be injured before we start.'

'It's all that sport when we were young. There's always a payback when you're older.'

'My father used to say, "All that physical activity you're playing will come home to roost when you're my age".'

'What do you mean? My pigeons come home to roost every day.'

'Ha ha, you haven't changed, Gray, as you've got older. There's always a smart answer,' declared Algy.

'Stepping out of the lift onto platform 2, there was a large crowd of people.'

'Are all these waiting for the London train?' Graham asked.

'You know why?'

'No, I haven't got a clue.'

'It's the first cheap train of the day. The earlier ones are "top whack". They're used by businessmen going to London for important meetings.'

'Bloody cheapskates,' joked an indignant Graham.

'Just like us, Gray. That's the reason we booked this one.'

'It's different for us, we're international jet setters!'

'What we can do is get a seat in first class and pay an excess to the guard. It's usually cheap but you get tea, snacks and newspapers.'

'Good idea, Algy. I don't fancy standing all the way to Reading.'

The 9:40 am arrived on time. To avoid a crush, Algy and Graham dragged their cases to the first-class carriage at the front of the train and boarded.

'Leave your case here, Algy, in the storage area.'

'I'm worried it might get nicked. That would be a great start to this adventure.'

'We'll use our heads and sit on the first seats so we can keep an eye on our luggage.'

'Don't give the guard a chance to ask for our tickets. He might think we're trying to get a free ride in first class. We should offer to pay straight away.'

'I've always said you're too strait laced. Far too moralistic and virtuous for your own good.'

'That's all we want is to get arrested for taking a free ride.'

'You make us sound like one of those American hobos who take rides on the freight trains for nothing. You worry too much, Algy.'

Graham looked straight at the guard, blurting out, 'My mate thinks you're going to arrest us for sitting in first class.'

'We'll pay the difference,' exclaimed a distressed Algy.

'No problem, boys. It's good to see you using your head. Second class is rammed.'

'See, Algy, you worry for nothing.'

'Where are you going, boys?'

'Barbados,' exclaimed Algy.

'You're having a laugh, aren't you?' We don't even go to Barrybados,' Graham intervened.

'He means Reading.'

'I see you're getting the Heathrow Express. Well, boys first class is great value at £10 excess each. I'll be around with the tea in a minute.'

'Algy might need some sedative in his tea to calm him down.'

'We don't serve tranquillizers but I've got camomile tea. That'll chill him out.'

Algy saw the funny side of his faux pas and the three men burst out laughing.

'There we are, Algy. I told you it would be okay. Just don't go and sit in first class on the plane. That could cost us £10,000.'

Arriving at Reading Station, Algy and Graham transferred to the Heathrow Express for the 45-minute journey to the airport. Disembarking at Terminal 5, the friends went to the queue for the British Airways desks. Getting close to the front, Graham took out his ticket.

'There we are, Algy, my ticket to Barbados. Where's yours?'

'I haven't got one,' exclaimed Algy.

Determined to pay Graham back for winding him up on the train, Algy began to play the game.

'What do you mean? You haven't got one,' muttered Graham.

'What I said, Gray.'

'It looks like I'll be going solo.'

Graham was convinced Algy had lost it up top. He'd been worried about sitting in first class on the train with a second-class ticket. He was now trying to get on a plane without one. Algy gently nudged Graham, then removed his phone from his pocket. Graham wondered what he was doing.

Turning to Graham with a wry smile on his face, Algy announced, 'You don't need a paper ticket. They are a thing of the past, except for technophobes like Mr Graham Murrell.'

Algy presented his phone at the counter then put his luggage onto the scales. Glancing towards Graham, he said, 'I really am a clever goody two shoes.'

'No, you're a clever dick,' whispered Graham.

'Have a nice flight, gentleman,' said the British Airways employee.

Settling for a one all draw, both friends decided to call a truce and went for a drink as there were a few hours to kill before their flight departed.

Chapter 43

The overhead seat belt sign came on and the captain announced, 'We'll be landing in about 20 minutes. In a few minutes, those sitting on the left-hand side of the plane will have a great view of the island and then you should be able to see Grantley Adams Airport.'

'Why is it named Grantley Adams Airport?' Algy asked.

'The original name was Seawell Airport before its name was changed in 1976 to honour the first Premier of Barbados, Sir Grantley Adams. He won the Barbados Scholarship and attended Oxford University to become a lawyer. While he studied there, his political views were influenced by the Liberal Party.'

'These liberal views shaped him as a politician and he rejected the socialism of the British Labour Party. Although, he spurned Labour Party views when he was installed as a politician in Barbados, he was pro working class.'

'Gray, you sound like you've got a doctorate.'

'I have. It was awarded by Doctor Google.'

'I should have guessed.'

'I just thought I'd better do a bit of research before we travelled.'

Algy and Graham looked out of the window as Barbados came into view. From the air, it looked roughly triangular in shape and completely surrounded by the Atlantic Ocean. Every beach was stunningly white with turquoise waters. Descending swiftly, the boys could see a variety of yachts on the ocean.

They started as dots but as the descent continued each vessel enlarged. The vista presented some exclusive looking craft confirming that Barbados is a playground for the rich and famous. Suddenly, there was a clunking noise causing Algy to exclaim, 'What's that noise?'

'No need to panic. The landing gear's just come down,' replied Graham.

Being a nervous flyer, take-off and landing were the worst parts of the flight for Algy. When he was in the sky, Algy was okay. Suddenly, the wing flaps lifted, causing him to experience further palpitations.

'What's happening to the wings, Gray?'

'The wing flaps lifting help the plane to slow down.'

'That's okay then.'

'Algy, just relax. In about 15 minutes, we'll be in the terminal.'

Having landed, one of the cabin crew opened the aircraft door and the passengers began filing out. As Graham and Algy passed through the door, they were hit by the Caribbean heat and humidity. This was so strikingly different from the temperate May conditions at home.

'We'll have to get our luggage from the carousel,' said Algy.

'We then need to get a taxi,' remarked Graham.

'That'll be no problem because there's plenty outside.'

'What's the name of the hotel we're staying in?'

'I booked the South Beach Hotel,' explained Algy.

'It's obviously next to the sea.'

'Quite right, Gray. It's right on the Caribbean Sea. We can hopefully do some sunbathing.'

'The main reason we're here is to find my relatives.'

'That'll take priority. Hopefully, we'll have some time to relax.'

'I suppose so. We've got five days.'

South Beach Hotel was in a stunningly beautiful place located right next to the Caribbean Sea. Seeing the white sand and azure sea gave Algy and Graham a truly luxurious, unforgettable view that they might not be able to fully benefit from. This part of their mission was to find Graham's relatives. Any relaxation or frivolity would be insignificant by comparison with the reason for them being in the Caribbean.

Sitting in their hotel room, Algy took the complimentary detailed map of Barbados from the table and opened it.

'Graham, have you any idea where your relatives might live?'

'My grandfather said to me it was a religious name, I think.'

Algy began to study the map in great detail.

'The only place name I can see that is linked to religion is Bathsheba.'

'Where is it?'

'On the east coast.'

'I do remember that name from Sunday school.'

'And I do,' added Algy.

In a moment of inspiration, Graham remembered what he had been taught in Sunday school about Bathsheba. Determined to reveal his knowledge he remarked, 'David, the greatest king of Israel saw the woman, Bathsheba, bathing in the nude on the roof of her house.'

'I know why you remembered that.'

'You've got a one-track mind, Algy. Let me finish.'

'Go on then, enlighten me.'

'He fancied Bathsheba but she was already married to Uriah the Hittite.'

'If David was the greatest king of Israel, I dread to think what the worst one was like.'

'Everyone makes mistakes, Algy.'

'I can't imagine Gill or Sarah being very sympathetic if we made that mistake.'

'You're right but the story of David was a long time ago.'

'What did he do then?'

'To get his own way, he put Bathsheba's husband right in the front of a battle where he was bound to get killed.'

'That's terrible. He must have been a right devious waster.'

'All human beings can be but there's a moral to the story.'

'Did he get killed?'

'Of course, he did. Then David took Bathsheba to be his wife.'

'I'm not being funny, Gray, if we did that we'd go to prison for years. What's the moral of the story? I must say I can't see one?'

'God forgives those who are truly sorry.'

'You'll have to tell me how he was sorry. He had just killed a man.'

'Bathsheba had a child by David and the child died.'

'That means the child was punished, not David.'

'David realised he'd done wrong by setting up Bathsheba's husband to die. He loved the child and God was punishing him. Being truly sorry for what he'd done wrong, God forgave him.'

'I've made mistakes but I've never killed anyone.'

'Enough of the religious education. Let's start by looking for my relatives in Bathsheba.'

'It seems a good place to start. We'll go on the bus tomorrow.'

The following morning, Algy and Graham walked from their hotel to the bus station. Whenever they asked a local for directions, they were impressed by how courteous they were, always addressing them as sir. One man even walked the last half mile with them because the bus station was concealed behind a building. They were aghast at how well-mannered and helpful all the local people were.

A few people boarded the bus for Bathsheba at Bridgetown bus station. As they journeyed to the east coast, more and more people jumped on board. Smartly dressed school children, looking a real picture in their school uniforms boarded and sat in the seats opposite the boys.

Two women hopped on, giving Algy and Graham a glimpse of life for most people in the Caribbean. They were carrying two cages each with chickens in them. How different this was to the clientele on Cardiff buses. It was a real eye opener for Algy and Graham.

35 minutes later, Algy and Graham left the bus, to be greeted by a coastal landscape which was very different to the one in Bridgetown. This was the Atlantic Coast. Looking its resplendent best, here was a magnificently exquisite landscape with Atlantic rollers. Nobody was swimming here because of the dangerous currents.

It was in complete contrast to the Caribbean Sea on the other side of the island, where large numbers of people cooled off in the tranquil waters. Algy and Graham were bewitched by a coastline which reminded them of some of the Pembrokeshire beaches. As they gazed at the ocean, two schoolgirls approached them and tapped Graham on the shoulder to catch his attention.

'Hello there,' said Graham.

'Please, Sir, will you buy us an ice cream?'

'There's nowhere to buy an ice cream here,' answered a stunned Graham.

'We're in the middle of nowhere,' said Algy.

The smaller of the two girls pointed out, 'There's an ice cream parlour behind these trees.'

'Come on then, I'll buy one and Algy will buy the other.'

Both men thought to themselves that this would never happen at home. Children were told not to speak to strangers. It became obvious that the girls had realised that Algy and Graham were not Barbadians but British. As a result of property in the Caribbean being expensive, it was only wealthy foreigners who could afford to purchase these luxurious villas.

Many of the locals didn't benefit from these affluent foreigners visiting their Caribbean second homes and many were impoverished. The journey to

Bathsheba had passed through villages where a number of the dwellings were tin shacks. It was glaringly evident that many Barbadian residents had little money.

After entering the shop, the girls chose two flavours each. Algy and Graham handed over Barbadian dollars. Their generosity left the girls ecstatic. Thinking quickly, Graham said, 'Is there a local church in Bathsheba?'

'We've just come from there.'

To prove their point, the girls pulled out their bibles to show the boys.

'Have you been to Bible study?' Graham asked.

'We have, Sirs. All you need to do is turn left and walk for about half a mile and then you'll come to Saint Joseph's Anglican Church,' replied the elder of the girls.

'Does it have a graveyard?' Graham remarked.

'It does and all the locals are buried there.'

'Thanks, girls,' said Algy.

Having walked half a mile to the church, the boys could see the gravestones. Entering the cemetery, they spotted a woman in uniform. They wondered if this was a local policewoman and if so, she might be able to give them some new information about whether there were any Murrells living on Barbados. The woman stood solemnly looking at a gravestone.

Quite obviously her dignified manner showed she was paying her respects to a family member. Sensing someone behind her, she turned to see Algy and Graham.

'Can I help you, Sirs?'

As he was looking for his relatives, Graham answered. 'Do you know if there are any Murrells buried here? I'm trying to establish whether I have any relatives on the island. My grandfather and father were both called Joey Murrell. While my father was born in Cardiff in Wales, my grandfather came over from Barbados to fight in the World War I.

'He fell in love with my grandmother and never went back to Barbados. I was told that they came from a place with religious connotations in the name. Bathsheba was the only place with any link to religion that we could see, that's why we came here.'

'I understand why you were looking for a place implying a religious name. However, nearly all the Murrells live in St Michael's Parish in Bridgetown. The island is divided into parishes named after saints. Every region of Barbados is named after a religious character. Faith is important to most of the people.'

'You haven't really made a mistake, how were you expected to know. As the mother of King Solomon, Bathsheba was an important woman in the Bible. Bathsheba is the only place with a religious name shown on the map.'

'Blow me down, we've just come from Bridgetown,' exclaimed Algy.

Graham looked dejected at the thought of wasting time by coming to Bathsheba.

'That's a pity.'

'By the way what's your names?'

'I'm Graham.'

'And I'm Algy. We're both from Cardiff in Wales.'

'I'm Inspector Thomas of the Barbados police and it's really great to meet you, boys.'

Wanting to appear grateful, Graham exclaimed, 'The feeling's mutual but we'd better catch the bus back to Bridgetown.'

'Hold your horses, boys. I said nearly all the Murrells. There's one who lives in Bathsheba having moved here recently to live with his daughter. He's a centenarian but he's as sharp as a razor and as fit as a fiddle.'

'Where does he live?' Graham asked.

'See that White House over there, that's where he's now living. His age meant he was finding it difficult looking after himself.'

'Will he mind us visiting him?' Algy asked.

'He loves people visiting him and can he talk! If there was a West Indian Championship for talking, he'd win it hands down.'

'By the way, what's his name?' Graham asked.

'He's Clarence Murrell.'

'We'd better get over there,' said Graham.

'Good luck, boys.'

Chapter 44

Algy and Graham left the churchyard and headed towards the big white house. Graham's mind was in a state of bewilderment but he hoped that he would find out something about his family history. His body quivered at the thought of possibly meeting a Barbadian relative for the first time. He was uncertain as to how Clarence Murrell would greet him.

It wouldn't be long before he'd find out. Apprehensively putting his finger to the doorbell, he hoped that the occupant would be a long-lost relative. Would he be greeted affectionately or would he be shown short shrift. Graham was about to find out.

A Barbadian woman in her fifties answered the door. Her dark skin tone contrasted with the snow-white dress she wore. Looking at Algy and Graham, she remarked, 'Good day, Sirs. How can I help you?'

'This is Algy Foster and I'm Graham Murrell.'

'That's very interesting. My grandfather is called Clarence Murrell. He is elderly and although he's sharp witted and very competent, I spend time looking after him.'

'That's why we're here. By the way what's your name?'

'My name is Rosie Lewis. Before I married, my maiden name was Murrell.'

'We've come from Cardiff in South Wales and I think we could be related.'

'I won't be able to help you establish whether we're related but my grandfather definitely will. He's the font of all knowledge when it comes to family history.'

'Would it be possible to see him?'

'Of course, he loves showing off his knowledge about our family history. Come on in. He's sitting on the veranda looking at the garden and the ocean.'

Rosie led Algy and Graham through the hall to the back of the house. Here an elderly, distinguished gentleman sat looking at the Atlantic Ocean. He was a venerable elder statesman displaying a pleasant welcoming disposition.

Stepping onto the terrace, Algy and Graham were awe struck at the thought that they could be on the verge of starting to unravel their past and give them an even better insight into reasons why people of colour have endured racism. Rosie approached her grandfather and introduced the two guests.

'Grandad, this is Algy Foster and Graham Murrell. They've come from South Wales.'

Clarence looked at Graham and said, 'Ah, Graham Murrell. Hopefully, another member of the sophisticated Murrell clan. What are you hoping to achieve by coming to see me,' remarked Clarence in an animated voice belying his great age.

'I was hoping to discover if I had any relations in Barbados.'

'It seems you've just found one.'

Rosie interrupted and asked, 'Gentlemen, would you like a cup of tea and some cake?'

Algy was parched and peckish and jumped at the opportunity.

'We'd love a cuppa.'

'What about you, Grandad?'

'That'll be lovely, Rosie. I can see us talking for some time.'

Turning to Graham, Clarence asked, 'What was your father's name?'

'Joey Murrell, who was born in Cardiff, but my grandfather was also called Joey.'

'Graham, I was born in 1919, the son of Lewis Murrell. I've been lucky to live to such a great age.'

'May I say you're fantastic for your age,' declared Algy.

'Do you realise there are more centenarians in Barbados than virtually every other country in the world?'

'That's amazing,' remarked a flabbergasted Algy.

'Not really because this beautiful island has a great climate, good food and a stress-free lifestyle. These contribute to a number of people making it to one hundred years of age. However, the most important factor is the religiosity of the people.'

'What does that mean?' A puzzled Algy remarked.

'It means that many of the islanders are very religious, which helps alleviate stress. We put our trust in Jesus rather than things like money. It helps us to be contented with our lot in life.'

'That's really interesting because church attendance in Britain has declined. Most people enjoy a good standard of living which makes many complacent about their wealth. This has resulted in Britain trusting less in God and taking their wealth for granted making us a more secular society,' declared Algy.

'By the way, we've just seen two little girls who had come from Bible study at the local church. In Britain, you don't see many children going to Bible study,' exclaimed Graham.

'Trusting in the Lord is most important for us Barbadians. All things come from the Lord.'

'Even ice cream!' Algy added.

'Yes, it came from Lord Graham and Lord Algy's pockets,' explained Graham.

'Let's get back to the Murrells. I've got some good news for you, Graham.'

'I'm all ears. Go on, hit me with it.'

'As I said I was born in 1919, the son of Lewis Murrell. My dad was born in 1895 and had an older brother called Joey.'

'Was that my grandfather?' Graham exclaimed.

'Almost certainly because my father told me his brother left Bridgetown in 1914 to fight in the World War I.'

'Have you any other information?' An excited Graham declared.

'Let me finish.'

'Go on, I'm listening.'

'My father told me Joey left on a tramp steamer called the Pontwen bound for Cardiff.'

'That's definitely my grandfather!'

'My dad, Lewis, never saw Joey again.'

'Clarence, I can tell you he married a Welsh girl called Annie Sleeman. Do you know, I can't believe I've found a relative? That must make you some sort of uncle but there's no way I'll work that out.'

'It doesn't matter. Neither can I,' said Clarence.

Algy sat in the room stunned that Graham had found a relative. He hoped that his luck would be in when they went to St Kitts. Clarence was determined to enlighten Graham about his ancestry. Though he was one hundred and one years old Graham was astounded at how astute he was. He was definitely a man blessed by God. He was so clear-thinking that he could have been sixty years younger.

'We have a remarkable family history, Graham.'

'How do you know that, Clarence? The Murrells came to Barbados many moons ago. Our ancestors were brought here during the days of the slave trade.'

Algy had just remarked that Britain had changed to a more secular society. Clarence continued, 'Change is inevitable within all cultures. Not too long ago, every Barbadian family had someone who learned their family history from the time their ancestors first came to this island.'

'You mean there are still people here who can recite a family's history,' exclaimed a gobsmacked Graham.

'It's a dying tradition unfortunately and there are only a couple of people left in Barbados who can do this. Fortunately, from your perspective I'm one of them.'

'You just take your time, Clarence. I'm listening.'

'Let me just tell you both that this expertise is known as the oral tradition. People from Africa who came to the islands as slaves adopted their master's religion. Tribal beliefs were dispensed with and many became devoted Christians.'

'The slaves learnt that stories about Jesus circulated in the early Christian communities and were handed down by word of mouth to be later written down. These are what we call the Gospels in the New Testament. Slaves copied this tradition as a way of handing down their family history to their descendants. Remember they couldn't read or write.'

'Why are there only a few people left who can do this?' Graham questioned.

'The youngsters on the island don't want to devote their time to it. Unfortunately, if they can afford a computer, they spend too much time on them and the oral tradition heritage is dying out. If I was to relate the whole Murrell family history, I'd be here until next year.'

'Can you go back to the days of the slave trade? I'd love to know where I came from.'

'Of course, I can. The Murrell family came from Nigeria. Our ancestors were taken as slaves in 1780 and marched to Benin where they were put on an English slave ship, then transported to Barbados.'

'Why did you say ancestors? I'd always been taught that slaves were transported in single sex boats.'

'On this occasion, some couples were transported across the Atlantic together. However, there's a really grim story attached to our ancestors' capture. The earliest Murrell ancestors were called Adedamola and Abedi. They had a young baby.

'African men working for the slave traders raided their village taking them captive. Adedamola and Abedi had the baby snatched from them. The raiders shot the child and then threw the infant's corpse on the village fire.'

'Oh my God,' shouted Graham.

Algy covered his face with his hands, distraught at what he'd just heard.

Clarence continued, 'They were chained with the other villagers and marched to the slave market at Ouidah in Benin where they became the property of Felix de Sousa. He was a ruthless Portuguese slave trader who became very wealthy as a result of the slave trade. Adedamola and Abedi were put on an English ship bound for Barbados.'

'They were forced to work on a large sugar plantation. Growing sugar cane eventually became the biggest industry in Barbados. All of our ancestors worked on these plantations until slavery ended in 1834.'

'What I find incredible about this was the involvement of other Africans in the capture of slaves,' announced a despondent Graham.

'Sadly, they were just looking after their own interests, making sure they didn't become slaves themselves.'

'Some people will do anything to look after their own ends,' interjected Algy.

Graham commented, 'You've been fantastic, Clarence. With your knowledge I've not only found out where my ancestry lies but it's enlightened me that what happened centuries ago has led to racism in so many countries. White superiority dates back to the days of the slave trade. Whites were the masters then and some people today are desperate to retain this dominance.'

'They just want to retain the whip hand,' explained Algy.

'It's incredible that those African tribesmen burned a baby,' declared a visibly upset Graham.

'The baby would have been of little use to the slave traders. There was no way the child would have survived the Middle Passage across the Atlantic,' explained Clarence.

'At the end of the day, slavery was all about money,' declared Algy.

'Enough of the negativity, boys. My daughter will contact our relatives who all live in Saint Michael's Parish in Bridgetown to arrange a big Caribbean party in your honour. We'll have a ball.'

'Clarence, you've been God sent. I can't thank you enough for what you have told me,' said an ecstatic Graham.

Chapter 45

25 May 2020

Following the Murrell family reunion at St Michael's Parish church hall, a reinvigorated Algy and Graham arrived at the airport for their 360-mile flight to Basseterre on St Kitts. Algy was praying that he'd be able to discover his family ancestry as Graham had done. An announcement came over the communication system calling passengers to embark for the flight to Basseterre.

Algy and Graham made their way to the departure point. Much to Algy's surprise there were only ten passengers. Turning to Graham, he exclaimed, 'There will be lots of room on this plane.'

'Don't you bet on it.'

'What do you mean?'

'Don't think we'll be going on a big jet.'

Being diffident about flying, Algy took one look at the plane and said, 'It's like a tin can. I'll be bricking it.'

'Don't worry, they're built to withstand turbulence but I don't know about a Caribbean hurricane.'

'Oh my God, I hadn't thought of that.'

'You need to think straight, Algy. It's not the hurricane season.'

'Stop winding me up, Gray.'

The flight to St Kitts took about an hour and as they came through the clouds the outline of the island came into view. Looking out of the window, the boys could see cloud shrouded mountains. The dormant Mount Liamuiga volcano presented itself with its crater lake prominent.

As the plane banked Graham remarked, 'There's another island there.'

'That's Nevis, Gray. There are fantastic sandy beaches on the island. It's supposed to be superb for diving as the waters are so clear.'

'Hopefully, we'll have some free time to go to the beaches.'

'First thing is we've got to try and find some of my family. We had great success on Barbados with your ancestors.'

'Is the airport just called Basseterre or is it named after someone?'

'It's named after Robert L Bradshaw, the first Premier of Saint Kitts and Nevis. In 1996, he was awarded the title of First National Hero. National Heroes Day is celebrated on 16 September, which is his birthday.'

'There you are, it's Dr Google again.'

'No wrong, I read it in Encyclopaedia Britannica when I was working.'

'You swot.'

As the plane landed, the banter ceased. Taxiing to the terminal building the boys disembarked. Entering the building, Algy turned on his phone to be greeted by a double ping. He had an alert. A forty-six year old black man had been murdered in the United States City of Minneapolis.

'Graham, there's been a black man murdered in Minneapolis. It's just come up on the phone,' exclaimed Algy.

'I bet a policeman murdered him.'

'I'll look now at the news story.'

'It happens regularly in the States.'

'You're right, Gray. He was murdered by a white policeman called Derek Chauvin.'

'It's almost forty years to the day when I was in Miami and a black man was murdered by the police. That murder sparked the Miami riots. I bet this one will kick off riots again. In some ways, it's justified because extreme civil disorder is the only way the authorities in America will sit up and take notice of the injustice blacks have to face.'

'I'm just reading that a black man called George Floyd was arrested over suspicion of using a counterfeit $20 bill. It says here that he was handcuffed, forced face down on the floor and Chauvin had his knee on his neck for over 9 minutes.'

'That's another racist copper attaching little value to a black life. It's disgusting.'

'The Black Lives Matter movement started a few years ago. They'll surely have something to say about this.'

'I hope they do. There's tourist information over there. Let's ask if they know anything about anybody named Foster, living on the island. It's not a big place. I've no doubt everybody here knows everybody else.'

Dragging their cases, Algy and Graham made their way to the tourist information. A pretty lady behind the counter politely asked in a broad Caribbean accent, 'Is there anything I can do for you, gentlemen?'

'We're from Britain and I'm trying to find out if I have any relatives on St Kitts. My father grew up here.'

'It's almost certain there will be someone. What's your name?'

'I'm Algy Foster and this is Graham Murrell. His father was from Barbados and we managed to find his relatives. Now it's my turn.'

'I know most things about people on the island and there's a Robert Foster who's a well-known multi-millionaire.'

'I doubt that he'd be a relative of mine. None of us have ever made any money.'

'Robert Foster is the richest man on Saint Kitts. He owns the Carlton Hotel and Beach Resort, just north of Basseterre. Get a taxi, everyone who lives on St Kitts knows where it is.'

'If it's a resort, it must be a whopping place,' commented Graham.

'Gentlemen, it's huge and exclusive. The place is frequented by wealthy Americans who are not afraid to part with their dollars. I would definitely go to see Robert first.'

'We're staying in the Marriott,' remarked Algy.

'The Carlton's on the way. You'll be able to stop off first. Robert is very amenable. I'm sure he'll see you.'

Walking outside, Algy and Graham hailed a taxi. Graham asked, 'Could you possibly take us to the Carlton Hotel and Beach Resort?'

'Man, I thought the only people rich enough to stay there were Yanks. Not too many Brits stay in that place. You must be well heeled.'

'We're as poor as church mice,' exclaimed Algy.

'What are you doing going there?'

'I'm hoping a long-lost uncle or cousin owns it and he'll give us a freebie.'

'I've heard of a frisbee but what the heck is a freebie?'

Answering quickly with a grin, Graham said, 'It means we're a pair of scroungers.'

'That Robert Foster is a shrewd businessman and so was his grandfather who raised all the money to set up the hotel. It's amazing what you can do with sugar.'

'I thought growing sugar cane had stopped on this island.'

'It has but there were some savvy operators in the Foster family. Jump in it will only take 2 minutes.'

'Pulling up outside the hotel, the boys paid the taxi driver and thanked him with a tip. A man in a blue uniform opened the door of the car. Doffing his cap, he said, 'Good day, gentlemen. Reception is just inside. You can't miss it.'

Algy and Graham went up to the counter to speak to the receptionist.

'Good day, have you made a reservation?'

'No, we haven't but we were hoping to speak with Robert Foster,' remarked Algy.

'He's a very busy man but I'll ring his personal assistant. Who should I say is asking for him?'

'Mr Graham Murrell and Mr Algernon Foster.'

Picking up the phone, reception informed Robert Foster's PA that two Englishmen wanted an audience with him. They thought it best not to take umbrage at the receptionist's failure to identify them as Welsh. To people in this part of the world, everyone from the United Kingdom was English. When the PA told Robert that Algernon Foster wanted to see him, he insisted they came straight up.

Conveying Robert's message, the receptionist said, 'Go straight down the corridor. Mr Foster's office is the third door on the right. Knock and the PA will call you in.'

Following the instructions given by the receptionist, they knocked the door and the PA answered. 'I'll take you through to Mr Foster now.'

Mr Foster was sat at a huge marble table surrounded by many different technological devices. These enabled him to scrutinise the work in the hotel. In this way, he could keep his finger on the pulse of this superb resort. Algy and Graham's mouths dropped open when they saw the high specification of the equipment he was using. They'd never seen an office like this. In school their offices were little bigger than a broom cupboard.

'How can I help you two gentlemen?'

'I'm Algy Foster or if you want to be more formal Algernon. My friend is Graham Murrell. Mind you, I call him Gray.'

'Don't worry about formality. I'm not into it. I'm Rob and you'll be Algy and Gray.'

'We're trying to find out if we have any family on the respective islands our fathers came from.'

'We had great success on Barbados. I found an elderly relative who was actually a centenarian. He knew the history of the Murrell family from the time that they were taken there as slaves,' exclaimed Graham.

'Why are you doing that?'

'Over the years in Britain, there's been a multitude of racist instances and we were taught in church that "all men are equal". However, during recent times there has been some improvement in attitudes, particularly amongst young people,' proclaimed Algy.

'I'll give you an example. When I was young, a group of us boys would be standing outside a cafe in Butetown, which was where we were brought up in Cardiff. Just because we were black and mixed race, the police would clip us over the head and move us on. We were good boys but they were only doing it because they thought black kids cause trouble,' explained Graham.

'I've been stopped and searched,' said a disconsolate Algy.

'For what?'

'For knives and other weapons but they don't do it to white blokes. They think blacks are troublemakers,' exclaimed Algy.

'We obviously don't get that problem here because we have a largely black government. I realise that I'm a product of the Slave Trade but we are an independent nation now. How can I help you?'

'You're Robert Foster and my father was Ronald Foster. I wondered if you knew anything about your ancestry.'

'I haven't learnt my family history from slavery to the present day because it's never been a tradition on St Kitts. However, my father is still alive but my grandfather James died a few years ago. What I do know is he had a brother Ronald. He was the most academic member of the family and became a newspaper editor on the island. He decided to leave St Kitts and go to Britain on the Windrush.'

'My God, that's my dad. Thanks, so much Robert. It's unbelievable that I've found a relative.'

'What I'd like to do, boys, is offer you a suite at the Carlton and it's on the house. We'll have dinner later on when I'll be able to give you more information about the Foster family history.'

'The trouble is we booked to stay in the Marriott,' interjected Graham.

'My PA will sort that out and if they want any money, I'll pay for it. We'll meet at 8:00 pm for dinner.'

Algy and Graham were shown to an executive suite. Such stylish luxury was something they could only dream about. Staying at the Carlton for a fortnight would not just cost an arm and a leg but it would break the bank. There was no doubt they would have to default on any payment here.

Algy appreciating the cost of such luxury, declared, 'We'd be doing the washing up here for a year if we had to pay for this.'

Graham nodded in agreement with Algy's assessment of the situation.

At first, Algy and Graham thought dinner suits would be the order of the day at such a prestigious hotel. However, Algy remembered that when he went to the United States Americans dressed casually in restaurants. Hopefully, this would be the case in the Carlton because the boys had not banked on eating in such an esteemed establishment.

Luckily, Algy's appraisal of the American dress code proved correct. Robert was at the table waiting for them both. They were told to order anything from the menu. Prices were eyewatering making Graham think that he wouldn't have spent this much money on a year's worth of meals.

Lobster, steak and crème brulee were exquisite dishes, leaving Algy and Graham well stuffed. Following the meal, Robert asked for a bottle of the best port to be brought to the table. Pouring three glasses, he declared,

'We've established that we're related, Algy, but there's a fantastic family story behind all this opulence.'

'I'm ready and waiting, Robert.'

'My great grandfather was also called Algernon Foster and was born in 1898. He was a determined character who worked incessantly hard on a sugar plantation saving as much money as he could to buy his own place. To begin with, he grew sugar cane and managed to make a reasonable profit. He had a real business acumen but his methods were dubious.'

'What do you mean, Robert? Nobody called Algernon could possibly be a shady character.'

'My great grandfather realised there was an opportunity in the United States to make oodles of money.'

'Did he move there?'

'He didn't have to.'

'How could he possibly make money if he didn't move there?'

'Algernon was a shrewd old boy. He grew sugar cane which he turned into molasses. He then installed a number of stills on the plantation. His next move was to begin distilling rum. This was a masterstroke because between 1920 and 1933, it was the alcohol prohibition era in the United States.'

'People there were crying out for alcohol and great-grandfather Algernon set up a smuggling racket. He used fishing boats from these islands to transport rum to Florida. It would be landed at the Florida Keys and distributed around America. The fishermen were only too glad to support his enterprise. It provided them with a second income.'

'By all accounts this fishy business was so profitable that he couldn't make liquor quickly enough. Eventually, Algernon made millions of dollars. The Yanks were desperate for alcohol and they were prepared to pay high prices to get hold of rum.'

'Algernon was a real rascal and when he retired, my grandfather took over the plantation and stills. By then, rum could be legally exported to the United States. Eventually, sugar cane production became uneconomic and the Foster family moved into tourism. This was when the resort was built. The family owed everything to Algernon for creating the initial wealth.'

'He was a bit of a boy,' exclaimed Graham.

'What I don't understand is how he got away with it,' asked a perturbed Algy.

'I've got a letter here which the family found when great grandfather died. I'll show you.'

Taking it from his top pocket, Robert handed the letter to Algy. The letter, although slightly yellow through age, was generally in good condition. Algy read the contents relating to a huge consignment of illegal rum which had been landed by a number of fishing boats at Key West. The recipient was delighted by the shipment because the liquor would furnish countless American speakeasies.

The sender of the letter said that there would be a fleet of lorries to bootleg the rum around the United States. Lifting his eyes from the letter, Algy had a few questions.

'What's a speakeasy.'

Graham seized on the opportunity to display his knowledge of 1920s America.

'These were illegal bars set up during prohibition. Algernon was obviously supplying them with rum.'

'Do you know what bootlegging is?'

'I think it means they used to conceal rum in lorries with other goods. It was all designed to fool the authorities.'

'Spot on, Gray,' exclaimed Robert.

Algy returned to reading the letter and focused on the signature.

'It's signed by Alphonse Gabriel,' remarked Algy.

'Gabriel was not his surname,' explained Robert.

'Well, it doesn't help us to throw light on his surname,' said Graham.

'Boys, there's only one Alphonse Gabriel.'

'What do you mean, Robert?' Algy asked.

'It's Al Capone.'

'Bloody hell, your family knew some rogues. He was the most famous mafia boss in the States. Your halo's really slipped now, Algy.'

'Great grandfather made millions out of this racket. Al Capone had the cops in his pocket. Corruption was endemic in the police and they were scared to death of him. Al Capone was only arrested when the FBI (Federal Bureau of Investigation) became involved. To his credit, he never grassed Algernon up,' explained Robert.

'I can't understand why your old man didn't stay here, Algy. You'd have been a multi-millionaire,' remarked Graham.

'Anymore of your banter, Graham, and I'll call in the boys from Chicago. They'll sort you out.'

The three men laughed at Algy's comment. Robert decided to explain what he knew about Algy's dad.

'Your dad was an academic who won an island scholarship. He could have gone to university if he had the money. Ronald was a sharp cookie and went on to become the newspaper editor on the island. He never disclosed it but I don't think he liked the mafia connection. The rest of the family all thought it was the reason why he left and went to Britain.'

'There you are, Gray, I told you I was from good stock.'

'The trouble is, Algy, roguish behaviour is in the genes. It's always there.'

'I knew you'd want the last word.'

'It's really great to be able to entertain you boys and in particular to be able to meet you, Algy, a long-lost member of the family. Is there anything else I could help you with?'

Deep in thought, Algy put his hand to his forehead and said, 'There is something you might be able to help with.'

'What's that Algy?'

'I don't know if there's any way I could find out where my earliest ancestors came from. Graham found a relative who was able to relate his family history through the oral tradition.'

'As I told you, we don't do that in Saint Kitts. When many of the slaves came here, the island was ruled by the French. Many of the slaves were forced to convert to Roman Catholicism.'

'How will that help, Robert?'

'Let me finish, Algy. The Catholic Church kept detailed records of these conversions. There's a Catholic Cathedral in Basseterre and the Archbishop is a hell of a character. He's progressive and allows things like modern music in his services. By the way he loves a tipple.'

'What's his name?'

'You don't need to worry about his name, Algy. He only answers to the name Arch. Why don't you go and see him?'

'He sounds a real star. Will he see us?'

'Of course, he will. I'll tell you what we'll do. You need to take a bottle of our best deluxe rum with you.'

Graham's eyes lit up.

'You're not still bootlegging, are you?'

'Don't be daft, Gray. You don't need to bootleg today,' exclaimed Algy.

'There's always Iran. The Ayatollah could be a rogue,' remarked Robert.

'This families got some history. It's no wonder dad hopped on the Windrush.'

'Old habits die hard boys.'

'It looks like we're going to see the Arch if I'm to find out some more about my ancestors.'

'I'm seeing him on Saturday,' remarked Robert.

Algy had his eyes opened at this meal and he asked, 'Why is that?'

'So, he can hear my Confession.'

'You Foster lot need it,' remarked Graham.

Chapter 46

26 May 2020

'That was a very interesting meeting with Robert,' said Graham.

'It was very revealing but it just goes to show how loyal to the family my dad was. He never divulged to me about his grandfather's bootlegging.'

'In some ways, it's ironic what happened.'

'What do you mean, Gray?'

'On so many occasions, black people have been discriminated against. Algernon managed to beat the system. He generated wealth from dealing with one of the most notorious gangsters in history. In the 1920s and 30s, racism would have been rampant in the States. Most wealth would have been in white hands but here was a black man who joined the party.'

'I suppose that wealth is being put to good use today because the hotel is staggeringly impressive. Robert is providing work for lots of local people and he pays them very well. Algernon raised the living standards of the fishermen who transported the rum and gave work to the people who made it. It might be wishful thinking but I'll always remember him in the future as the St Kitts version of Robin Hood.'

'I suppose in some ways that's right. He was taking from the rich to give to the poor. Turn the telly on, Algy. We'll have a look at the BBC World News.'

Algy went over to the telly and switched it on. Graham was astounded at the scenes being televised from the United States. He exclaimed, 'Look at this, there's riots in Minneapolis. People are really upset at the death of George Floyd.'

'We live in the twenty-first century, yet racism is still a problem today as it was in years gone by.'

'I couldn't get over Clarence telling us about my earliest ancestors from Nigeria and how their baby was heartlessly shot and thrown on the fire.'

'Our ancestors were unfortunately being seen as no better than animals. The slave traders used and then just disposed of people when they had no more use for them.'

'The awful thing about what happened in the village was that it was carried out by African tribesmen.'

'People from all ethnicities are prepared to sink to the lowest level possible to make money. There's nothing more sickening or degrading than killing a baby.'

'Those Africans debased themselves.'

'I've got a funny feeling that people are so upset with the death of George Floyd that these riots are going to spread.'

'I'm going to phone the Archbishop to see if we can meet with him today.'

The Archbishop was delighted that two men from Wales wanted to see him. He invited Algy and Graham to the Cathedral of the Immaculate Conception, situated at Independence Square in Basseterre. The hotel reception ordered a taxi for the boys and the taxi driver with a beaming smile asked, 'Where are you fellas going?'

'We're going to meet the Archbishop at the Catholic Cathedral.'

'Boys, nobody calls him Archbishop or My Grace which is the usual way to address an Archbishop. He's a real quirky character, a proper one-off, popular with everyone.'

'Make sure you've got the rum, Algy.'

'I have.'

'He'll love you giving him that. You'll find out he's not averse to having a couple of drinks.'

Stepping from the taxi, the boys paid the driver and went into the Cathedral. Sitting approximately halfway down the nave in a pew was a man wearing a biretta, the traditional headdress worn by Roman Catholic clergy. Sporting this item of clothing, the boys immediately knew it was the Archbishop. Walking down the nave, Algy and Graham approached him.

Eager to show respect for his lofty position in the church, Algy said, 'Good morning, Your Grace.'

'Nobody calls me that. I'm the Arch,' exclaimed the indignant clergyman.

Algy had remembered what Robert had said but he was still flabbergasted by the Bishop's disgruntled response. Anxious to adhere to this unusual convention,

Algy proclaimed, 'Well, Arch, we've come to see you because we've been told you might be able to help me find my ancestors.'

'We'll see what we can do. We've got extensive diocese records here.'

'By the way, Arch, this is a gift from Graham and me.'

Taking a look at the bottle, the Arch's eyes lit up.

'This is not just the best rum on the island but it's the best in the world. Algernon Foster started distilling this liquor many years ago. He was supposed to be an old scallywag but everyone says he was a really cracking bloke who worked hard to raise the standard of living of the islanders he employed.'

'I'm Algy Foster and this is Graham Murrell.'

'If you're named after and related to Algernon, you must be worth a fortune.'

'We were both teachers, and although we're not multi-millionaires, we're very comfortably off. We've no complaints about our lifestyle.'

'I'm going to get three glasses for us to have a glug of rum.'

'Where do you want us to go, Arch?' Algy exclaimed.

'Stay right here. I will be back in a minute.'

'This one's got a head like a box full of frogs,' remarked Graham.

'He's definitely different, that's for sure.'

The Arch returned with three glasses and opened the rum. He put about six shots into each glass. The boys looked at each other in disbelief. Graham was in shock at the thought that they were about to drink rum in a church. Algy didn't drink a lot and to be confronted with a huge tot of rum and consuming it in a church disconcerted him.

'Are we okay to do this in the Cathedral. It's a holy place and we'll be desecrating it?'

'Everywhere is a holy place. God made it all.'

'As far as I'm aware, Robert Foster made the rum.'

'Let me tell you something. There's a part of God in everything. God made Robert Foster so he also had a big part in making the rum. I think the Lord will be very pleased with us appreciating such an appealing and intoxicating creation of His.'

Refusing to waste time, the Arch drank the rum down in one and poured another.

'Come on, you two, swill it down.'

Algy and Graham were at a loss to know what to make of this totally nutty clergyman. They'd never met a cleric like him. They were compelled to comply with the Arch's request.

'We need to get down to business now. I'll phone the archivist and he'll look through the Cathedral records. Have you any idea when your ancestors might have come here as slaves?'

'I've no idea,' said Algy.

'We'll need the earliest Cathedral record book.'

Taking out his mobile phone, the Arch asked the archivist if he could bring the earliest baptismal record book from the vault. Every record was in numerical order. The archivist brought a brown, dusty book and handed it to the Arch.

Dating back centuries, this book could potentially be a treasure trove of information. Whether it would throw any light on Algy's earliest ancestors remained to be seen. Opening the metal clasps holding the book, the Arch then turned the cover. Algy and Graham were disappointed when they saw the first page.

'It's written in French,' observed Algy.

'What's the problem?' The Arch retorted.

'Neither of us speak any French,' commented Graham.

'You mean teachers can't speak French,' exclaimed an indignant Arch.

He continued, 'Well, that won't matter because I spent five years in France. It's no problem. If I recall, you said you didn't know when your ancestors first came to St Kitts.'

'Not a clue about it, sorry, Arch.'

'Let's assume they came on the first slave ship that arrived in St Kitts. We'll look at the earliest entry in the register. We'll read this first page from 1780. It says Akin and his wife, Bimpe, were brought to St Kitts on a slave ship. They had been eighty days at sea.'

'Graham's ancestors from Africa came as husband and wife. We were told that this was unusual,' commented Algy.

'It was unusual but let me continue. When they arrived in St Kitts, their master insisted, they were baptised into the Christian faith. His name was Monsieur Henri. Akin and Bimpe were the first African slaves in Saint Kitts to be baptised.'

'What a coincidence that they came as husband and wife just as my earliest ancestors did,' remarked Graham.

Algy listened intently and the Arch continued, 'Akin and Bimpe were christened Jean and Francois. Believe it or not, slaves were branded with a red-hot iron at the slave market before they were transported and this was classed as a form of baptism.'

'How cruel was that?' Algy exclaimed.

'A Catholic priest was always present at the slave market to recite the baptismal vows. This left a stain on the soul of the Catholic Church. Church teaching today expresses the equality of all men and women, not the superiority of one ethnic group over another.'

'Is there anything else written down there?'

'There's a second entry in darker ink, meaning it was almost certainly added at a later date. It says that the couple came from a Nigerian village where their friend's baby was murdered and thrown into the fire.'

Algy's legs wobbled at what he'd just heard and he dropped onto his knees. Graham looked startled at what he'd just learnt. Such a mind-boggling revelation meant that Algy and Graham's ancestors had come from the same village. What happened had a similar impact on both men to that of a divine manifestation. This was an unprecedented moment in both men's lives and they were in shock.

Astounded, Algy and Graham were rooted to the spot. Nonplussed it was difficult to process what they had been told. Their stomachs were knotted and it was as if they were frozen in time. Still on his knees and finding what he had just learnt unbelievable, Algy wanted to double check that he'd heard correctly and asked, 'Where were they put on a slave ship, Arch?'

'It was in Ouidah, the largest slave market in Benin.'

'That's where my ancestors sailed from,' exclaimed Graham.

'Praise the Lord. This has been an epiphany for you both.'

Algy and Graham weren't practising Christians but what they had just discovered left them stunned. Both experienced shivers down their spines at the thought that their families were interconnected. In their wildest dreams it would have been inconceivable that their ancestors came from the same village. Arch could see that the boys had been knocked sideways.

'Are you both okay?'

'There's just one thing, Arch. My name is Foster but the slave owner was Monsieur Henri. It was usual for slaves to take their master's name.'

'You're missing a trick here, Algy, because you are in shock. Saint Kitts was a French island but the British later captured and ruled it as one of their colonies. No doubt the slaves changed masters and their names were altered.'

'I'm so totally flabbergasted by what I've been told that I couldn't even work out something as simple as that.'

'I think we need another drink, Arch,' exclaimed a normally abstemious Graham.

'That's a great suggestion. Charge your glasses, boys.'

'It looks like Benin here we come,' said Algy.

Part 7
No Sense of Loss

Chapter 47

Following their meeting with the Arch, Algy and Graham were exhilarated at being able to trace their families' ancestry to Benin. Both were badly affected by Adedamola and Abedi's baby who had been shot and thrown into the fire. Although, the perpetrators of this criminal act were Africans, these men had committed this repulsive immoral misdemeanour through their lust for money and wanting to protect their own liberty.

Nevertheless, Algy and Graham saw this action as symbolic of the little value attached to black lives throughout the centuries. Inequality in society had caused institutional racism, affecting both their lives. Although, there had been improvements, race discrimination was still an issue needing to be addressed.

A little baby had been killed in 1780 at the time of the Slave Trade through having no market value. On 25 May 2020, George Floyd was murdered because a policeman had decided his life was worthless. The ending of his life by a white policeman because he was suspected of using a counterfeit 20$ note was not just a travesty of justice but a crime against humanity.

From the inception of the slave trade until the present day, so many black people had lost their lives through racist attitudes. Algy and Graham were distraught at what had taken place in Minneapolis and fully understood why people had rioted to demonstrate their support for the Floyd family. This indiscriminate action against a human being was certain to provoke a violent response from people affected by the barbarity of the police action.

Returning to the hotel, Algy and Graham were planning how they were going to get to Benin. They went to Robert's office and his PA ushered the boys in. Robert was anxious to know if they knew anything at all about the Foster family, prior to their arrival in St Kitts.

'Did you find visiting the Arch useful?' Robert asked.

'What a character he is,' exclaimed Algy.

'I told you so.'

'He had us drinking rum in church claiming God had made it,' remarked Graham.

'That's the Arch for you. He's a total one off.'

'We thought he had a head full of toys in the beginning but we soon realised he's all there,' said Algy.

'What was he able to tell you?'

'He sent his archivist to get the earliest baptismal records from the Cathedral's vault. Lo and behold, the Foster's earliest ancestors came from Benin. The most remarkable thing was that they lived in the same village as Graham's ancestors.'

'Are you certain about that, Algy?'

'Absolutely certain because they were baptised when they arrived. At a later date when they had learned French, there was a second entry into the Cathedral records stating that they had been captured at the same time as a couple whose baby was shot and thrown on the village fire. Those people were Graham's earliest ancestors in Barbados.'

'You mean that our ancestors came from the same village in Benin! That is truly remarkable and I'm astounded.'

'We're going to go to Benin to visit the site of the slave market. We want to see for ourselves the place where they were traded,' said Graham.

'Boys, I've got a vested interest in what you're doing. I'm really impressed with what you've found out and I'll be paying for your trip.'

'Robert, you can't do that,' exclaimed Algy.

'My PA will look after the booking for you. Where was the slave market in Benin?'

'Ouidah and there were more slaves transported from that port than any other place in Africa,' said Graham.

'You'll have to fly to Miami to get to West Africa. My PA will get onto it immediately. There's only one thing I want in return, Algy, and that is for you to keep in touch with me.'

'No problem, Robert. It's been great to meet you and I'll be out here again.'

'There's always a bed here for you.'

'We've had a bit more than a bed, Robert. Your hospitality is second to none,' commented Graham.

'By the way, boys, just to let you know the murder of George Floyd has sparked demonstrations across the world. Britain has taken a lead in protesting about the killing of an innocent man.'

'That's pleasing to hear because large numbers of young people in particular want the inclusivity of all ethnic groups,' declared Algy.

'Today, there is more intermarriage in Britain which over time will lead to a greater intermingling of the races. Many older people might be "dyed in the wool" but most youngsters will not put up with discrimination,' claimed a perceptive Graham.

'Right, boys, you need to get ready for the last part of your odyssey. I hope you get from your visit to Africa exactly what you're looking for.'

Chapter 48

3 June 2020

'My secretary has finalised the details for your trip to Benin. You'll be taking a flight to Miami from St Kitts, where you will have an overnight stay. She's booked you into the Hilton. It's the best hotel in town. On 5 June, you have a flight to Lagos in Nigeria and she's arranged for a chauffeur driven car to take you to Ouidah.'

'Don't worry about the return journey. I've arranged for the car and driver to be available for you on 10 June. We will give you the phone number. All you have to do is call and they'll come from Lagos to get you. There's nothing to worry about because they are a highly reputable company.'

'But, Robert, Lagos is in Nigeria,' exclaimed Algy.

'It's only 85 miles from Ouidah and it's the nearest international airport.'

'We can't thank you enough for what you've done.'

'It's nice to be able to help family, particularly after what you've unearthed. Oh, and by the way, Gray, you're now one of the extended family. Our ancestors were next door neighbours and you never know we could have been blood relations!'

'It's a good thing to think like that, Robert.'

'Very true, Graham. All the best, boys.'

Robert's word about financing and transporting Algy and Graham was a copper bottom guarantee. After spending a night in Miami, they flew to Lagos in Nigeria on a Nigeria Airways flight. Over 15 million people populate Lagos, making it the second largest city in Africa. By comparison, Ouidah was tiny, with less than 100,000 inhabitants.

As Robert had promised, there was a chauffeur driven car waiting at Lagos Airport ready to transfer Algy and Graham to Ouidah.

Although, a journey of only 85 miles, it took 4 hours because of the volume of traffic in Lagos and the inferior infrastructure. Algy and Graham saw high levels of urban poverty as they were driven out of Lagos causing them to reflect on how fortunate they had been in life. Their driver informed them that two thirds of the city's population lived in informal housing.

Throughout the city, there were 380 slum communities and altogether 112 million people were living in poverty in Nigeria. He was quick to point out that the country has an expanding economy with the potential to lift millions out of poverty. Upset by the situation for millions of unfortunates, he stuttered when he said the government needed to work at freeing millions of Nigerians from poverty by building a new political and economic system, because much of the wealth was in the hands of a small minority of very affluent individuals.

During the eighteenth century, Ouidah was a densely populated, prosperous city located on West Africa's Slave Coast. The city grew to prominence during the seventeenth century as a slave market to export blacks to the Americas. Ouidah became the most active slave trading port in Africa. Europeans called it the Bight of Benin and the surrounding area the Slave Coast.

This name was given because of its importance in supplying the Americas market with slaves. It is thought that Ouidah itself exported over 1 million Africans. It was from this port that Graham and Algy's ancestors were transported to Barbados and St Kitts.

Ouidah was renowned as a slave trading centre but also became known as the most important centre in Africa for voodoo. This was a belief system where tribal beliefs amalgamated with Christian doctrine. In Benin, voodoo is recognised as an official religion followed by forty percent of the population. The country has a public holiday called Voodoo Day and there is a national museum dedicated to voodoo.

Algy and Graham knew little about this West African nation but after being dropped by their driver at the San Miguel Hotel, they were determined to find out about the city's role in the slave trade.

'Let's go into the city, Gray, to look for confirmation of the slave trade.'

'We'll just put our clothes away and get going.'

When they were ready, the boys walked into the city coming across a square with a statue taking pride of place there.

'Let's go and have a look at this,' exclaimed Graham.

'I think I know whose statue that is.'

'Who do you think it is, Algy?'

'I bet it's Felix de Sousa.'

'I've heard of him but surely the Benin government wouldn't allow a statue of someone who treated Africans in such an appalling way to have a prominent spot in a Benin Plaza.'

'Let's go over and read the inscription.'

Fixing their gaze on the statue, they could see it was de Sousa. Graham was flabbergasted.

'It says on here he was the father of the city. I find it unbelievable that someone who caused so much sadness is being revered in this way.'

'Not only is there a statue, Graham, but there's also a museum dedicated to his family and a Plaza named after him.'

'Don't they realise that this man was the principal slave merchant in the history of the slave trade?'

'I've read that the Benin government is going to build two museums solely devoted to the slave trade.'

'No doubt the descendants of de Sousa who still live here downplay the presence of this statue. If the government are building museums to the Slave Trade, they could start by putting that statue in there.'

'I've read that this monster took many African women as his wives and had up to eighty children. Although, these descendants are African, they can't see that what Felix de Sousa did to their fellow human beings was awful.'

'It's understandable that the descendants of the slaves have a completely different point of view and they deplore what the Benin government are doing.'

'What this government here are failing to realise is that de Sousa and his henchmen took Africans from rival tribes.'

'The sad part of all this is the Benin government's complicity in slavery.'

'We know what they're doing is making money out of the suffering of over one million people.'

'Sadly, de Sousa's family remain among the most influential people in the country. It's these people who control how Benin's history is portrayed to the world.'

'The Benin government seems to have forgotten the misery de Sousa caused and they present him as a founding father of the country.'

'Because he made money for Benin from the abuse of African people, they are putting money before the horrific treatment of our forefathers.'

'That makes the Benin government duplicitous in the slave trade.'

'This lot here need to start telling it as it is, Gray.'

'That de Sousa was a ruthless slave trader who was only interested in creating a fortune for himself.'

'Gray, there's a tour guide over there. Let's go and see him. I'll ask him what he thinks about this statue.'

Walking across the square to a bench, Algy and Graham wondered what sort of reception they might get from this escort.

'Good day, Sir. We can see that you're a tour guide and we'd like to ask a question,' remarked Graham.

'I'll be pleased to answer any questions you might have. It's another 10 minutes before my party arrives.'

'Our ancestors were slaves transported from Benin during the eighteenth century. We'd like to know if you agree with the exaltation of Felix de Sousa,' asked Graham.

'I'd like to know if you think it's right for Benin's government to make money out of such a harrowing business as slavery?' A confused Algy asked.

'I run a small business here but the government don't appreciate the history of what happened in Benin. In particular, they forget that de Sousa was one of the worst people involved in the slave business. Unfortunately, this statue helps make the country a lot of money, superseding the human misery caused during that dreadful period of African history.'

'If you feel so strongly about this villain on the plinth, why do you continue to take tours around these sites?' Graham exclaimed.

'I don't make a fortune from what I do but be assured, I tell people how bad Felix de Sousa was. We can't wipe out the slave trade from Benin's history but we need this statue to come down because de Sousa was wicked.'

'We sort of get what you're saying because Britain has statues that have been left up in our cities,' remarked Algy.

'There's one in Bristol of Edward Colston which has been left in place even though members of the public have demanded it be taken down. He was an English slave trader who made a crock of gold from slavery,' exclaimed Graham.

'They even named a concert hall after him but the word is that the trust running it are going to remove the name from the building. Colston Hall is a huge music venue and naming it after a slave trader does not go down well with artists, many of whom are champions of social justice. Oh, I've just remembered there's also a school named after him and that name will have to change. Having a slave trader's name attached to a building which is supposed to promote inclusivity is not on,' added Algy.

'In 1999, our President Mathieu Kerekou visited a Baltimore church where he apologised to African Americans for Benin's role in the slave trade. He was so traumatised by what had happened those years ago that he fell to his knees as he made the apology. Although, Kerekou genuinely apologised it meant little to African Americans and those in other countries when they see statues of Felix de Sousa in this square.

'Some of Benin's most distinguished scholars are battling with the government to get them to investigate the part that de Sousa and other Africans played in the slave trade.'

'I just don't get why the government won't act and remove this monument of a hideous human being. Glorifying somebody like de Sousa is an affront to all descendants of the Slave Trade,' said Graham.

'What you must try to understand is that the Benin people are divided on this issue which is the reason why the statue stays here.'

'You'll have to explain that to us,' remarked Graham.

'Many of the ruling elite in Benin are descended from Felix de Sousa. He had numerous wives and children, so of course his descendant's hero worship him making them revere the statue. We are now a democratic country and they see de Sousa's story and the history of slavery as a means of bringing tourists to the country.'

'I've got to say, I've a major issue with that statue. How an image of such a barbaric man is allowed to stay on that plinth I just don't understand,' added Algy.

'I promise you, boys, I tell the story of slavery as it is. There's no way I'll gloss over such a terrible period in African history.'

'It's been really eye opening to talk with you but keep on fighting for justice for the 1 million. Thanks very much,' proclaimed a grateful Algy.

'I agree with Algy that you've given us a greater understanding of what has happened in Benin but keep persevering for justice.'

Algy and Graham returned to the hotel with an enhanced knowledge of the political situation in Benin and the discord between de Sousa's descendants and the victims of slavery. There was so much more for them to learn about this distasteful past episode in Benin's history.

Chapter 49

'Tomorrow we must visit the monument named "the Door of No Return",' suggested Graham.

'It's a special monument in complete contrast to the statue of Felix de Sousa, because for many Africans it was their last glimpse of their homeland,' explained Algy.

'You're right, Algy, it's a memorial to more than 1 million enslaved Africans deported from Ouidah.'

'Our courageous ancestors were marched in chains from the town's slave market to the nearby port for transportation to the New World.'

'How must these African peoples have felt being put on ships to an unknown destination. Fear of the unknown must have been their overriding emotion as their time in Africa came to an end.'

'Do you realise slaves were often blindfolded as well as chained.'

'Why did they do that? They must have been terrified,' asked Graham.

'Obviously, the chains were to stop them escaping but being blindfolded was symbolically getting the slaves to forget where they came from. It was a bizarre thing to do.'

'How cruel was that? The slave traders were trying to clear their minds of any African memories.'

'We'll visit it tomorrow in memory of our ancestors and the other Africans whose liberty was removed by these avaricious monsters.'

Algy and Graham woke early on the morning of 7 June, and took themselves off to the coastline for what would be a momentous, thought-provoking occasion. Both men were deep in reflection about what they might see on this visit but Graham was first to speak.

'Do you realise that our ancestors would have to walk from the slave market in Ouidah to the coast.'

'What a difficult thing to do. After walking miles from their village, our ancestors would have been crammed into small rowing boats probably for transportation to the large slave ships. Any indiscretion would almost certainly have led to their death,' remarked Algy.

'I'd have just jumped overboard and tried to escape rather than be tethered in a slave ship.'

'Graham, we'd have all felt the same way but an escape attempt would have led to certain death. Remember these people's spirits would have been broken by having to endure the mistreatment of their captors. There would have been little chance of Africans escaping when both spirit and flesh would have been broken at that point.'

Arriving at the largest memorial to the slaves erected by the Benin government, this bronze shrine would create the greatest impact on any morally principled tourist. Both sides of the archway were covered in male and female African slaves ready for despatch to the Americas. As Algy and Graham approached the memorial, they could see images of enslaved people walking towards the sea.

This depiction triggered an emotional response when they thought of how their ancestors had been treated in such an appalling manner. Walking to the "Door of No Return" and looking back at the side facing the sea, they could see a mural portraying slaves walking away from their homeland. There was a simple single tree on the memorial, symbolising the homeland they would never set eyes on again.

Algy and Graham stood staring at this bronze tribute to their ancestors. They saw it as a commemoratory mausoleum to the Africans who had been forced into slavery. Algy was moved to comment, 'When you look at these images it makes you want to weep at the way human beings were treated by their fellow man.'

'It helps me to understand why some people still think black people are an inferior entity of the human race.'

'What happened here in Ouidah explains why some people today think they are superior to black people.'

'Racism in society has its roots back in West Africa. Sadly, white men decided to treat and traffic Africans as a human commodity who could be bought and sold.'

'Every ethnic group has to confront human weakness. Unfortunately, survival instinct led to certain African tribesmen wanting to make sure they weren't enslaved. To do this, they did the dirty work for the European traders. They were prepared to sell their souls to the Devil.'

'The main motivation was self-preservation and money but there would have been a few good people who wouldn't have succumbed to this temptation. Throughout the ages there have been some morally good people who have been prepared to sacrifice their own life rather than indulge in injustice.'

'The Door of No Return is a wonderful symbol of the misery that a million Africans had to endure. That statue of Felix de Sousa is something that needs to be taken down and put in a museum.'

'Every ancestor of the Benin slaves needs to come here to appreciate the distress and hardship their forefathers suffered.'

'Looking at this memorial has the potential to induce a sense of despondency within me. However, I think that's a negative reaction and I'd rather focus on the doughty human spirit of the African slaves who showed the resoluteness needed to survive this tragedy.'

'They were definitely special human beings to have survived after being chained and marched to Ouidah. Then there was the Middle Passage, a hazardous journey across the Atlantic. All this was a testimony to their resilience and strength of character. I can only stare at this monument and admire them.'

'I agree wholeheartedly with you, Gray, but that de Sousa statue needs to come down.'

'At the moment, there's no chance of that, Algy, because there are conflicting interests among the Benin people. You've got a large group of people who see de Sousa as some kind of hero.'

'I know they might be related to him but they need to think straight and realise that he was a money grabbing monster who enslaved Africans. Any who disobeyed de Sousa had their lives ended.'

'I've seen enough in Benin to make me realise that the racial problems we've experienced throughout our lives are due to people like de Sousa, who tried to reduce our ancestors to the level of an animal. Our descendants were human beings who couldn't aspire to fulfil their potential but were forced to serve the white men, who thought they were superior.'

'By making our ancestors subservient, European slave traders could enjoy great wealth. Money was at the root of all this evil but what they didn't bargain for was that the spirit of our ancestors lived on in subsequent generations. We are continuing the fight for equality and our children will carry on after we're gone. It is gratifying to know that victory over the injustice of racism will be achieved in the end. The problem is there's still a considerable minority today who cling to the ideals that their race makes them superior.'

'It will happen but it'll take time. I think we've seen enough. It's time to go back to Wales, Gray.'

'You're right, let's get back to the hotel and raise a glass to the bravery of our ancestors.'

Chapter 50

'I'll make a cup of coffee, Algy. Could you turn the telly on? Let's have a look at the BBC World News.'

The George Floyd murder had sparked unrest in many parts of the world. Black Lives Matter had acted against the barbaric death of an African American citizen in Minneapolis. There were protests in countless countries but the BBC World News was showing the statue of Edward Colston in Bristol being torn from its plinth, then rolled down the road and deposited in the harbour. Elements in British society had become active by taking the lead in showing the world that black lives do matter.

Edward Colston was the deputy governor of the Royal African Company. He had overseen the transportation of 84,000 African slaves to the New World. Approximately a quarter of these human beings died on the slave ships during the Middle Passage crossing. These unfortunates succumbed mostly to disease and failed to reach the plantations of the new world.

Corpses were treated with total disdain by sailors following Colston's contemptuous orders. Bodies were thrown overboard, providing food for sharks following the slave ships, instinctively knowing dead African bodies would be thrown from vessels.

Bristol had been built on the wealth created by Colston's brutality. Inhabitants ignored the fact that this money had been created by the savagery of a man who lacked any sense of morality. His sole aim was to generate finance at the expense of his fellow human beings.

Disappointingly, it had taken one hundred years for people in Bristol to realise that Colston's unscrupulous business ventures were the unethical actions of an unprincipled individual. Ironically, Colston's statue was pulled from its plinth, with protesters symbolically inflicting pain on his bronze effigy by kicking and stamping on it.

In a final symbolic gesture, Colston's fall from grace was completed by the statue being rolled into the harbour. The protesters' actions were reminiscent of the slaves' fate when they were thrown into the sea as shark fodder.

Algy and Graham couldn't take their eyes away from the screen. The silence was interrupted when Algy said, 'There are people of all races involved in Colston's statue being toppled.'

'It's a lesson to the City Council. Why didn't they listen to the many requests for the statue to be removed?'

'They're out of touch with people's feelings that is why. Some of the young people protesting are the descendants of African people who were chained in the holds of Colston's ships.'

'Algy, one man has placed his knee over Colston's bronze throat.'

'Isn't it ironic that this individual is acting in the same way as the cop who killed George Floyd?'

'This should never have come to this. That statue should have been removed peacefully and put in a museum, not in a public place as an exalted figure. Colston had people in Bristol who defended his actions because of the money he spent developing the city.'

'Having that statue in Bristol for years has cast a dark shadow over the city. It will definitely be a better place without it. There'll be people in authority calling for the protesters to be tried as criminals. Remember what we were taught in Sunday School when Jesus turned over the money changers' tables in the Temple.'

'We were taught it was "righteous anger". The Holy Temple needed to be treated with reverence but it had been turned into a marketplace.'

'Surely what has happened in Bristol is righteous anger when people of colour have had to walk past that statue on a daily basis knowing Colston's cruelty had been inflicted on their ancestors. What's more he'd made shedloads of money from his barbarism.'

'I'd love to go into the square where Felix de Sousa's statue is and pull it from the plinth.'

'I feel the same way, Gray, but there's a couple of problems. Do you really think the two of us could do it? It's been a long time since we did any weight training and there's no doubt we would spend a long time in a Benin prison if we did succeed!'

'The statue of de Sousa and the monument for the Door of No Return are in complete contrast to one another. One glorifies a tyrant while the other is a memorial to the 1 million African people sold into slavery from Ouidah.'

'Hopefully, the Benin Government will eventually take de Sousa's statue down.'

'I wouldn't bet on it. Nevertheless, during the last few weeks, we've found out so much about the capture of our ancestors by the slave traders. We've also been made aware of the role played by a monster like Felix de Sousa. Most important of all is that we've found out how our ancestors survived and prospered. It's a testimony to their resilience and we should draw pride from their achievements.'

'Attitudes in society are definitely changing around the world. Young people are looking to change viewpoints and treat people of all races equally. It's something we've wanted throughout our lives.'

'We're definitely ready to go home, Algy.'

Chapter 51

Algy and Graham went to bed that evening secure in the knowledge that their trip to the Caribbean and Africa had produced results. The quest to find their ancestry had thrown up interesting facts leading to their search ending in Benin. The images on the monument known as "The Door of No Return" were heart rending for both men, making them appreciate the dreadful suffering inflicted on their forefathers.

Responsibility for this suffering lay at the door of Felix de Sousa. Despite the brutality of his work, he had been immortalised in a statue located in a Benin plaza. Algy and Graham had been incensed at seeing this monument given pride of place in a supposedly democratic African nation. Having watched the toppling of Edward Colston's statue on the television, they wholeheartedly wished the same could happen to the de Sousa image.

People like de Sousa and Colston had seen African peoples as inferior. Their superior attitude led to the enslavement of black people. When the slaves were eventually freed, hostility to black people continued. Organisations such as the Ku Klux Klan in the United States, and fascist bodies like the National Front in Britain, promoted the idea that black people were second class citizens who were not needed in their respective countries.

Algy and Graham had both suffered because this attitude had pervaded British society. However, by the twenty-first century, the British perspective on racism had slowly started to change, particularly amongst younger people whose sentiments were towards inclusivity and equality.

During the 1970s, Algy had difficulty entering the teaching profession because his colour made him superfluous to requirements. By the time he had retired, his work for the Education authority made him a real asset who would be difficult to replace.

Over time, the Christian churches moved from a position where African slaves were seen as only fit for subservience. They were viewed as savages being rescued from eternal damnation. Having pagan beliefs was seen as a barrier to entering heaven. During the early days of the Slave Trade, church and state were seen to be partners in this detestable transatlantic business.

Justification for this barbarism was given impetus through literal interpretation of Biblical evidence. Contradictory scriptural material helped legitimise the subjugation of people regarded as inferior. The Book of Leviticus expounded the teaching that Israelites could buy and keep slaves. It also taught that the Israelites could enslave foreigners as permanent property.

Originally, this notion derived from the idea of God making a covenant with the ancient Israelites where they judged themselves to be God's chosen people. Later, Jewish teaching by the rabbis presented the Jews as a light to the nations and not as a superior people.

In the New Testament, the Apostles had never asked that slaves be emancipated because slavery was legally accepted as part of ancient society. Such tenuous evidence enabled church and state to justify slavery as a divinely prescribed institution.

Pope Nicholas V had allowed the Portuguese to enslave pagan African peoples, seemingly giving Felix de Sousa the right to abuse these individuals. Not before time and after the violation of countless thousands of African lives, church attitudes began to change. The treatment meted out to these people contravened the teaching that there is equality in creation.

Algy and Graham could see by looking at Felix de Sousa's statue a sadistic monstrosity of a person whose work had infiltrated society, creating racist attitudes which were still prevalent in the twenty-first century. They fell asleep content in the knowledge that they now had a fuller understanding of the history, inclination and self-interest of one ethnic group to dominate another.

Their last thought before falling asleep was that they were disappointed at not being able to emulate the actions of the demonstrators in Bristol by tearing down Felix de Sousa's statue.

Shortly after 2:00 am, Algy and Graham's hotel room was suddenly lit by a luminous, dazzling light causing them to momentarily open their eyes. The light was so bright it engulfed the room. This blazing, vivid luminescence lasted only a split second. It was followed by an ear-piercing crash, causing the hotel room to violently vibrate.

'Was that an earthquake?' Graham exclaimed.

'It couldn't be because tremors last longer than that. What about the bright light? That's nothing to do with an earthquake.'

'You're right. It was over so quickly. Get your shorts and T shirt on. We need to go and look.'

'Bring your phone, Algy. We can use the torch on it if we need to.'

'Surely other people will have heard that.'

Opening the door of their hotel room, they went down the stairs and out into the warm tropical night air. Being in such a hurry, they began to perspire. They were nervous and their hearts were pounding in their chests. Both were tense and nervous because they were fearing the worst. Their physical symptoms were making them feel lightheaded.

'Graham, there's a commotion in the square next to the statue. Let's get over there,' urged Algy.

Their running days over, Algy and Graham walked as quickly as they could to the furore in the square. People were clamouring to see what pandemonium had been created. Being extremely well lit, the boys had a good view of the area.

'Graham, de Sousa's statue's gone.'

'What do you mean? How could it?'

'I don't know. But let's go and look.'

People were looking at a huge, strange, black, smouldering rock on the ground, prompting Algy to remark, 'Where's de Sousa's statue?'

'It looks like that lump of rock hit it. Obviously, the collision caused the noise we could hear.'

'But there's nothing left of it.'

'The only thing that could cause this level of damage is a meteorite from outer space which explains the dazzling light we saw. Most of them burn up when they enter the Earth's atmosphere.'

'This one's got through and done what we wished we could have done.'

'Look, Algy, there's a group of men gawking at two bits of the statue.'

Algy and Graham walked across to look at the remnants of the statue. Staring hard Algy exclaimed, 'There's a number of men obstructing our view but it looks like all that's left of it are the hands. The rest has been smashed to smithereens.'

'Algy, I couldn't have done a better job if they'd given me a pile driver.'

Felix de Sousa's hands had come to rest on the grass, palms up.

'Look, Graham, the hands are starting to turn red.'

'The protesters in Bristol put red paint on Colston's hands to symbolise the blood of the slaves.'

'Graham, I don't think it's red paint.'

Seeing the hands emitting red fluid traumatised the Beninese causing them to hastily back away from the fragments of de Sousa's statue. Running in all directions, they appeared revulsed by what they had witnessed. Their fright originated from their voodoo beliefs giving rise to their repugnance at these haemorrhaging remnants.

Their first instinct was that this red liquid was blood. Voodoo worshippers believed that blood was used to cast spells and even curses. Human blood was the most potent force in this type of magic. The men having scarpered for their lives allowed Algy and Graham to examine de Sousa's mitts.

'You're right, Algy, this looks like real blood.'

'What's more, it's beginning to create some patterns on both hands.'

'It appears to be taking the form of a message.'

'You're quite right. There are letters forming.'

'No wonder the Benin men recoiled at seeing the hands on the floor.'

'Graham, it says, *Not in My Name.*'

'What do you think it means?'

'This meteorite was no accident. Normal space debris often falls to Earth but the message is no coincidence. It might have hit the statue but the writing is a communication.'

'Are you trying to say that God is at work here, Algy?'

'Graham, there's no other explanation.'

'We're like most people and take God for granted.'

'We used to be church goers when we were young. This is a definite sign that God is in control of the Universe.'

'Why did God allow such terrible things like slavery to happen?'

'Men and women have Free Will but humans fail to use it properly.'

'Unfortunately, we're all born with Original Sin.'

'You mean the potential to sin. Some people have the ability to evaluate between right and wrong.'

'Disappointingly people can behave in an appalling way because of money.'

'Slavery brought crocks of gold to people like de Sousa and Colston but unfortunately there was a high price paid by Africans taken into slavery.'

'Their descendants have continued paying the price ever since.'

'One thing we've learned from seeing these hands is that the church might have been involved in legitimising slavery but God had nothing to do with it. At the time of de Sousa, the church and governments had got it wrong. All humans are tainted by sin.'

'We were taught in Sunday school that we're all created equal.'

'People like de Sousa and Colston failed to take that on board through greed and went their own way.'

'They ended as statues on plinths because many people revered them for investing their money in developing cities and countries.'

'We were also taught the golden rule for all time, "Do to others as you would want done to you". Let me tell you, Gray, they were statues because they had hearts of stone.'

'Well said, Algy. Remember Lot's wife, she disobeyed God when they fled from Sodom and Gomorrah. She was told not to look back but she did and was turned into a statue.'

'It's amazing what we've remembered from Sunday school.'

Epilogue
A Black Rose Between Two Thorns

29 September 2021 The Betty Campbell Statue

'Remember you said that Felix de Sousa and Edward Colston had hearts of stone,' recalled Graham.

'You said Lot's wife disobeyed God and was turned to a statue,' retorted Algy.

'Betty Campbell's statue is different. We're here today to pay tribute to a woman who against all the odds did nothing but good. The glowering de Sousa and Colston resting on their plinths were nothing but egotistical and obnoxious human beings.'

'One thing is certain, Betty didn't have a heart of stone.'

'Quite right. Hers was a heart of gold.'

'She succeeded against all the odds to be the first black headteacher in Wales. She was such a determined woman.'

'She aspired to succeed after she was told by a teacher when she was a pupil that black people couldn't be teachers, particularly a headteacher.'

'I had difficulty in getting into the profession but Betty broke the mould and gave me a chance when it seemed I'd wasted three years in college.'

'Betty's statue was commissioned following a BBC Wales poll winning great public support.'

'Wasn't it called the Hidden Heroines Poll?'

As Algy finished his comment, Prof. Uzo Iwobi, founder of Race Council Cymru said, 'Wales has shown that this black woman matters to us all.'

Geraldine Trotman, the Black History Patron for Wales, added, 'The unveiling of the statue of Mrs Campbell will be one of the greatest moments for Butetown and everyone who lives in Wales.'

'I know everyone in other parts of Britain knows Butetown as Tiger Bay but people like Betty have changed the perception of the place from the time when we were young,' remarked Graham.

'It lost its reputation as a place where prostitutes touted for business as sailors left their ships,' exclaimed Algy.

'There's so much more to our former home than the one you've described. Nobody's done more than Betty to change it.'

'I can't wait for them to unveil her statue so we can see what the sculpture looks like.'

Prior to the unveiling, Algy and Graham stood and listened to a performance by the Oasis One World Choir. Speeches followed by the leader of Cardiff City Council and the Welsh Minister for Social Justice. When these dignitaries finished praising Betty, there were video messages from Prince Charles and the actor, Michael Sheen.

Graham whispered, 'They're extolling Betty's virtues and she deserves all these plaudits.'

Algy and Graham were particularly moved by the Mount Stuart Primary School's rendition of the song *Something Inside So Strong*. This had been Betty's favourite song and the school children did it justice. Betty would have been so proud of that performance.

Finally, the moment that Algy and Graham were waiting for had arrived. The sheet covering the statue was pulled back by Mrs Campbell's family. Algy and Graham's mouths dropped open when they saw what had been created.

The sculptor, Eve Shepherd, had designed and sculpted a mother tree with Mrs Campbell's head and shoulders forming a canopy beneath which ten young children stood. Betty Campbell was being presented as a maternal tree within her community. This depiction showed her protecting her children, her school and community.

'This is a staggering piece of work, Algy.'

'You were right. De Sousa and Colston had hearts of stone but the roots of a tree extend a long way creating stability.'

'Betty created security for the Butetown community. Her work was exceptional.'

'I could easily be one of those under that canopy, Gray. She gave me my first teaching opportunity. Her mantra was to make other people's lives better. This statue is an iconic piece of work because the structure is unique.'

'Didn't you say earlier that you wondered if John Actie and Tony Paris would come to the unveiling. I think there's two men standing in the distance.'

'I can see them but their faces are obscured.'

'I think I might be seeing things. It's a cloudy day but there's a bright light emanating from the sky and it's shining on those two fellas faces.'

'It's a strange phenomenon for sure. The bright light in Ouidah was followed by a destructive bang.'

'Then there were de Sousa's hands. I found it unbelievable and wouldn't have believed it if I hadn't seen it with my own eyes.'

'Do you think this curiosity could be a divine message conveying another communication that God knows the Cardiff Five were treated unjustly? Men might try to cover up the truth but nothing can be hidden from God. In the end, justice will prevail.'

'The Lord sure works in mysterious ways, Algy.'